JEANNE WHITMEE

GIVE ME TOMORROW

Complete and Unabridged

CHARNWOOD
Leicester

First published in Great Britain in 2015 by
Robert Hale Limited
London

First Charnwood Edition
published 2017
by arrangement with
Robert Hale
an imprint of
The Crowood Press
Wiltshire

The moral right of the author has been asserted

Copyright © 2015 by Jeanne Whitmee
All rights reserved

A catalogue record for this book is available
from the British Library.

ISBN 978–1–4448–3395–9

Published by
F. A. Thorpe (Publishing)
Anstey, Leicestershire

Set by Words & Graphics Ltd.
Anstey, Leicestershire
Printed and bound in Great Britain by
T. J. International Ltd., Padstow, Cornwall

This book is printed on acid-free paper

SPECIAL MESSAGE TO READERS

THE ULVERSCROFT FOUNDATION
(registered UK charity number 264873)
was established in 1972 to provide funds for
research, diagnosis and treatment of eye diseases.
Examples of major projects funded by
the Ulverscroft Foundation are:-

- The Children's Eye Unit at Moorfields Eye Hospital, London
- The Ulverscroft Children's Eye Unit at Great Ormond Street Hospital for Sick Children
- Funding research into eye diseases and treatment at the Department of Ophthalmology, University of Leicester
- The Ulverscroft Vision Research Group, Institute of Child Health
- Twin operating theatres at the Western Ophthalmic Hospital, London
- The Chair of Ophthalmology at the Royal Australian College of Ophthalmologists

You can help further the work of the Foundation
by making a donation or leaving a legacy.
Every contribution is gratefully received. If you
would like to help support the Foundation or
require further information, please contact:

THE ULVERSCROFT FOUNDATION
The Green, Bradgate Road, Anstey
Leicester LE7 7FU, England
Tel: (0116) 236 4325

website: www.foundation.ulverscroft.com

Jeanne Whitmee studied speech and drama, followed by a career in the theatre, until her marriage and the birth of her two daughters. Before turning to full-time writing, she taught speech and drama. She is the author of over thirty books, some written under pseudonyms, many having been issued in large print and translated into various languages, both European and Eastern. She still takes an active interest in the theatre and arts and her hobbies are watercolour painting, gardening and cooking. She lives in Cambridgeshire with her husband, and has four grandchildren.

GIVE ME TOMORROW

When Frank Davies marries a younger woman, Susan, his ten-year-old daughter Louise feels pushed out — and even more so when baby Karen arrives. Neither her father's outrageous spoiling of her, nor the drama school to which she is sent to pursue her dream, is enough to distract Louise from the void left by her absent mother. Now, years later, with her father gone, Louise is obsessed with finding her mother, while distancing herself from her family and spitefully making trouble for Karen whenever the opportunity arises. Karen has her own family problems to deal with, while Susan longs to see her girls reconciled and to pick up the threads of her own life again. Eventually each woman, in her own way, is shown the path to happiness. But will they take it?

Books by Jeanne Whitmee
Published by Ulverscroft:

ORANGES AND LEMONS
THE LOST DAUGHTERS
THURSDAY'S CHILD
EVE'S DAUGHTER
BELLADONNA
KING'S WALK
PRIDE OF PEACOCKS
ALL THAT I AM
THE HAPPY HIGHWAYS
SUMMER SNOW
POINT OF NO RETURN
THE WISE CHILD
YOU'LL NEVER KNOW . . .
TRUE COLOURS
TO DREAM AGAIN

1

'Excuse me, madam, I must ask you to accompany me to the manager's office.'

Karen stared in amazement at the dark-suited man standing at her elbow. 'Why? I don't understand,' she said.

The man put his hand on her arm. 'If you'd just come back into the store with me . . . '

Karen shook the hand off indignantly. 'Just tell me what the problem is.' She felt her cheeks warming and her heartbeat quickened as the curious eyes of other shoppers turned towards her. 'What do you want? Who are you?'

The man leaned towards her and lowered his voice. 'Come along now, madam. We don't want to make a scene, do we?'

'I'm not making a scene.' Karen could hear the rising note of alarm in her voice. 'I just want to know why you're asking me to go to the manager's office with you.'

The store detective glanced round him. 'Very well. If you insist, I have reason to believe you are concealing goods for which you have not paid.'

'*What?*' Karen caught her breath. 'You're accusing me of shoplifting?' She thrust her handbag into his hands. 'Here, look for yourself. My sister will tell you . . . '

She turned around to Louise, who had been following her out of the store, only to find that

1

her sister was nowhere to be seen. Bemused, she looked around her. Where on earth had she gone? Turning back to the detective, she saw that he had unzipped her bag and to her horror, the hand he dipped inside emerged holding a fragment of black lace with a store label attached to it. He looked at her triumphantly.

'I think you had better accompany me at once,' he said. 'If you refuse I shall be obliged to call security.'

Karen stared at the man. 'But — that's not *mine*! I've never even seen it before. I didn't . . .' Panic-stricken, she looked around again for Louise, who seemed to have vanished into thin air. Acutely aware of the eyes of other shoppers boring into her back, she followed the detective back into the store. As they walked through the ground-floor departments and through a door into a corridor, he was speaking on his mobile phone.

Neville Smith, the store manager, was a small man with an inflated awareness of his important position as manager of Hayward's department store. He wore a baggy grey suit and rimless glasses, and his thinning hair was carefully combed over his bald patch. He looked up sternly as Karen was presented to him.

'I must inform you here and now that it is the policy of Hayward's to prosecute shoplifters,' he said without preamble. 'We have suffered so much loss over recent months that we have to be stringent.'

'There is some mistake,' Karen said shakily. 'Those things in my bag — I didn't take them. Perhaps you should look at your CCTV footage.'

The manager gave a sardonic little smile and pushed his glasses further up the bridge of his nose. 'May I point out that the fact that they are in your possession is more than enough to prove your guilt.' He glanced at the store detective. 'Did you witness the theft, Marshall?'

The store detective cleared his throat. 'A member of the public alerted me,' he replied.

Karen turned to him. 'Then whoever that was has made a grave mistake.'

Neville Smith treated her to another of his scornful little smiles. 'I'm afraid that's an all too familiar line, madam.'

Karen turned to the store detective. 'So where is this member of the public?'

Smith looked at the store detective. 'I take it you asked her to wait?'

Marshall looked a little flustered. 'I — er — no.'

Smith sighed. 'How many times must I tell you that any witnesses should be asked to wait?'

'She may still be in the store,' Marshall said quickly. 'I think she was on her way to the coffee lounge. I could probably find her.'

'Then I suggest you do so immediately.' As the detective left the room, the manager turned his attention to Karen. 'In the meantime, madam, would you be good enough to empty your handbag onto the desk?'

'No. I would not be good enough to empty my bag,' Karen said stubbornly. 'Not until you have proved that I am guilty. As I suggested before, surely you only need to view the tape in your CCTV to clear this whole thing up.' She opened her bag and pulled out what she now saw was a set of black lace designer lingerie which she laid on the manager's desk. 'These items are not mine but I did not steal them. Anything else in my bag is private.'

'I must warn you that once we have verified that the witness actually saw you conceal the goods, I shall be obliged to send for the police.'

Karen sighed. Her heart was hammering in her chest but she was determined not to let it show. 'Perhaps I can be permitted to sit down,' she said. If this woman insisted that she saw her take the goods what was she to do? *Louise.* This was Louise's doing. It had to be. She'd caused plenty of problems in the past but this was the last straw. Where on earth *was* she? How dare she land her in a mess like this and then just disappear?

'You may be seated,' the manager conceded pompously.

Karen sat down gratefully and an uncomfortable five minutes passed as they waited. Then the office door opened to admit Marshall and a flashily dressed woman with magenta hair. Karen stood up and moved aside. Marshall introduced the woman.

'This is Mrs Jones, sir. She is a regular customer here at Hayward's.'

'Quite so.' Smith's beady eyes assessed the woman's appearance. 'I understand that you witnessed an act of theft this afternoon, Mrs Jones.'

'That's right,' the woman said self-righteously. 'I hate to see a lovely store like Hayward's being taken advantage of. When I saw it I felt I had to report it at once.'

'Very public-spirited, I'm sure.'

'But I don't really want to be involved in any legal action,' she added guardedly. 'I don't want to be called to give evidence in court nor nothing.'

'All I need you to do for now is to identify this person as the one you saw taking the articles.' The manager glowered at the store detective. 'Marshall — would you be good enough to step aside and allow Mrs Jones to see the accused?'

Marshall stepped smartly to one side and Karen and the woman came face to face. Karen looked directly into the other woman's eyes and immediately saw her confidence fade.

Mrs Jones bit her lip. 'Ah — well — she was certainly wearing a red coat like this person's got on,' she said. 'And I'm fairly sure that was the bag she stuffed them into — or one like it. But the woman I saw take the knickers was a blonde.'

The manager looked irritated. 'Are you now saying that you are unsure?'

'Well, I definitely saw someone take the knick — er — undies and stuff them into a bag,' she said. 'But — I'm sorry but I can't say for sure that it was this person, just someone in a red coat. Unless — er . . .'

'Unless what, Mrs Jones?'

'I suppose she could be wearing a wig,' she said.

Karen looked round at the other three people in the office. 'Perhaps one of you would like to try to test my hair,' she suggested, leaning forward.

'That will not be necessary.' The little man at

the desk seemed to have diminished in size. His face flushed an unbecoming beetroot shade as he glared at the store detective. 'Thank you, Mrs Jones,' he said through clenched teeth. 'Perhaps next time you could make sure you are reporting the right person.'

The woman looked apologetically at Karen. 'I'm sorry if I caused you any bother,' she muttered.

'Oh, please don't worry yourself about it,' Karen said, trying not to sound sarcastic. She resisted saying, *Maybe you should have gone to Specsavers.*

Mrs Jones left the room hastily and Karen turned to the manager. 'Perhaps you would like to confirm what the witness has said by viewing your CCTV tape as I suggested?'

'There will be no need,' Smith said. His colour had now faded to a sickly grey. 'It is obvious that there has been a mistake. You are free to go.'

'Thank you.' Karen stood her ground. 'But first I'd like an apology,' she said. 'It's not every day one is named as 'the accused' or threatened with prosecution.'

Smith cleared his throat. 'I think you will agree that it was a natural mistake.' Karen waited, saying nothing and Smith cleared his throat again and continued, 'Please accept my apologies for any inconvenience and — er — embarrassment caused.'

Karen picked up her handbag and as she left the office, she heard Smith upbraiding his store detective.

'Marshall! How many times must I tell you to

make sure those tapes are regularly changed and running!'

★ ★ ★

In the car park Karen climbed gratefully into her car. It was only then that she realized that she was still shaking. What a horrible experience. Suppose she had been seen being apprehended by one of her pupils' parents? It would only take one! Simon was going to be furious about this. If the store had insisted on pursuing the case and the papers had got hold of it, they could both have lost their jobs. It was so irresponsible of Louise — and so typical.

Louise Davies, or Louisa Delmar as her half-sister liked to call herself, was fourteen years Karen's senior. Although they shared the same father they were as different in temperament and character as it was possible to be. Louise was an actress. Touring around the country and never in the same town for more than a few months, she always turned up on her married half-sister's doorstep whenever she was between jobs. Recently, the summer show she had been appearing in down in Devon had come to a close and she was waiting for her agent to arrange a pantomime for her.

Delving into her handbag, Karen took out her phone and clicked on Louise's number. The call went straight to voicemail. Furious, she left a message: 'Louise! Where the hell are you? What did you think you were playing at? You've just almost had me arrested for shoplifting. Please ring me as soon as you get this.'

She started the car and backed out of her space. She was almost halfway home when she heard her phone ringing in her bag. Pulling over, she stopped and took the phone out. It was Louise calling.

'Louise!'

'Darling, I've just got your message. What's the matter?'

'Don't play the innocent with me. You know bloody well what's the matter. You put those things in my bag in Hayward's, didn't you?'

'Things? What things?'

'Designer lingerie ring any bells? Simon and I could have lost our jobs through this. I could be ringing you from the police station right now for all you know.'

Louise gave a maddening little giggle at the other end of the line. 'Oh, come off it, sweetie, don't exaggerate. You're not at the police station, are you?'

'No, no thanks to you. More to the point, where are *you*?' Karen demanded. 'And where did you disappear to? You left me to face the music on my own.'

'Look, it's all too silly for words. I can explain everything.'

'Then I think you'd better start. Where are you, Louise?'

'I'm in the park. It's such a lovely day I thought I'd have — '

'Whereabouts? I'm coming right now.'

'The little café by the lake. Look, there's no need to be so stuffy.'

8

Karen didn't reply, she just ended the call and thrust her phone back into her bag, then, turning the car, she headed back in the opposite direction.

★ ★ ★

The park was looking lovely in the autumn sunshine. The trees were turning to gold and the sky was blue and cloudless. The sound of children's voices filled the air as they played on the swings, making the most of their half-term holiday. But Karen hardly took any of it in. She had only one aim in mind: to find her half-sister and let her have both barrels. She spotted Louise as soon as she came through the yew archway at the lakeside. She was sitting on a bench, her elegant legs crossed and her short skirt pulled up, displaying several inches of thigh as she calmly nibbled at a choc-ice. Karen had never in her life wanted to hit anyone as much as she did now.

Louise looked up and gave a cheery wave. 'Hello, darling! There you are. Would you like one of these?' She held up the half-eaten choc-ice. 'They've always been my weakness.'

'I remember,' Karen said drily, sitting down on the bench next to her. 'I don't want a choc-ice. It would probably choke me. What I want is an explanation — now, please.'

'Oh, all right.' Louise sighed and popped the last of the ice cream into her mouth and screwing the wrapper into a ball, tossed it into the bushes.

9

'You put those things in my bag when I went to the loo, didn't you?'

Louise shrugged. 'OK — yes, but why not? I'm sure Hayward's can afford to lose a few pounds a damned sight more than I can.' She glanced sideways at Karen. 'I couldn't resist those sexy, black lace undies. Gorgeous, weren't they? What a pity you had to go and get yourself caught.'

'It's *theft*, Louise. Against the law, and it was despicable to involve me in it and then just disappear.'

Louise frowned. 'I knew you were going to be bloody boring about it. You're so damned buttoned up, Karrie.'

'I don't think you understand how serious this is. If I'd been charged, Simon and I could both have lost our jobs.'

'Oh, don't be so melodramatic!' Louise said dismissively.

'I'm not. It's true. Do you imagine that the school governors would allow either of us to continue after shoplifting charges and all the publicity that would have ensued? Why did you do it, Louise? You were seen taking the things and if it hadn't been for the difference in our hair colour, I'd be in custody right this minute.'

'But you're not. So what are you going on and *on* about?'

'You still haven't explained why you took these things.'

Louise shrugged. 'I fancied them — simple as that.'

'You *fancied* them!' Karen shook her head. 'So

10

why put them in *my* bag?'

Louise grinned impishly. 'I couldn't resist winding you up. You always take the bait so beautifully. Oh, come on, darling. I couldn't know you'd get nabbed, could I?'

Karen's fingers itched to smack her sister's face. It was useless arguing. They could go round and round for ever. It was obvious she was going to get no more sense out of Louise. She could be completely amoral at times. She tried a different tack. 'Have you heard from that agent of yours lately?'

Louise chuckled. 'You're not terribly subtle, are you, darling? What you're trying to say is that you've had enough of me.' She pouted. 'Don't tell me I've outstayed my welcome.'

Karen shrugged. 'What do you think? After this afternoon — yes, you have!'

'Pity.' Louise sighed. 'I'll call Harry tomorrow morning if you're really going to insist on punishing me.' She glanced at Karen. 'I haven't said anything but there could be something quite exciting in the pipeline.'

Karen raised a cynical eyebrow. 'Oh yes? I've heard that one before. But then I suppose there's bound to be a panto coming up in some remote corner of the country.' She looked at her sister. 'You could always get a proper job, you know. The department stores will be taking on extra staff for Christmas soon.'

'Thanks for the vote of confidence, darling. Anyway, as I told you, there's a possibility of something really big in the offing.'

'Well, let's hope it comes off this time.'

'OK, don't go on about it. I'll get on to it in the morning.'

'Good,' Karen said without conviction.

Louise looked at her half-sister sheepishly. 'Look, there's no need to mention any of this to Simon. You know what he's like. He's so po-faced. He wouldn't see the funny side.'

Karen raised an eyebrow. 'Strangely enough, I know the feeling.' She turned to Louise. 'I'll make a bargain with you. I won't tell if you promise you actually will move out.'

Louise stared at her. 'You *what*? Where else can I go?'

'You could find yourself a flat or a room somewhere. I've had enough, Lou. Whenever you're around there's always trouble. This afternoon is the last straw.'

For a moment Louise looked crestfallen. 'I suppose I could try Susan.'

Karen looked at her. 'Mum? You know she only has a one-bedroom flat.'

'I could doss down on the sofa.'

'Why are you always so hard up? Where did all the money go to that you got for the house?'

Louise sighed. 'Trust you to bring that up again.'

'So — you should have quite a healthy bank balance. You could easily afford to rent a flat.'

'Perhaps.'

'I hope you think it was worth chucking Mum out for.'

'It was my house,' Louise said stubbornly. 'You were married and I had no one. Dad left it to me and I needed the cash. Susan wanted to

12

downsize anyway. The place was far too big for her.'

'You got a good price for it so you can't be short of cash.'

'A girl has to put something away for a rainy day.'

'Really? Well, this is it, Lou. This is the rainiest day I've seen for a long time, so get your umbrella out.' Karen got up from the bench and began to walk away. Louise jumped up and followed her.

'I suppose I'd better come home with you and start packing, then?'

'I suppose you better had.'

2

Karen watched from the window as Louise walked down the path and out through the gate and into the waiting taxi without a backwards glance. Why did she always feel so guilty? Louise took advantage quite outrageously and this afternoon she had really overstepped the mark, but still, perversely, she couldn't help feeling bad about telling her to go, especially when she knew she'd be landing herself on poor Mum.

'You still haven't told me what that was all about.' Simon had come into the room and was standing behind her.

'You don't want to know,' Karen said without turning round.

'I do actually.' Simon dropped an arm across her shoulders. 'Whenever she's around, you look really stressed but when you came in this afternoon, I could see you were at the end of your tether.'

Karen turned to look at him. Most of the time, Simon put up with Louise's visits without saying a word, although he had never liked or approved of her. In her turn, Louise made no secret of the fact that she considered Simon dull and boring. She was always making cutting remarks to Karen about his clothes and hairstyle, his taste in music and cars, most of all, his job as head teacher of St Luke's Primary School, which she considered mind-numbingly dreary and bourgeois.

14

'She overstepped the mark,' she said non-committally. 'Suddenly I'd had enough.'

'What did she do? Come on, you might as well tell me. I'll find out in the end anyway.'

Karen took a deep breath. 'She shoplifted some underwear in Hayward's.'

Simon shrugged. 'Why doesn't that surprise me?'

'But she put the stuff in *my* bag and then disappeared when the store detective stopped me.'

'Oh my God!' Simon's eyes widened in horror. 'What happened?'

'Luckily I was able to prove that I didn't do it. But not before I had the humiliation of being stopped and frogmarched through the store to the manager's office.'

'My God!' Simon's face flushed angrily. 'Do you realize what that might have meant for me?'

'For *you*? I think you mean *us*! Of course I do. I eventually found Lou calmly eating ice cream in the park. She made light of the whole thing as though it was some hilarious prank. That's when I saw red and asked her to leave.'

Simon frowned. 'For God's sake! When I think what the outcome could have been. I would never have worked again if you'd been charged. So where's she off to now?'

'To Mum's, unfortunately. I rang ahead to warn her and I was hoping she'd say no but you know what a soft touch she is. I just hope Lou doesn't take advantage.'

'That's a fond hope. Seriously, Karen, something will have to be done about your sister.

15

We can't allow her to keep on scrounging on us, especially as she must be rolling in cash since she sold the house. It's quite preposterous. No one else would stand for it.'

'Well, let's hope Susan is able to knock some sense into her.'

'I doubt that.' He looked thoughtful. 'Speaking of sense — have you given any more thought to what we talked about last night?'

'About me giving in my notice at school? No, I haven't. I've only been back at work for two terms. What's that going to look like? The governors will think I can't cope.'

'It doesn't matter what they think. You know my feelings on the matter. I've always thought you should be at home with Peter at least until he goes to school.'

Karen sighed. 'We've been through all that. He's quite happy with Mum and in a few months, he'll be old enough for nursery.'

'Well, I happen to think that your mother isn't a fit person to be bringing him up. She spoils him rotten with ice cream and chocolate and all the wrong food.' He spread his hands. 'And frankly, Karen, since you've been back at school the house is a tip.'

She stared at him. 'A *tip*, is it? Well, if you gave me a hand now and again, maybe it wouldn't be.'

He looked outraged. 'Gave you a hand! My job doesn't finish at half past three as you well know. Even when I get home, there's a pile of paperwork to be done and then at the weekend there's the garden. I can't possibly do more.'

'Of course I realize all that, but I have

16

preparation to do too — *plus* the housework and Peter.'

He smiled smugly. 'My point exactly. You're taking on too much.' As she opened her mouth to protest he ran an exasperated hand through his hair. 'Oh, for Christ's sake, Karen, why don't you just admit it and give in? Peter's almost two. In three years he'll be off to school. The time will fly by.'

'Other new mothers go back to school even sooner than I did,' she protested. 'As I said before, he'll be going to nursery soon and I'd be twiddling my thumbs all day.'

'You could always fill the time by doing some housework and cooking some decent meals. I'm getting a bit tired of supermarket ready-meals.'

She gave him a withering look. 'Well, I'm not giving my job up just because you say so. If you want me to go you're going to have to fire me.' She smiled defiantly up at him. 'And I don't think you'd like what the governors would make of *that*!' She turned towards the door. 'I'm off to bathe Peter now. As you don't seem to be up to your neck in paperwork at the moment, perhaps you'd like to peel some potatoes for tea.' She was halfway up the stairs when she heard his infuriating parting shot:

'As it's half-term next week, perhaps you could spend it tidying up a bit. I'm told that's what other working mothers do. And by the way, it's *dinner* — not tea!'

3

Susan replaced the receiver and sighed. Karen had sounded apologetic.

'I'm really sorry, Mum, but Louise is on her way over to you. We've had a bit of a falling-out and I'm afraid she's going to ask if she can stay with you. You don't have to say yes,' she added hurriedly. 'If you've got anything planned don't put it off for her. She's got absolutely no consideration, so stick to your guns.'

Susan sighed. 'Yes, dear. I will.'

'I thought I'd just warn you.'

'Thanks. Just leave it with me. It'll be fine.'

She closed the balcony doors and drew the curtains reluctantly. Soon it would be winter. Next weekend the clocks would go back and the nights would lengthen. She sighed. It was no fun, being on your own. Sometimes she was glad she had no one to please but herself, but at others — when she felt down or depressed, she longed to have someone to talk to, to share a meal or a cup of tea with, someone who'd be nice to her when she was feeling low. Not that Louise exactly filled that description, but she was company at least, and Susan didn't see her stepdaughter very often.

She looked around her at the things she'd managed to salvage from her marital home. It was easier, of course, having a smaller place to look after. It was quite a nice flat and she could just about afford it on her pension. But it had been a shock when Frank died and she found that he'd left the house to Louise. An even greater shock when her stepdaughter announced that she was in desperate need of the money and intended to sell it. At first she had felt as though the rug had been pulled out from under her feet. Karen had been furious and offered her a home with her and Simon, but Susan valued her independence too much to accept. After all, she wasn't in her dotage yet and Frank hadn't exactly left her destitute. He'd left her a small legacy which she'd invested in the hope that she'd be able to afford a better home in the not too distant future.

Frank had always spoilt Louise. It was understandable in a way. His first wife — Louise's mother — had walked out when her daughter was barely more than a toddler and Frank had never stopped trying to make it up to her.

Susan had been twenty-four when she'd met Frank. She worked as manageress at the Blue Bird Café. Frank worked for the local council as a highway surveyor. His office was just a few doors away from the café and he was in the habit of dropping in for his morning coffee. They got to chatting and eventually he asked her out. She learned that his wife had walked out and left him with a four-year-old daughter and her heart had gone out to him. By that time, Louise was ten and for the last six years Frank had had no social life at all; hurrying home from work each evening to pick Louise up from the childminder or school, make her tea, and put her to bed.

'But now she's beginning to get a bit more independent,' he told her with a smile. 'So maybe I'll be able to get a bit of time to myself.' Not that he ever did. Louise was very demanding. And she always came first. Often when he and Susan had arranged to go out he'd have to ring her and cancel; the reason invariably being something to do with Louise. He'd got into the habit of giving in to her and he couldn't let go.

It was a whirlwind courtship. She and Frank married just six months after their first date. Susan had no family and she looked forward to having a home and family of her own; someone to care for who would care for her in return. But sometimes it seemed that Frank cared only for his daughter.

When Karen arrived things improved. She was such a sweet-natured little baby and Susan was overjoyed to have a baby to love and care for. Louise took little interest in the baby, though Susan told herself that it was understandable. The fourteen-year age gap meant that the girls had little in common.

Karen met Simon at college, and Susan and Frank were delighted when they got engaged. He was a pleasant, steady young man with good prospects in the teaching profession and when baby Peter came along a couple of years later, Susan had been overjoyed. Naturally, Karen wanted to return to her work as a teacher as soon as she could and Susan was thrilled to be asked to step in and care for her little grandson on a regular basis once Karen's maternity leave came to an end. It made her feel useful and needed again now that she was on her own. There was plenty of time for her to do other things in the school holidays and catch up with her hobbies and social life, such as it was.

Susan knew that Louise often visited Karen when she was between acting jobs and although Karen never complained, Susan felt that she took advantage. Not that there was anything she could do about it. Karen never said anything, although she did let drop the occasional telling remark. Privately, Susan thought that although she would never admit it, Louise was envious of Karen's settled lifestyle. She'd made her choice when it seemed she had acting talent and begged to go to drama school. Susan often wondered just how much talent Louise actually had. She certainly hadn't got very far in her chosen career, picking up the odd part in a touring play, a place in the company of a seaside summer show and then of course the inevitable pantomime for a few weeks at Christmas. It all added up to less than a third of the working year and when she was 'resting' as she liked to call it, she fell back on her family's generosity and came to visit.

★   ★   ★

Susan switched on the electric fire. The evenings were getting chilly now. Karen had been looking forward to spending time at home with Peter. Not that she'd been able to enjoy it as she'd hoped. Louise had landed on her doorstep a week last Monday and showed no sign of moving on any time soon. Her stepdaughter hadn't paid her a visit, but then that was par for the course. Susan sometimes felt that she was at the bottom of Louise's list when it came to priorities.

Picking up the *Radio Times*, she saw that there was a gardening programme on in ten minutes' time. She missed her garden sadly, and she still hoped that one day she'd be able to afford a little bungalow with a bit of garden for her to tend. She switched on the TV and settled down to watch. But the opening credits had barely finished when there was a ring at her doorbell. Picking up the entryphone, she heard Louise's voice.

'Hi, Susan. It's me. I'm here on a flying visit and I couldn't leave without coming to see you.'

'Oh, how nice.' Susan pressed the door release. 'Come on up.'

Louise appeared a few minutes later and flung out her arms in her usual affected manner. 'How lovely to see you and how well you're looking.' She enveloped Susan in a hug. 'It's so *good* to see you.'

'It's good to see you too, Louise,' Susan said, extricating herself from Louise's embrace. 'It must be almost a year,' she added pointedly.

Louise looked shocked. 'No. Really? Time flies so, doesn't it? And of course I've been so busy.'

Susan knew perfectly well that Louise had been to stay with Karen at least twice since Louise had last visited her but she let it pass. 'Well, now that you're here, come in and tell me all your news.' She led the way through to the sitting room and Louise took off her coat and sat down on the settee.

'Karrie has been telling me how marvellous you are with little Peter,' she said. 'Rather you than me. Babies have never been my thing as I'm sure you know.' She laughed. 'As a friend of mine puts it — noisy, messy and smelly. It's so good of you to be a free childminder for her. She's so lucky.'

'I'm not a *free* childminder,' Susan corrected. 'Karen insists on paying me the going rate, even though as Peter's grandmother I would willingly do it for nothing. He's such a dear little boy and I adore looking after him.'

'Well, anyway, she's lucky to have you.'

'You must sometimes feel that you'd like a more settled, conventional life, Louise.'

'Me? Good heavens, no!' Louise gave a brittle little laugh. 'Life in suburbia looks like a living death to me. I love living on the edge; the excitement of never knowing what's round the corner.'

'I see, and is there anything round the corner for you at the moment?'

'I'm expecting to hear from my agent any day now,' Louise said. 'There might be something exciting coming up for me.'

Susan had heard all this before. 'Really, so are you going to tell me about it?'

Louise shook her head. 'Not till it's confirmed. I'd hate to jinx it.' She cleared her throat and glanced sideways at her stepmother. 'Actually, Karrie has a bit of a crisis on at the moment. I can see it's a problem for her — me staying there, and I don't want to be a nuisance. So I wondered — could you put me up for a few days?'

23

Susan took a deep breath. Karen had already prepared her but she had always been so bad at saying no. She cleared her throat. 'You realize that I only have one bedroom, don't you, Louise?'

Louise shrugged and patted the seat beside her. 'This sofa is very comfy. I could manage beautifully on it for a few nights.'

'What do you call a few nights?'

Louise's eyebrows rose. 'Susan, just say if it's inconvenient. I just thought that with you being family . . .'

Susan took a deep breath. Karen would be so cross with her if she caved in so easily. 'Forgive me for reminding you, Louise, but you're not hard up, are you? Surely you could afford to rent a small flat for a few weeks, until your agent comes through with this wonderful job?'

'It wouldn't be worth taking on a flat,' Louise told her. 'I'm expecting a call from him any day.' She frowned. 'And actually I *am* quite hard up,' she said. 'Money goes nowhere these days.'

'But you got a good price for the house.'

'You always have to bring that up, don't you? Then you wonder why I don't come to visit you. You don't understand, Susan, an actress has to keep up appearances. I need to buy clothes. Not just any old clothes but designer fashion. I have to be seen around town in all the right places — have my hair done and watch my looks. It would be fatal to let myself go.'

Susan took in what Louise was wearing and told herself that if that was designer wear, standards must have dropped. 'It all sounds quite exhausting,' she said dryly. 'But of course, none of us are getting any younger.'

Louise bridled. 'I'm thirty-five but I think I look at least ten years younger if I do say it myself.'

Susan knew perfectly well that Louise would be forty next birthday but she kept her mouth shut on the subject. 'So you're saying that all of the money you got for the house has gone on clothes and keeping up appearances?'

Louise bridled. 'Quite a bit of it, yes. I do have a nest egg of course but I don't want to touch that. No one knows what the future might bring.'

'Indeed,' Susan said. She didn't bother to add that that was exactly how she had felt when Frank died and the house had been sold from under her. 'I take it you sign on for Jobseeker's when you're not working,' she said.

Louise nodded reluctantly. 'Yes, but you know what a pittance that is.'

'I suppose there's always temporary work.'

'You sound just like Karrie,' Louise said. 'What do you expect me to do, *scrub toilets?*' When Susan smiled and shook her head she added, 'Anyway, I told you, there's a strong possibility of something really exciting coming up any day now. I don't want to miss it because I've taken on some mundane job, do I?'

'I suppose not.'

'Right, so getting back to the point — can you put me up?'

Susan frowned. 'You mentioned that Karen is going through a crisis. What's happened? Should I be worried?'

'No, nothing like that.' Louise paused. 'OK — we've fallen out. It was all about something trivial and I'm sure it will soon blow over, but in the meantime . . . '

'If, as you say, it's only for a few days.'

'At the most.'

'Then I suppose you'd better go and collect your stuff.'

'As a matter of fact, I left my case outside on the landing.'

* * *

Susan loved order and she always felt that when Louise was staying, it was as though the flat was full of people. Although she was sleeping on the sofa, she didn't get up until halfway through the morning. When she did, she used up all the hot water and made full use of the washing machine. The flat was strewn with her belongings and the bathroom was festooned with her drying tights and underwear. It never occurred to her to give a hand with the cleaning or cooking and in the evenings, she hogged the TV remote control, dismissing Susan's taste in programmes as 'boring'. She made absolutely no attempt to help with the shopping, nor did she offer to contribute towards the food bills.

Once the half-term week was over, Susan suggested to Karen that she babysat Peter at her house. It was a relief to get out of the flat although she dreaded the state the flat would be in on her return each evening. She also tried not to think about the heavy telephone bill Louise was running up. She used the landline all the time. It never seemed to occur to her to use her mobile. The worst of it was that most of her calls were long-distance ones to her agent and various other people.

When she ventured to ask if there was any news about the so-called 'exciting prospect', Louise merely shrugged and muttered something vague about 'these things taking time'.

Susan asked Karen why she and Louise had fallen out but her daughter was cagey, shrugging it off as a 'storm in a teacup'.

'If she's taking advantage, Mum, just kick her out,' she said, and although Susan agreed that she would, they both knew that it was easier said than done.

★　★　★

Louise had been at the flat for ten days when Susan began to have a suspicion that the marvellous job she had been so effusive about was either a non-starter or all in her mind. She became quiet and preoccupied and jumped every time the phone rang, racing to be first to pick it up. Then suddenly one evening, her mobile phone trilled out. Rummaging for it in her bag, she listened in breathless anticipation to the voice at the other end and slowly a look of excited relief lit her face. The call seemed to last forever but eventually Louise said goodbye and ended the call and looked at her stepmother, her face wreathed in smiles. Her whole demeanour had changed.

27

'I'll be off tomorrow morning, Susan,' she said cheerily. 'It's been lovely staying with you and I really appreciate it. Thanks a lot.'

Susan's heart leapt. She was going at last! 'Was that your agent?' she asked. 'Was it about the job?'

Louise nodded. 'Well, fingers crossed. There are some details to iron out yet. But anyway, I'll be out of your hair tomorrow.'

She left soon after breakfast, before Susan had left for Karen's.

'Thanks for everything, Susan. I'll be in touch,' she said, pecking her stepmother on the cheek.

'Where will you be staying?' Susan asked.

'With Dianne, an old friend from drama school. She's got a flat in Earl's Court and she's always happy to put me up for a few days. I rang her last night. Would you just ring a taxi for me while I gather my stuff together?'

As she disappeared into the bedroom, Susan lifted the receiver. One more call and it would all be over.

Ten minutes later, she watched from the window as Louise stepped into a taxi down in the street.

She was bursting with her news as she took off her coat later at Karen's.

'She's gone,' she said briefly, knowing there was no need to elaborate.

'Louise — gone? Just like that?'

'Just like that. She had a phone call yesterday evening and announced right after it that she was leaving this morning. She's gone already.'

'So — is it a job, or what?'

'I asked that. She just said something about an exciting possibility.'

'I take it she'll be sponging on her friend, Dianne, again.'

'She did say she'd be staying with her, yes.'

'Oh well, at least you've got your home to yourself again. I'm sorry, Mum. I'm afraid it was partly my fault you got saddled with her.'

'I wish you'd tell me what you quarrelled about.'

'Maybe I will one of these days,' Karen said, putting her coat on. 'For now, just be thankful that she's gone. If you've got any sense you'll say no next time she asks to stay. I'm going to. It's time we left her in no doubt about how we both feel, Mum. She's always ridden roughshod over us and it's time we called a halt to her freeloading. After all, she can't be hard up.' She kissed her mother's cheek briefly. 'Thanks, Mum. I'll have to dash now.'

What Karen said made good sense. It was high time they told Louise a few home truths. But she had the distinct feeling that Louise would find a way to be the injured party when they did. Somehow she always did.

4

It was my fourth birthday that day. I'd had a party and I was really sleepy when I went to bed but something woke me. Rising up the stairs, I heard my parents' raised voices. I couldn't make out the words, just the frightening tone of their voices, sharp and ugly with anger; Mum's shrill and Dad's hoarse and rough. They were rowing again. I felt my heartbeat quicken and my tummy churned sickeningly. Pulling the covers over my head, I stuck my fingers in my ears. I must have gone to sleep again because suddenly it was morning and I was awake. Slipping out of bed, I padded through every room on my bare feet, searching the whole house for Mum. When I couldn't find her, a wild panic filled my chest.

'*Mum!*' I heard myself screaming. 'I want Mum!'

'Lou — *Lou*, wake up!'

Someone was shaking my shoulder.

'Lou, you're dreaming again. Wake up now, love, everything's all right.'

I opened my eyes to see Dianne standing beside the bed. My heart was still pounding but I took a deep breath and sat up, shaking my head. 'Sorry, Di. Did I wake you? Was I shouting again?'

'Yes. I don't know what those nightmares are about but they certainly seem to terrify you.' Dianne sat down on the side of the bed.

'I've had them on and off for most of my life,' I admitted. 'They usually recur when I'm nervous about something.' I pulled myself up into a sitting position. 'My parents used to have these horrendous rows when I was little and I'd wake and hear them.'

'They must have scared you pretty badly if they're still affecting you.'

'They did. Then one morning my mum wasn't there any more. I never saw her again.' I shuddered, my stomach still churning at the memory of the dream. 'When I was about eight I started getting bullied at school. The other kids said my dad had killed her and buried her body in the garden. That gave me even worse nightmares. Then, on my ninth birthday I got a card from her so I knew it wasn't true. She'd written her address on it. I managed to keep the card but I never got to see the letter she enclosed with it; Dad tore it up and wouldn't let me read it.'

Dianne laid a hand on my shoulder. 'Shall I make you a cup of tea?'

I shook my head. 'No. I'll be OK once the dream has faded.'

'You're seeing this mystery guy tomorrow, aren't you?' Dianne observed. 'Is that what you're nervous about? You didn't tell me much about it last night.'

'There's a lot hanging on it.'

'You've never really told me much about him — or this project he's planning.'

'It's not really a mystery. I haven't said anything because I didn't want to jinx it. You

31

know how superstitious I am. I didn't mention it to anyone at home. They don't have a very high opinion of me or my talent and they probably wouldn't have believed me anyway. When I was down in Devon in the summer with the Sunshine Follies, Harry came down and brought this guy along. His name is Paul Fortune. He's a musician and composer and he's written this musical called *Oh, Elizabeth*. It's based on Jane Austen's *Pride and Prejudice*. Harry brought him backstage afterwards and apparently Paul had been quite impressed by me in the show. He said that he saw me as the perfect actress to play Elizabeth Bennet.'

'Wow!' Dianne's eyes widened. 'So is it him — this Paul Thingummy that you're meeting tomorrow?'

'Yes, I'm having lunch with him and Harry. There was some ground-laying work he had to do before going ahead, like booking venues and rehearsal rooms — setting up advertising and so on, which is why it's taken so long, but now it seems it's all systems go. The show kicks off in the provinces and then — fingers crossed — eventually moves into the West End.'

'It sounds like a great opportunity,' Dianne said. 'And I do wish you the best of luck. You're sure there are no strings attached, aren't you?'

I laughed. 'No, of course there aren't. Harry's hinted that he might ask me to put up a small amount of the money, but that's not a problem. I've still got most of the cash I got for the house stashed away.' I looked at Di. 'You know how old I am and how long I've been waiting for a break.

32

This could be it; my last chance at making the big time.'

Dianne looked doubtful. 'Mmm, I'd be a bit careful if I were you. How much do you know about this guy?'

'Basically just that he's someone my agent knows. But Harry and I go back a long way and I trust him.'

'I see. What was your initial gut feeling when you met him — this Paul Fortune?'

'Frankly, wow, what a hunk!' I giggled. 'The three of us went out to dinner after the show and Paul and I hit it off like a house on fire right from the off.'

'Are you saying you slept with him?'

'Oh come on, give me *some* credit. They were only there the one night. Even I don't work that fast.'

Dianne wrinkled her nose. 'Just be careful, Lou. I know how much you want to grab what looks like a great opportunity and I also know how impulsive you can be. Just how much of your money is he after, if you don't mind me asking?'

'I've no idea, he might not want much at all,' I hedged. 'Anyway, it seems that every cast member will be putting a share in and we'll all get it back, plus dividends when the show takes off.'

'*If* the show takes off.'

'Oh, come on, Di, don't pour cold water on it. What makes you such a cynic? I don't understand you. You were one of the most talented students in our year,' I told her. 'With your looks and talent, you could have been a star by now if you hadn't given the idea of a stage career the elbow.'

'Or I could have been penniless and homeless. The theatre is far too precarious for my liking, Lou, and in spite of what you say I never really felt I had any real talent. As it is I've got a good steady job that I enjoy, a nice flat and a reliable income and I still enjoy a bit of amateur work.'

I grinned at her. 'Bor-ing. Still, whatever floats your boat, I suppose.'

'Do you think it's a subconscious anxiety about this project that's causing you to have these nightmares about your childhood?'

'No. I get them from time to time. As for this new musical, I can't wait.' I paused, wondering whether to voice the thought that was in my mind. 'I think I know what is causing them, though. Since Dad died I've been thinking a lot about my mother, wondering if she's still alive and what she's doing. I've had this really strong feeling that I'd like to find her again.'

'Why, when she let you down so badly? It's an awful long time ago and after all, you've got Karen and your stepmum.'

I shook my head. 'They've never felt like a real family to me. I've always felt like the odd one out. As a kid I felt resentful that they'd stolen Dad away from me. I think he understood that. It was probably why he left me the house. And I've never been able to shake off the feeling that the split might have been my fault.'

Dianne shook her head. 'You were only a little kid. How could it have been your fault?'

'I don't know. It's just a feeling. I suppose all kids from broken marriages feel like it. Anyway, I'd like to know the real reason for the split and only she can tell me.'

'OK, so if you want to try and find her why don't you go ahead? It shouldn't be that difficult.'

'I wouldn't know where to start.'

'They say that the Salvation Army is good at finding people. You could try them for starters.'

'Well, maybe,' I said. 'But she could have married again — have a different name. Thinking about it and doing it are two different things. Anyway, my main priority right now is my meeting with Paul tomorrow.'

'Have you ever talked to anyone about it?'

'Trying to find my mother, you mean?' I shook my head. 'Susan and Karen wouldn't understand. Neither of them ever met my mum. Dad married Susan when I was ten and there are too many years between Karen and me for us to feel like sisters. Anyway, she's as different from me as chalk from cheese. She and her precious Simon are so bourgeois and horrendously smug with it. They always make me long to shock them out of their complacency.' I bit my lip at the memory of the shoplifting episode. I'd never gone over the top quite that far before. It was a lot worse than a wind-up and I baulked at telling Dianne about it. She'd never understand. 'I'm afraid I can't resist rattling her cage,' I said lightly. 'Old habits die hard.'

'Mmm.' Dianne smiled ruefully. 'I remember the practical jokes you used to play at drama school; quite merciless, some of them. But going back to your family — Susan's always been a good stepmum, hasn't she?'

'I suppose so. She's a bit of a pushover though. She never comes out with what she's really thinking — just makes bland comments.'

'Which — if I know you — makes you even more secretive?'

I couldn't help grinning. 'You're right. I try to keep in touch. I visit whenever I can but quite frankly, I don't think any of them would give a damn if they never saw me again.'

'I'm sure that's not true.' Dianne glanced at the alarm clock. 'Look, it's past one. Maybe we should both get some sleep now.'

★   ★   ★

Dianne looked in before she left for work at eight o'clock the following morning.

'Here, I've brought you a black coffee.' She put the cup on the bedside table. 'Don't go back to sleep.'

I emerged from under the duvet and tried to force my eyes open. 'Thanks, Di, you're an angel. I'll get up and have a cold shower when I've drunk it. That should wake me up.'

'Well, good luck.' Dianne hesitated in the doorway. 'Lou — if you get a few spare minutes before you leave, could you tidy up a bit?'

I bit my lip. 'Sorry, Di. I know I'm a slob. If I get time I'll put some of my stuff away.'

'Great. And while I remember, there isn't a scrap of food left in the fridge so maybe on your

36

way home you could pop into the supermarket and get something for tea. I'll have to dash now. Bye for now.'

When I'd showered I did my best to tidy up the stuff I'd left lying about in Di's living room. It wasn't that bad and I felt slightly resentful that she'd actually asked me to do it. I'd have sorted it eventually, and this morning I had other things on my mind.

Once I'd stuffed the last pair of tights down the back of the sofa and hung the towels back on the bathroom rail, I set about preparing for the coming meeting. In spite of what I'd told Susan, I actually only possessed one decent designer outfit, a classic black suit by Chanel. I washed my hair and borrowed Di's hairdryer to blow-dry it. Twisting it up into the French pleat I peered at the roots. I should really have had them touched up but it was too late to worry about it now. It would have to do. Five years ago, a brightening rinse would have been enough to revive its vitality but now the dreaded greys were all too evident and I was till trying to ignore the faint lines that had begun to appear round my mouth. Sitting at the dressing table, I half-closed my eyes and regarded my reflection, thinking about Jane Austen's Elizabeth Bennet, the part I was hoping to get. It would mean dropping almost twenty years. The one and only time Paul Fortune had seen me on stage I was wearing a glamorous evening gown and full stage slap, then later at the restaurant seated opposite him at a candlelit dinner table. When he saw me in the cold light of day, would he change his mind about offering me the part?

I took a deep breath and reached into my bag for the little sapphire necklace that I'd relieved Susan of. It had belonged to my mother. I remembered seeing her wearing it and it should have been mine by right anyway, so when I saw it lying on her dressing table I had no feeling of guilt about taking it. I decided to wear it now — for luck. Fastening it round my neck, I slipped it inside the neck of my top. Then I laid out the collection of concealers, foundations and blushers that would hopefully bring about the necessary transformation.

★ ★ ★

The table for lunch had been booked at an Italian restaurant in the Strand. In my eagerness I arrived too early. Anxious not to appear too keen, I disappeared into the ladies' and lost some time reapplying my lipstick and fussing with my hair. When I decided I was just late enough to appear relaxed yet not impolite, I gathered up all my courage and made my way to the bar.

I spotted them at once and sighed with relief. At least they had turned up. Pausing, a little out of their line of vision, I assessed them both. They looked an unlikely pair; bald, bespectacled Harry in his usual formal dark-grey suit and tie; Paul in jeans and a black roll-neck sweater, his dark hair longish and flopping slightly over his brow. I took a deep breath and breezed in.

'Hello, you two. I'm so sorry I'm late. I had such a job finding a taxi.'

Paul stood up and offered his hand. 'How nice to meet you again, Louise. What can I get you to drink?'

I hardly tasted my lunch. In fact I can't even remember what I ordered. I was too busy assessing Paul's thoughts and wondering if he still felt the same about offering me the part. As soon as the dessert had been served, Harry made his excuses.

'I hate to eat and run but I'm afraid I'm going to have to leave you two now,' he said, getting up from the table. 'I've got an important meeting at two. But I'm sure you can manage without me.' He smiled. 'Let me know how your meeting goes,' he whispered in my ear as he bent to drop a formal kiss on my cheek.

'I'll be in touch.' I smiled up at him.

When he'd gone Paul asked if I'd like a liqueur. I shook my head. 'I won't, thanks. It's a bit early in the day. But don't let me stop you.'

'I don't want any more to drink either,' he said. 'I prefer to keep a clear head.' As he glanced at his watch I wondered if, like Harry, he was about to make an excuse to leave, but he looked at me enquiringly. 'Look — if you're not doing anything else this afternoon, would you like to come back to the flat with me? I could play you some of the numbers I've written for the show and you could have a copy of the script to take home and read. What do you say?'

What did I *say*? I was absolutely thrilled. He hadn't written me off after all. 'That would be lovely,' I said, trying not to appear too keen. 'I'd love to hear some of your music.'

His flat was on the top floor of a fashionable block in Kensington. He opened the door into the living room, which contained a grand piano and a couple of black leather sofas. I tried not to let him see how impressed I was. Going over to the piano he picked up a copy of the music, complete with words, and handed it to me.

'Have a seat. I'll run through a couple of songs and then perhaps you'd like to try them out.'

My heart was thumping as he ran his fingers over the keys. If this was an audition it was the most unusual one I'd ever had. He ran his hands over the keys and then broke into the first theme. I don't read music so I tried hard to memorize the tune. Luckily, it was quite a simple melody and the words seemed to fit well. When I got up to stand beside him at the piano, my knees were trembling but I got through the first verse without stumbling and he looked quite pleased.

'That was great, Louise. Shall we try another? There's a nice duet between Elizabeth and Darcy. I'll take Darcy's part if you like, though I warn you, I'm no Pavarotti.'

The duet was pleasant and although I was nervous it seemed to go quite well. When it was over Paul smiled up at me.

'I know it's early days but I've got a really strong feeling that we're going to have a hit on our hands.'

My mouth was dry as I asked, 'Is this an audition, Paul?'

He looked surprised. 'I think we've passed that stage. I already knew you could sing. The part is yours — if you want it, that is. I thought that was a foregone conclusion.'

I felt my colour rise. 'I see. Well, of course I want the part.'

'Right, that's settled, then.' He got up from the piano. 'Shall we break for a cup of tea?'

'I'd love one. Can I do anything to help?'

The kitchen was very modern and minimalist with every labour-saving gadget imaginable. While he put the kettle on I found cups and saucers and laid a tray.

'This is a beautiful apartment,' I remarked.

He nodded. 'It's nice and central. It suits me very well.'

'I love the songs,' I said. 'What I've heard so far, that is. Have you gone very far with the casting?'

'It's almost complete,' he told me. 'I'm producing myself as well as being musical director, naturally. I do still have to get a director but I have a very good one in mind. I can't tell you who yet. It's always difficult to get a big-name director when you don't plan to put a big star in the leading role.'

I looked at him. 'Yes, I was going to ask you about that.'

'*You* are going to be my star, Louise,' he said. 'If the show really takes off, as I believe it will, your face is going to be on the front of all the magazines.' He left me for a moment to absorb this heady prospect and for a second I wondered if he could hear my excited heart drumming from across the room. Then he asked casually, 'Did I tell you that I've arranged a read-through for next week?'

'No,' I said, my mouth dry. It was all gathering momentum even faster than I'd expected.

'I hope you'll be free to come.'

'Of course I will. Just tell me where and when.'

Over the tea and biscuits he asked me about myself and I outlined my career, trying to boost it up and make it sound better than it actually was. He asked me about my family too, which surprised me. I told him how my mother had walked out when I was very young and how I intended to try to find her again. He was sympathetic.

'Well, once you're a West End star I've no doubt she'll want to know you,' he said with a smile. As he poured a second cup of tea for both of us he asked, 'Louise — there was some mention of you putting some money into the show . . .'

I nodded. 'Yes. I'm not wealthy but I could manage a little.'

'The rest of the cast are chipping in,' he went on. 'It's because at the moment I don't have a backer. Again it's the start thing, but I hope to get someone interested very soon. It's just to get the ball rolling and the loans will all be paid back as soon as possible — with interest of course.'

'Naturally.'

He paused, biting his lip. 'I hate to ask, but have you any idea how much your input might be?'

I did some quick sums in my head. 'I take it there'll be no salary during the rehearsal period,' I said tentatively.

'Well, no, I'm afraid not.'

I gave him the figure that was in my head. 'Don't take that as positive,' I added. 'I'll have to work out what I'll need to live on. I'll do it later this evening when I get home.'

He looked pleasantly surprised. 'That — or something like it — would be very generous,' he said. 'But think of it as an investment. Once we get into the West End the cash should start rolling in.'

★ ★ ★

I couldn't wait for Di to get home. I was longing to tell her that all her misgivings were unfounded and that the new musical was going to be a hit. The moment she got in I began.

'I've had the most exciting day,' I told her. 'It was perfect. After lunch, Paul took me back to his flat. You should see it, Di. It's in Kensington; the last word in luxury and it . . . '

'Great,' she interrupted as she took off her coat. 'So what did you get for tea?' She shook the raindrops off her coat and hung it up without looking at me. 'I'm starving. I didn't have time for lunch and . . . ' She turned and caught my expression.

Tea! I'd completely forgotten about the supermarket. I bit my lip. How could she expect me to think about mundane things like food after the exciting day I'd had?

'Oh — I'm sorry, Di,' I mumbled. 'I forgot.'

She stared at me. 'You forgot! Oh, really, Lou. Surely it's not asking too much for you to pop into Tesco on your way home for a few bits.'

I was shocked at her response. 'I *said* I'm sorry. Surely you can rustle up something just for tonight.'

'Well, no, I can't actually. The fridge is completely empty, thanks to you and your constant snacking while I'm out at work. Perhaps you could pop out now and get something. I don't care what, just as long as it's edible.'

I stared at her. 'But it's raining!'

'Yes, oddly enough I noticed that on the way home when I got soaked,' she said with unnecessary sarcasm.

'You're serious, aren't you?'

'Never more so.'

Furious, I reached for my coat. 'There's a mini-market up the road,' I snapped. 'Will that do for you?'

She shrugged. 'Like I said — as long as it's edible and *you*'re paying, it's fine.'

On the way to the corner shop my temper cooled a little. It was good of Di to let me stay and if she decided to throw me out it would make life difficult; that, I had to admit. Maybe I should have made more of an effort; after all, if I had to find other accommodation now before the provincial tour began, it would be expensive and with my contribution to the show I was going to have to watch the pennies. Reluctantly, I acknowledged that I was going to have to pocket my pride.

At the corner shop I bought a packet of pasta and a jar of sauce; a tin of peaches and a carton of cream. Then, on second thoughts, I bought a box of chocolates. Keeping on the right side of

Di seemed the diplomatic way to go under the circumstances.

Back at the flat she seemed to have calmed down too. My purchases seemed to satisfy her and when I gave her the chocolates and apologized for forgetting to shop earlier, she shook her head.

'Thanks. It's all right, Lou. I'm sorry too if I was a bit sharp but I've had a pig of a day at the office.' She put a pan of water on for the pasta and opened the jar of sauce. 'I know you're dying to tell me all your news but there are a couple of things I'd like to clear up first.'

'OK, like what?' I said, my back to her as I began to lay the table. I had the distinct feeling I wasn't going to like what she was about to say.

'Well, if you're planning to stay on for a while that's fine. You know you're always welcome, but I'm going to have to ask you to contribute to the bills — food and so on.'

'Oh — OK then.' Fair enough, I thought. Maybe I had been taking advantage a bit.

'And — maybe a little towards the rent.'

'Right.' *The rent!* What else was she going to ask for?

'And — I hate having to mention this, Lou, but do you think you could try and be a bit tidier around the place?'

I bit back a sharp retort. I'd always thought of Di as my best friend. Now all at once she was behaving more like some sort of nanny. But I didn't really have a choice but to agree to her terms if I wanted to stay. I forced a smile. 'OK, Di,' I said through clenched teeth. 'Sorry if I've been making your home look like a tip.'

She didn't argue, seeming to miss the irony. Smiling, she said, 'Well, that's got that out of the way. Now — are you going to tell me about your day while we wait for the pasta to cook?'

Somehow she failed to see that she'd just taken most of the shine off it.

5

'Come into the kitchen and sit down, Mum. I've got something to tell you.'

Susan had just brought Peter home from a trip into town to see Father Christmas. It hadn't been a success. To her horror he'd been terrified and ran screaming from the scarlet-clad figure into his grandmother's arms, without even waiting for his gift. All the way home on the bus he'd been inconsolable and now he stood clutching Susan's hand, his lip trembling. She was shocked that Karen hadn't even noticed his distress.

'Can we just get Peter his tea first?' she asked. 'He's a bit upset.'

For the first time Karen looked down at her son. 'What's the matter with him?'

Susan frowned and shook her head in an attempt to play the situation down but Karen persisted. Crouching down to the little boy's level she asked, 'What's the matter, baby? Don't you feel very well?'

Peter shook his head. 'Don't like man,' he said, a tear rolling down his cheek.

Karen looked up accusingly at Susan. 'What man? What happened?'

Susan sighed. 'I took him to Harvey's to see Santa but Peter was afraid of him.'

Karen picked Peter up and dried his tears. 'Really, Mum,' she said over his head. 'What were you thinking? He's far too young for that kind of thing.'

'I remember taking you at that age and you loved it. I'm sorry. I did tell him beforehand where we were going and he seemed to be looking forward to it.'

Peter soon cheered up at the promise of a boiled egg and soldiers and it was while Karen was tying on his bib that Susan asked, 'So — what was it you wanted to talk to me about?'

'Oh, yes.' Karen looked up, a finger of wholemeal bread halfway to Peter's open mouth. 'I just wanted to say that we won't need you to babysit Peter after next week.'

'Oh!' Susan was stunned. 'So have you decided to go along with what Simon wants?'

'What do you mean?'

'I take it you're giving up work till Peter is older?'

'Good heavens, no, I'm not!' Karen said firmly. We're getting an au pair.'

Susan's eyebrows rose. 'An *au pair* — from abroad, you mean? To live in?'

'That's what au pair means, yes. She's Dutch. I always think they're very homely people, the Dutch, don't you?'

'I don't think I know any,' Susan said faintly. 'Where did you find her?'

'Online, but of course we've spoken on the telephone.'

'Since when have you been able to speak Dutch?'

'I don't, of course, as you very well know, Mum. Adrey — that's her name — speaks

48

perfect English. I'd hardly be employing someone Peter couldn't understand, would I?'

'So I'm to be surplus to requirements after next week, then, am I?'

Karen sighed. 'Oh dear, I did hope you wouldn't take it like that, Mum.'

'How else did you think I'd take it? I thought you were happy with our arrangement. Have I done something wrong?'

'No, of course you haven't and I — we are really grateful for all you've done. It's just that Simon has been really stuffy about me going back to work so soon. As you know, he's always been adamant about Peter going to a nursery while he was still so young and he's got all these archaic ideas about a woman's place.'

'So you're making a stand?'

'I suppose you could call it that, yes.'

'And Simon's all right with this au pair thing, is he?'

Karen wiped Peter's mouth and replaced his empty plate with a bowl of mashed banana which she began to spoon into his eager mouth. 'We've come to an agreement. He's been complaining that the house isn't as spick and span as it was before, and he says he's fed up with convenience food although we only have ready-meals very occasionally. Adrey will do the housework and some of the cooking as well as taking care of Peter, so he could hardly argue on those counts.'

'Can you afford it?'

'As long as I'm working, yes.'

'And what about your privacy?'

'We're going to make the spare room into a bedsit.'

'And suppose you don't like each other or she proves to be unsuitable? Once she's here it'll be difficult to get rid of her, won't it?'

Karen had the grace to look slightly embarrassed. 'As a matter of fact, she came over last weekend for that very reason and we all got along very well. She's a lovely girl, very practical and down to earth. And most important, Peter seemed to take to her right away.'

'I see, so it's all set in stone, then?'

'Oh, don't be offended, Mum. I didn't want to tell you until we were sure it was the right way to go.'

'Until *you* were sure it was the right way to go,' Susan corrected. 'I'm still not convinced that Simon approves of your plan. It doesn't sound like his kind of thing at all to me.'

'Well, it'll have to be and that's that!' Karen said. 'Anyway, I reminded him that if the spare room was occupied we wouldn't be able to accommodate Louise any more.' She smiled. 'It was my trump card and it seemed to seal the deal.'

'I suppose that means *I'll* have to put her up.'

Karen wiped Peter's mouth, took off his bib and lifted him out of his highchair. 'There you are, darling. Off you go and play for a while till bath time.' As he scampered away she looked at Susan. 'I had a text from Louise last week. It seems she got that part she was hoping for in this new musical show so I don't think we'll be seeing her again for a while.'

'A text, eh? That's more than I got — not so

much as a phone call or a postcard. Did she mention anything about Christmas?'

'Not a thing.'

'Well, at least that's a relief.' Susan stood up. 'I'd better be getting home. It's dark so early these evenings and the buses get full up at the rush hour.'

'I'd run you home but Simon's not in yet and I can't leave Peter.'

'Of course you can't. I wouldn't dream of putting you out.'

Karen shot a quick look at her mother as she walked to the door with her. 'Mum, please don't think we're not grateful for all you've done since I went back to work. I couldn't have managed without you. But you know, you're not getting any younger and an energetic toddler must be tiring for you.'

Susan bridled. 'I'm not *ninety*, Karen. If Peter had been too much I'd have said.'

Karen bit her lip. 'I'm not sure that you would. Anyway, you know what I mean, Mum.' She laid a hand on Susan's arm. 'You should be enjoying life — making new friends, joining things.'

'Like bingo or a sewing circle, you mean?'

Karen chuckled and gave her arm a push. 'If that's what turns you on!'

Susan laughed in spite of herself. 'Well, I hope this new scheme of yours turns out well. But if it doesn't you know where I am. I'm not one to bear grudges. At least, not where my grandson is concerned.'

Karen kissed her cheek. 'Thanks, Mum. You're a real treasure.'

* ★ *

Susan queued in an icy drizzle for fifteen minutes before a bus finally turned up. As she climbed aboard, she saw that it was standing room only and she gave a resigned sigh as she grabbed a strap.

'Please, do have my seat. I'm getting off soon.'

A distinguished-looking man with thick silvery hair was easing himself out into the crowded aisle beside her. He wore a belted trench coat and carried a furled umbrella. Susan looked up into the smiling brown eyes and felt herself blush.

'Oh — well, thank you very much but there's really no need. I'm not going very far.'

He inclined his head. 'I insist.'

Susan sank gratefully into the seat and smiled up at him 'Thank you.'

Although he didn't speak again, Susan was acutely aware of him standing next to her in the crowded bus and to her surprise as she stood up at her stop, she saw that he was already alighting onto the pavement. Turning and noticing her, he held out an arm to help her down.

'Please, allow me. Do you have far to walk?' he asked.

Susan shook her head. 'I live in the flats; Snowden House. It's on the next corner.'

'Then please share my umbrella. I'm going the same way. I'll walk along with you. You can't be too careful after dark these days.' He looked down at her with a wry smile. 'Listen to me! No doubt you're wondering why you should trust a man you've never set eyes on before.'

Susan felt herself blushing again and was grateful for the dusky half-light.

'Not at all. You're quite right and I'm very grateful. You hear of so many muggings and handbag snatches that I don't venture out much in the evening, this time of year.'

'Very wise. I don't normally use the bus but my car is in for servicing today so I don't suppose you've ever set eyes on me before.' He smiled down at her. 'I've noticed you on several occasions though,' he confessed as they walked along the pavement. 'I've seen you with a little boy in a pushchair, at the corner shop and occasionally in the park.'

'That's Peter, my little grandson,' she told him. 'I take care of him while my daughter is at work. She's a teacher.' Suddenly she remembered that her services had just been discontinued and added, 'Well, that is to say I *used* to take care of him.'

'Used to?' He looked down at her. 'But surely he's too young for school?'

'My daughter and son-in-law are getting an au pair; a Dutch girl. Karen, my daughter, thinks I'm past it.'

He laughed out loud. 'Good heavens, these young people! *Past it*, indeed. The very idea!'

They reached the corner of the street and the entrance to Snowden House.

'This is me,' Susan said. 'Thank you so much for seeing me home. There aren't many gentlemen around nowadays, more's the pity.'

He looked up at the small block of flats. 'It looks very nice but I'm afraid I couldn't bear to

53

live in a flat,' he said. 'I love my garden too much.'

'I've only been here a year,' she told him. 'And I miss my garden too. One of these days I'm going to buy myself a nice little bungalow with a garden.' Remembering Karen's bombshell she added, 'Now that I won't be taking Peter out, I won't get enough exercise. I don't like going for walks by myself and I hate those jolly hockey sticks keep-fit classes.'

'I run a gardening club at the local college,' he told her. 'I know you don't have a garden yet but you'd be very welcome to join — ready for when you get one.' Reaching into an inside pocket, he took out a card and handed it to her. 'The details are on there along with my telephone number. Think about it and give me a ring.'

Susan stared down at the card, unable to make out any details in the rapidly fading light. 'Thank you. It sounds really interesting. But surely you'll be closing for the Christmas break soon?'

'We still have a couple of sessions to go. If you're interested you could treat it as a taster. No charge of course. Well, I mustn't keep you standing here in the cold any longer,' he said. 'Give it some thought.' He held out his hand. 'I'm Edward Mumford by the way — Ted.'

Susan took the proffered hand and found it large and strong. A typical gardener's hand, she mused. 'Lovely to meet you. I'm Susan,' she told him. 'Susan Davies.'

6

The venue for the read-through was in a run-down church hall in Stoke Newington and I had a hell of a job to find it. When I finally tracked it down, in a scruffy back street, I was fifteen minutes late, hot and out of breath. The door creaked like something out of a budget horror film as I let myself in, and the atmosphere of damp mustiness nearly took my breath away. I needn't have worried about being late. Paul clearly hadn't arrived yet. In one corner of the large empty space, an assorted bunch of out-of-work actors sat on a semicircle of chairs next to an ancient upright piano; all of them half-hidden behind newspapers. They barely looked up as I entered and I didn't recognize any of them.

As I crossed the hall in my high-heeled shoes, my footsteps echoed embarrassingly on the bare floor and one of the assembled group looked up from her paper.

'Hi there! Are you here for the read-through?' I forced a smile at the middle-aged woman, taking in the tatty fake-fur coat and jeans. Her hair, an unlikely flame colour, was tied back with a purple scrunchie. She didn't look much like Jane Austen material.

'Yes. I'm playing the leading part actually,' I told her. What part could *she* possibly be playing? I asked myself. Although it was only a read-through, I'd made a special effort with my appearance this morning but she looked as though she'd thrown on the first thing she'd picked up off the floor.

'Really? Good for you. Come and sit down. I'm Carla Dean and I'm playing Mrs Bennet.' She looked me up and down critically and chuckled. 'Odd, that, isn't it? Seeing that we're obviously about the same age.'

I chose to ignore the barbed remark. 'Is there any coffee?' I asked through clenched teeth.

She laughed. 'Coffee? You must be joking, darling. Don't know if you've noticed but this is hardly the Ritz. I'm afraid you'll have to wait till after. I think there's a café round the corner.' Her voice was deep and throaty and she exuded a powerful odour of tobacco.

'Is Paul here?' I asked as I took a seat.

'Not yet.' Carla opened her bag and took out a packet of cigarettes. 'I'm going to slip outside for a drag.' She offered me the packet. 'Join me?'

'No, thanks. I don't smoke,' I told her stiffly. 'I try to look after my voice.'

'OK, suit yourself,' Carla said good-naturedly as she stood up. 'Looks as though His Lordship's going to be late.' She crossed the hall, her scuffed trainers making no sound on the bare boards. As she reached the door, it opened to admit a man. Everyone perked up with a rustle of newspapers, but when they saw that it wasn't Paul they relaxed again. As he came closer my heart gave a leap of recognition.

'*Mark!*' I said. 'Mark Naylor!'

His face broke into a smile. 'If it isn't little

56

Lou Davies. What a lovely surprise. Bloody hell! I haven't set eyes on you since drama school. How long is it — twenty years?'

'Nowhere near! Don't exaggerate.' I glanced around, hoping no one else had heard his crashingly tactless remark. 'And actually, it's Louise Delmar nowadays,' I added, lowering my voice.

He pulled a comically apologetic face. 'Whoops — sorry — on both counts.' He fetched a chair from the stack in the corner and sat down beside me. 'Well, this *is* a surprise,' he said. 'How did you get involved in this little epic?'

'In the usual way — through my agent,' I told him. 'I'm playing Elizabeth.'

His eyebrows rose. 'The lead, no less. Wow! Good for you.'

'What about you?'

'Wickham,' he said. 'Not much of a singing part but then I'm not much of a singer.' He nudged my shoulder. 'So — what have you been up to all these years? I must say you look as if you've done all right. Come on, tell me all about yourself.'

'I haven't done too badly,' I told him non-committally.

He glanced down at my hands. 'Married?'

'Good heavens, no! You?'

'Need you ask? You blighted my love life forever. After you turned me down, I never looked at anyone else.'

I laughed. 'I don't believe a word of it.' Mark had been besotted with me when we were at drama school — used to follow me around like a

57

lost puppy. I'd been fond of him too. He was always such fun, but he didn't have a lot going for him. He wasn't blessed with looks and he had neither cash nor influence, all of which were important to me back then. Well, still are. When he asked me to marry him and I turned him down, he insisted in his over-the-top, flamboyant way that I'd broken his heart. To be honest, I was never all that certain that he was serious. Most people thought he was gay, although I knew from experience that he most definitely wasn't. Once we left our paths hadn't crossed again — till now.

I opened my mouth to answer him but before I could reply, the door creaked opened to admit Carla, accompanied by Paul Fortune. Feet shuffled and newspapers were hastily folded away as the rest of the cast came to life. Paul apologized for his lateness.

'Sorry, folks,' he said. 'Had a string of phone calls just as I was about to leave. Are we all here?' He looked round and his eyes alighted on me. 'Ah, Louise. Glad you could make it.'

Mark nudged me. 'Ooh! Looks like you're well in there, sweetie.'

'He saw me in a show I was in a couple of months ago and offered me the part on the spot,' I told him, massaging the truth slightly. 'We've had lunch together a couple of times — along with Harry, my agent, of course.'

'Oh, of *course*.' He treated me to his quizzical, lopsided grin. 'You'll be telling me next that you haven't been to his flat on your own.'

I gave him my enigmatic smile. 'Just the once.'

58

'Snap!' he said with a flash of his sharp blue eyes.

I felt my eyebrows shoot up. '*You've* been too?' I wanted to ask more but Paul was handing round the scripts.

'With your permission, I'll run through the songs for you before we start reading. Just so that you can get an idea of the melodies,' he said. He pulled a face as he lifted the lid of the piano to expose the discoloured keyboard. He placed his music on the dusty stand. 'I'd better apologize in advance,' he said. 'I've got a feeling this old girl isn't exactly a Steinway.'

'Or even a Yamaha,' Carla quipped. A half-hearted ripple of laughter went round the rest of the cast and I nudged Mark. 'She's playing Mrs Bennet,' I whispered. 'She thinks she's Judi Dench!'

Mark smothered his splutter of laughter behind his hand. '*Behave!*' he whispered back.

★ ★ ★

The read-through went off reasonably well and when it was over, Paul seemed quite pleased.

'Sorry, people, but I'm going to have to rush,' he said as he crammed his music into his briefcase. 'I've got all your addresses so I'll post you a rehearsal schedule as soon as. Do please start learning your lines. We'll start working on the songs once we all get together with a decent piano. It won't be till after Christmas now. Have a good holiday, all of you.'

As we packed up our scripts I turned to Mark.

'I don't know about you but I'm spitting feathers. Do you fancy a coffee?'

He nodded. 'You bet.'

I glanced across to where Carla Dean was deep in conversation with another member of the cast. 'Quick,' I said, grabbing Mark's arm. 'Let's get the hell out of here before we get stuck with her.'

We found a decent-looking pub and ended up ordering lunch from the tempting-looking menu. As we waited with our much-needed drinks, Mark took his coat off and for the first time I noticed his expensive, well-cut trousers and cashmere sweater. In our student days, he wore tattered jeans and T-shirts. As he reached out a hand for his drink, I also noticed the Rolex watch on his wrist.

'You look very prosperous,' I remarked. 'Have you been successful, or just lucky?'

He grinned and lifted his whisky and soda with a flourish. 'Here's to us, darling.' He took a sip and looked thoughtful. 'Successful or lucky? Mmm, I guess I've had a bit of both. I've had a few small parts in touring plays. You don't get rich on that but it was enough to keep me ticking over. No, the best break I had was when an uncle of mine died. He'd made a lot of money in his day — out of pet food, would you believe. He'd never married or had a family and he didn't leave a will, so as his next of kin I copped for the whole shebang.'

'Well, well! Pet food, eh?' I raised my gin and tonic. 'Congratulations. Here's to my very own pedigree chum!'

60

He laughed. 'Nicely put. I see you haven't lost your razor-sharp wit!'

'So — I expect you live in a stately home in Surrey or somewhere.'

'No.' He shook his head. 'Part of the legacy was my uncle's apartment in Stanmore. It was nicely furnished and equipped so I just moved in there. It's quite handy for the Tube. I can get up to the West End in half an hour.' He took a sip of his drink.

I studied him over the rim of my glass. 'So — now that you're in the money, why on earth are you still bothering to work?'

He gave me a whimsical smile. 'This business gets under your skin. You know; *the sound of the greasepaint, the smell of the crowd!* I know I'll never have my name up in lights. I'm not very good. I've always known that, but the whole thing — atmosphere, excitement — it's very seductive.' He smiled wryly. 'Being offered the part in this show has been a huge breakthrough for me.' He smiled. 'The West End, eh? I only hope I can hack it. I'm sure you remember my flair for fluffing lines.'

I laughed. 'I remember your genius for ad-libbing. More than once you were the cause of sheer chaos. By the way, what did you think of the rest of the cast?'

He grinned. 'Bit of a motley crew. Your Darcy's not bad-looking, though I'd swear he's wearing a wig. Nobody's hair is that perfect; either that or he spends a fortune on hairdressing.' He glanced at me. 'Speaking of which, have you been asked to put cash into this show?' When I nodded he asked, 'So how did you come by the necessary readies?'

'My dad died and left me the family home.'

'Wow!' His eyebrows rose. 'That must have been a blow to the rest of the family.'

'Oh, they're all right,' I told him airily. 'My sister is married to a guy with a fabulous job and Dad left my stepmother enough to keep her comfortable. They were fine about it.'

'Good! So you and I are in the money at last? A far cry from those hard-up drama-school days.'

'You could say that.'

As our food arrived, I took in Mark's appearance again. He'd changed quite a bit. The old Mark with his sense of fun and his flamboyant manner was just the same, but the brown hair that had once straggled down to his shoulders was now cut in a crisp, short style and frosted at the temples in the very best romantic novel fashion. His wiry, stick-thin body had broadened into quite a presentable physique and the few lines on his face actually improved his looks. He turned and smiled at me as the waiter walked away.

'Well, this looks pretty good to me. I'm starving.' He picked up his napkin and tucked it under his chin.

Yes, he's certainly improved with age, I told myself. Not to mention the fact that he'd come into money too. Maybe it was fate, our meeting up again.

'Where do you live?' he asked.

'Earl's Court. A little flat I keep for when I'm

up in town,' I told him glibly.

'Right, so will you be staying there for Christmas?'

I shook my head. 'Oh, no. I expect I'll be going home. I've had several invitations but you know how it is; Christmas is the time for families, isn't it? They'd be so disappointed if I cried off, especially Peter, my little nephew.'

He looked wistful. 'I see. You're so lucky. Unfortunately both my folks died a few years ago — within weeks of one another. And my sister lives in Australia, so for me it'll just be a solitary frozen dinner-for-one and *The Great Escape* on the telly.'

'Why don't you book into a hotel?' I asked, wishing I hadn't been quite so quick off the mark with the self-boosting lies.

He shook his head. 'I tried that once but the place was full of sad, lonely bastards like me; very depressing.' His eyes brightened into the warm smile I remembered so well. 'The best Christmas present I could have had is meeting you again,' he said, squeezing my hand.

As we parted on the pavement outside, we exchanged mobile numbers.

'See you when we start rehearsals,' Mark said. 'Take care and have a lovely time with your folks.'

I watched wistfully as he walked off down the street towards the Underground station. Why did I have to come out with all those bloody lies? I asked myself. If we were going to be seeing a lot of each other, the truth was bound to come out sooner or later, and I was going to have to think up a lot more fibs to cover myself. They rolled off my tongue without my even thinking. It was a defence method I'd learned as a child getting mercilessly bullied at school, and somehow it had become a habit I couldn't shake off. I never even stopped to think about the consequences — even fleetingly believing in my own fantasies at times. It had landed me in trouble more than once in the past. As I turned towards the bus stop, I mentally kicked myself.

'Why is it you never learn, you silly cow?' I muttered.

It really had been lovely meeting Mark again. No one except my dad had ever really loved me as he had and I'd chucked it back in his face. I'd been rotten to him back in our student days but he obviously held no grudges. As I boarded the bus, I resolved to make it up to him in the months that followed.

★ ★ ★

'I take it you're going home for Christmas?' Dianne asked as we prepared the evening meal together later. She hadn't even asked me about the read-through when she got in from work and I was feeling a bit miffed; too proud to bring it up myself. The only thing that seemed to concern her was that I'd remembered to do some shopping on my way home. I thought she'd have thanked me but she just seemed to take it for granted.

She glanced at me. 'Are you, then — going home, I mean?'

'I haven't actually been invited,' I replied. 'I had a text from Karrie to say that they've got this Dutch au pair living with them so that's obviously a hint that there won't be room for me.'

'Can't you stay with your stepmother?'

I shrugged. 'Her sofa isn't exactly what you'd call comfy. It's only a two-seater and lumpy with it. Anyway, I expect she'll be going to Karrie and Simon's for the day.'

'You could go too. And the sofa can't be all that bad — just for a few days.'

I looked at her. 'I thought you and I would be spending Christmas together,' I confessed. 'I was quite looking forward to it and I don't want to push in where I'm not really wanted.'

She looked uncomfortable, her head bent over the potatoes she was peeling. 'The thing is, Lou, my parents really want me to go home. My brother is getting engaged and they're planning a party on Boxing Day.'

'Oh, well you must go of course. I'll be OK here on my own.' Privately, I thought she might have suggested taking me along too.

Dianne frowned. 'I'm not allowed to sublet the flat, Lou,' she said.

I laughed. '*Sublet?* I'll only be staying here for a few days on my own, surely that doesn't constitute subletting?'

She dropped the potatoes into a saucepan of water and lit the gas under it, turning to me with a determined expression. 'To be brutally honest, Lou, I'd rather not leave you in the flat on your own.'

'Why not? I'll be OK.'

'Oh, I'm sure you would be, but to be frank, you're not the tidiest of house guests. Take today, for instance. I came home from a hard day at work to find your breakfast washing-up still in the sink, including a burnt porridge saucepan, and I found several pairs of your tights stuffed down the back of the settee when I was vacuuming the other day. You never even *think* of taking your turn with the cleaning and you leave wet towels all over the bathroom floor. If you're here for a week on your own, I dread to think what state the flat will be in when I get home.'

'Speak your mind, why don't you?' I sniped. I stared at her. 'Anyway, since when have you been so house-proud?'

'I'm not . . .'

'You sound positively paranoid to me!'

'I do like some kind of order.'

'OK, I'll get out of your hair,' I told her. 'As a matter of fact, I turned down an invitation just today because I didn't want to disappoint you.'

She looked slightly relieved. 'Well, maybe it isn't too late to change your mind.'

I turned to walk out of the kitchen. 'Well, we'll just have to keep our fingers crossed, won't we? Otherwise it looks as if I'll be spending Christmas in a cardboard box!'

★ ★ ★

I waited until Dianne had left for work the following morning, then I got my phone out and clicked on Mark's number. He sounded sleepy when he answered.

'Who the hell is this ringing me in the middle of the night?'

'It's me — Lou,' I told him, laughing. 'And as a matter of fact, it's half past eight.'

'Like I said — the middle of the night.' He cleared his throat. 'Only joking, Lou. It's good to hear from you any time. What can I do for you?'

'It's more what I can do for you,' I told him. 'How would you like me to come and cook you a traditional slap-up Christmas dinner in your own home?'

I could almost hear him blinking. 'Sorry, it's a bit early for riddles,' he said. 'I could have sworn you offered to cook me Christmas dinner in my own home. You did say you were Lou Davies, didn't you — not meals on wheels?'

I laughed. 'No, it's me all right — and it's *Louise Delmar*, cloth-ears! I'll explain — I had a call from my stepmum last night; they're all off to Sweden for a Scandinavian Christmas. Of course, they wanted me to join them but I don't fancy it. My flatmate is off home so I thought — why don't Mark and I team up? It could be fun.'

'That would be great, Lou!' He sounded fully awake now. 'A home-cooked Christmas dinner plus *your* company! How lucky could I get?' There was a pause then he said, 'Flatmate? You never said you had a flatmate.'

I bit my lip hard and forced a laugh. 'Didn't I? Well, it's only a recent arrangement. She had nowhere to go so I offered her a room.' Suddenly I remembered that he knew Di from our time at drama school, but I decided not to mention that.

'Right.' He lowered his voice. 'Hey — I hope you're a good cook.'

'The best,' I lied, crossing my fingers and thanking God for Aunt Bessie.

7

'You're not going to let *her* cook the Christmas dinner, I hope.'

Simon tutted irritably as he straightened the bottom sheet and punched his pillow into shape. 'Look at this. She doesn't even know how to make a bed properly!'

'Oh, stop finding fault with the poor girl. You haven't stopped since she arrived.' Karen slapped cleansing cream onto her face and whipped a tissue out of the box on the dressing table. 'She's an absolute treasure with Peter. He adores her. She's so patient and creative with him.'

'So she might be but you can't say the same about her cooking. It's abysmal,' Simon complained. 'Tasteless stodge in watery gravy.'

'Shhh! Keep your voice down. She'll hear you.'

'That's another thing,' he hissed. 'The only place we can actually have a private conversation is in bed and even then it has to be conducted in whispers. And as for doing anything else in bed . . . '

'*Simon!* Keep it down, for God's sake.' She turned to him. 'Look, if I keep working we'll be able to afford a bigger house in a couple of years. Surely it's worth a few sacrifices.'

'That's a matter of opinion. And I thought you said she spoke fluent English.'

'She does.'

'When *we're* around, yes, but when she's on her own with Peter she obviously speaks to him in Dutch. When I spoke to him the other day he came out with a mouthful of it and when I asked her about it, she said it was a nursery rhyme. I was horrified. It's coming to something when I can't even understand what my own son is saying.'

'Isn't it an asset for him to be growing up bilingual?'

'If it was German or French, yes, but where or when is he going to need Dutch?'

'You never know.' Karen drew back the duvet and climbed into bed. 'Why can't you think about all the advantages of having Adrey with us? You have to admit that the house is spotless and your shirts are beautifully ironed.' She turned to look at his unconvinced face and decided to play her trump card. 'Best of all, Louise won't be joining us this Christmas because we simply haven't a spare room any more.'

'Well, that is a plus, I suppose,' he said grudgingly.

'And aren't you pleased that I'm not so tired these days?' She reached across to kiss him and her hand crept under the waistband of his pyjamas. 'In fact I'm feeling really sexy tonight.'

He grasped her hand and firmly removed it. 'Well I'm *not*. How do you expect me to work up any enthusiasm when there's just a thin partition between us and her?'

'She's probably asleep. Anyway, we don't go in for all that noisy stuff.'

He turned his back to her and switched off his bedside lamp pointedly. 'I told you, I can't work up any enthusiasm and if I can't — well, surely I don't have to draw you a picture?'

'There's no need to be crude.'

'Just go to sleep, Karen, or you'll look like nothing on earth in the morning.'

Deeply hurt, she switched off her own lamp and turned over, a lump in her throat. Presently, a large tear slid down her cheek and she brushed it away with a corner of the duvet. After a few minutes she felt Simon turn towards her.

'I'm sorry, love. I didn't mean that,' he said quietly. When she made no reply he reached out a hand to rest on her waist. 'I've got such a lot of stress at school as you know, what with the coming festivities and everything. I know how hard you work too and I do appreciate it.' The hand crept up to cup her breast. 'Know what?' he whispered in her ear. 'I think I can hear Adrey snoring.'

Karen couldn't conceal the chuckle that rose in her throat. Taking his hand she moved it slowly down her body and lifted her face for his kiss.

8

Susan said goodnight to the rest of the group as they left the classroom in twos and threes and began to put on her coat. It was the second meeting of the Green Fingers Club she had attended and the last before Christmas. She was sorry. She had enjoyed the meetings so much. The other members were pleasant company and she had learned a lot from Ted's expertise. Her only regret was not having a garden of her own on which to practise some of the new skills and tips that she had scribbled down in her notebook.

'Can I give you a lift home, Susan?' Ted stood at her side, winding a scarf round his neck. 'It's freezing outside tonight.'

She smiled up at him. 'Thank you. That would be lovely.'

They walked along the corridor together and out into the frosty night air. As they walked across the car park he turned to her.

'I don't suppose I'll see you again until after Christmas, so would you like to come for a festive drink with me?' His brow furrowed. 'Or perhaps you don't drink and you'd prefer a coffee?'

Susan laughed. 'I do drink — moderately of course, but either would be nice. Thank you.'

They opted for the Coach and Horses, a comfortable pub almost next door to the college. Inside the lounge bar it was warm and comfortable, tasteful evergreens decorated the walls and there were red candles on every table. They chose a table near the log fire and Ted went to the bar for drinks, a pint of bitter for him and a gin and tonic for Susan. 'I got you ice and a slice,' he said as he joined her at the table. 'I hope that's all right.'

'Lovely. Thank you.' She raised her glass. 'Here's to a happy Christmas.'

Putting his glass down, he looked at her. 'So — do you think you'll be joining us next term, or did you find it unutterably boring?'

'Oh, no!' Susan said quickly. 'I mean about it being boring. I was fascinated. It was so interesting. And yes to your first question; I'd love to sign up next term. My only complaint is that it's going to be so frustrating, not being able to try out all your useful tips and advice.'

He leaned towards her. 'I've been thinking about that,' he told her. 'My garden is quite small. Only really big enough for a lawn and a few flower beds, so I grow my own vegetables on an allotment. The chap next to me is giving his up in the New Year. How would you feel about applying to the Council to rent it?'

Susan looked doubtful. 'An allotment? Do they let women have them?'

He laughed. 'Of course they do. Why not? The only people who are not allowed are those who have a bad track record for neglect.'

Susan sipped her drink thoughtfully. 'How big would it be? I'm not sure I could manage on my own.'

'You wouldn't be on your own. As I said, the

plot is next to mine so I'd always be there to help you out.' He paused. 'Look, sorry if I'm going too fast for you. Maybe I'm being presumptuous — taking too much for granted. If you hate the idea just say. It was only a thought.'

He looked so embarrassed that Susan reached out an involuntary hand to pat his arm. 'No, no, it's a lovely idea and so kind of you to think of me.' She sat back with a smile. 'Just fancy, home-grown organic vegetables. I could keep Karen supplied and still have lots left over.'

'You could.' Very softly he placed his hand over hers on his sleeve. 'And there's a farmers' market every other week in town. If we get a glut, some of us club together and rent a stall. It's great fun and quite profitable too.'

'It sounds it.' Susan felt her cheeks flush and she didn't know whether it was the gin and tonic, the heat of the fire, or the warm feel of Ted's hand on hers. Then a thought suddenly occurred to her. 'Oh, but where are these allotments? Could I get there easily? And what about gardening tools? I mean, I did have some when I had a garden before but I gave them to Karen and Simon.'

'You could always ask for them back,' he said, his eyes twinkling. 'I have a lock-up shed on my allotment and you could keep your tools in there with mine.' He took a drink of his beer. 'As for getting there — it's only fifteen minutes in the car; you could come with me.'

She smiled tentatively. 'How can I refuse?'

'Of course you can refuse!' His smile vanished. 'Please don't feel obliged to agree if you don't like the idea. I'd hate to bulldoze you into it.'

'You've given it so much thought.'

He gave her a wry grin. 'To be honest I've thought of little else.' He looked away. 'It's been a bit of a pipe dream. Meg and I never had children and although I've been on my own for five years I still can't get used to my own company.' He turned to look at her. 'I don't make friends easily. When I started the Green Fingers Club I thought I might meet some like-minded folk and I have, but they come in couples or pairs of friends and anyway, there isn't anyone who I'd say was on the same wavelength as me.' He raised an eyebrow at her. 'Does that make sense or does it make me sound stuffy and difficult?'

Susan shook her head. 'Of course it makes sense. I know what it is to be widowed and like you, I've never been someone who's happy as part of a group. I prefer one-to-one friendships.'

'Somehow I knew that instinctively. But there is a big difference. You have a family.'

'That's true.' On impulse she asked, 'Ted, what are you doing for Christmas?'

He shrugged. 'Sitting in front of the box and wishing it was spring.'

'Then come with me to Karen and Simon's for Christmas Day?' she invited.

'Oh, I couldn't impose on people I don't even know.'

'You wouldn't be imposing, and you'd soon get to know them. I always contribute my share of the food and I help with the cooking; we all muck in. You'd be very welcome and I'd like you

75

to meet my family.' She took in his hesitant expression. 'But it's only an idea. Don't say yes just because I've asked you.'

He smiled. 'I'd love to come. Thank you.'

★ ★ ★

'Really, Mum! Who is this old man and what on earth made you invite him without asking me first?'

Susan was shocked by Karen's reaction. 'To start with, he's not an *old man*; he's about the same age as me. He's on his own and he's lonely. I had no idea you'd be put out about it. One more can't make all that difference.'

'It could be very awkward, having some stranger in the house,' Karen said. 'Christmas is a family occasion after all.'

'What happened to *goodwill to all men*? And anyway, what about Adrey? She's not family.'

'That's different. She's away from her own family for the first time and I want to make it special for her. I've asked some of the neighbours for pre-lunch drinks so that she can get to know them.'

'*I* wanted to make it special for Ted too. He's been on his own for five years and he's terribly lonely.'

'That's hardly my problem. Anyway, what do you know about this Ted person? You want to be careful, Mum, picking up strange men on the bus. He could be some kind of conman.'

'Well, he's *not*!' Susan bristled. 'And I didn't *pick him up* as you so delicately put it. I haven't

76

lived as long as I have without being able to tell a genuine person from a crook. And if he's not welcome then I'm not coming either.'

Karen looked shocked. 'Oh really, Mum! Don't be so ridiculous.'

'I never ask you to do anything for me, Karen,' Susan said as she marched down the hall. 'But if you can be mean-minded enough to turn down a lonely person at Christmas, then you're not the daughter I thought you were.'

'Mum — wait!' Karen caught up with Susan at the front door and took her arm. 'Please, don't go like this. Bring your friend, Ted, if you like. I'm sorry I was snappy. It's just that there's so much to do, what with shopping — cards and presents and everything at home and all that's going on at school. You know how stressful Christmas is . . . '

'I don't want you to wear yourself out on my account.' Susan firmly detached her arm from Karen's grasp. 'We'll be fine. I'll invite Ted to spend Christmas with me at the flat and you can concentrate on making it a special Christmas for your Dutch au pair and the neighbours.'

★ ★ ★

'So, I hope you don't mind, Ted, but I thought we'd have Christmas Day on our own at my flat,' Susan said when she rang Ted the next morning.

There was a slight hesitation at the other end of the line. 'Susan — my dear, I hope you're not giving up the day with your family on my account.'

77

'Not at all,' she assured him. 'When I thought about it I realized that it might all be a bit overwhelming for you. They're having friends in for the evening and I know you don't like crowds of strange people. I don't know any of them so I'm not very keen either.'

'You're absolutely certain about this?'

'Absolutely.'

'Well, if you really are, then the answer is a resounding yes. As a matter of fact the prospect of it just being the two of us is very pleasing,' he said. 'It'll be an opportunity to get to know one another better.'

'Yes, it will.' Susan smiled, feeling a little flutter of anticipation. It was so long since she had planned a Christmas of her own. 'Right, then,' she said. 'I'd better get down to the supermarket before the last-minute rush starts.'

'Do you mind if I come with you?' Ted said. 'I absolutely insist on sharing all the expense with you.'

'There's no need, but it would be lovely to have your company,' Susan said. 'Then I won't have to guess what you like and don't like to eat.'

'And on the day I insist on helping,' he said. 'I'm a dab hand with Brussels sprouts.'

Susan smiled to herself, serene in the knowledge that she had made the right decision.

9

Mark was waiting for me as I stepped off the train, laden with bags of shopping.

'Wow!' he exclaimed as he took a couple of them from me. 'Looks as if you've bought enough to feed an army. It must have cost you a fortune. Come on, I've brought the car.'

'You've got a car?' I said, following him into the street.

'Of course. I don't use it for going up to town — too difficult to park but I do like it for holidays and days out and so on.'

The car turned out to be a Ferrari — sleek, black and shiny, and Mark's apartment was in a smart block of luxury flats built conveniently handy for the main shopping centre and the Underground station. Mark drove into the basement car park where he had his own numbered space, and then whisked me up to the penthouse apartment in the fastest lift I'd ever experienced.

The apartment was gorgeous, even more lavish than Paul's. The kitchen had every modern convenience. The furnishings were a little old-fashioned maybe, but I had to remind myself that an elderly man had lived here and Mark clearly hadn't updated anything.

The large living room had massive sliding doors, leading out onto a spacious balcony, and I stood in the middle of the room and spread out my arms.

79

'Oh, Mark, it's lovely. I have to say, you certainly fell on your feet, inheriting all this.'

He smiled. 'It is rather nice, isn't it? I suppose I really ought to change things round a bit — bring it up to date but it always feels like too much hassle. What do they say — if it ain't broke, don't fix it?'

'Well, there's nothing broke about this place.' I kicked off my shoes and threw myself onto the enormous corner settee. 'I'm surprised you can ever tear yourself away from all this to go on tour.' I sat up and looked at him. 'Er — what are the arrangements — where do I sleep?'

He laughed. 'Don't tempt me. Seriously, there are two bedrooms so you can take your pick. They both have their own en suite so we won't bump into each other in the nude first thing in the morning.' He grinned impishly. 'More's the pity!'

'In your dreams!' I said, laughing as I got up and followed him to the spare bedroom. Like the rest of the apartment, it was luxurious but I hazarded a guess that I wouldn't be staying in it for long.

I made spag bol for supper — the only dish I can actually cook from scratch — and we sat and ate it at the kitchen table. I'd hastily unpacked all the frozen Christmas fare I'd stocked up with at the supermarket and hidden them in Mark's massive freezer when he wasn't looking. The turkey was already defrosted (at least I know that much) and I slipped it onto a large serving dish and put it in the fridge. Luckily there was plenty of room. All it contained was a pint of milk and some cans of beer. Obviously Mark was no Gordon Ramsay and I guessed that he existed mainly on takeaways.

After clearing his plate, Mark leaned back in his chair and took a sip of the wine he had produced from a well-stocked wine rack. At least he didn't stint himself on that. 'That was delicious,' he said with satisfaction. 'This is really great. How long can you stay?'

'I think you could have timed that question a little more tactfully,' I told him.

He laughed. 'You know what I mean. Who would have thought a week ago that I'd be sitting here, looking forward to spending Christmas with the love of my life I'd given up hope of ever seeing again.' He drained his glass and refilled it, holding the bottle enquiringly towards my empty glass.

'Yes, please.' I took an appreciative sip. 'You're right. We never know what's round the corner, do we?'

'So — how long can you stay?'

Quickly, I calculated. Di was away till the day after Boxing Day. I'd give her a day to feel flat and miss me. 'Four days,' I said. 'That is if you can put up with me for that long.'

'I can put up with you for as long as you like,' he said.

'You might not be saying that a few days from now,' I warned him. 'You're still wearing those rose-coloured glasses you wore twenty years ago.'

'And very comfy they are too,' he said, holding up his glass. 'Here's to our meeting again and to our renewed acquaintance.'

'And to the new show.' I touched my glass to his. 'To it being a hit!'

Suddenly Mark was serious. 'About the show,' he said, putting his glass down. 'Isn't it usual for a show like this — heading for a West End theatre — to be backed by a consortium of people; you know, impresarios?'

'It will be,' I told him. 'Paul said that borrowing money from us to get off the ground is only temporary. He'd got someone lined up. And it's only been difficult because he hasn't booked a star attraction for the lead role.'

'OK, but where's the director?'

'He's been searching for the right person,' I explained. 'He has a really big-name guy interested.'

'Oh, yes — who?'

'He didn't tell me.'

'Well, I hope you're right.'

'I'm sure everything is in place,' I assured him. 'Harry Clay, my agent, is in on the whole thing. I've been with him for years and I trust him.'

Mark took a reflective drink of his wine. 'I was invited up to his flat to audition me for the part,' he said. 'My agent was as surprised as me. He — Paul — showed me the sketches for the sets; very impressive. He said they were already being built up in Yorkshire somewhere. After that we had tea and cakes and he asked me for money.'

'It was similar for me,' I told him. 'Although he'd already seen me in a show, I was in back in the summer. At his flat he played some of the songs for me and I sang one or two.'

'Then you had tea and he asked you for money?'

'Well — yes.'

'Are you with me in wondering if it's all completely kosher?'

'No. I told you; Harry, my agent, is in on it too. He's very shrewd. He'd never risk his money if he had any doubts and he certainly wouldn't let me be taken for a ride.'

Mark was shaking his head. 'It's all a bit odd,' he said. 'I mean, who's ever heard of Paul Fortune anyway — or any of those weirdos we met at the read-through the other day?'

'I told you, there are no big names.'

'Mmm.' He stroked his chin. 'You have to admit, Lou, it's one hell of a risk.'

'Well, that's up to Paul, isn't it? It's his risk and he seems confident enough.'

'I hope you're right.' He took a deep breath and smiled. 'Let's not be pessimistic. It's Christmas, you're here with me and tomorrow I'm going to have the first home-cooked Christmas dinner I've had in years with my first love cooking it for me.' He raised his glass. 'Here's to us!'

I clinked my glass to his. 'To us! And to being optimistic about the show.'

'Absolutely!' Mark said. 'What do I know anyway?'

Later, as I lay in bed — surprisingly alone — I couldn't help thinking about Mark's words. He was wrong, of course he was; he *had* to be. Paul had promised to make me a star. *Your face will be on the cover of all the magazines*, he'd said. He had to be on the level. I couldn't bear it if he wasn't. This was my very last chance.

* * *

Christmas dinner was a success — as much to my surprise as anyone else's. Though you have to be a complete loser to mess up a frozen, pre-cooked meal. Mark was delighted. If he suspected that it wasn't *exactly* home-cooked he didn't mention it. His pessimistic mood from the previous night had gone and instead he was on form in the style of the old Mark I remembered so well. After lunch, we watched TV and dozed in front of the realistic living-flame electric fire. After a couple of bottles of champagne, Mark grew amorous and we ended the day in bed together. He'd always been a good lover and he certainly hadn't lost his skills, making me ever so slightly curious about whom he'd been practising on in my absence.

84

10

Karen was up early on Christmas morning. Peter had wakened them at six, bouncing on the bed and dragging a pillowcase full of presents.

'Open, Mummy!' he demanded.

Simon groaned and turned over, squeezing his eyes tightly shut as Karen switched on the bedside lamp. 'Take him back to bed, for God's sake. It's the middle of the night.'

Karen slipped out of bed and put on her dressing gown. 'Come downstairs with Mummy, darling,' she said, taking Peter's hand and picking up the pillowcase. 'We'll leave grumpy old Daddy to sleep.'

When all the presents were opened, she left Peter playing with his new toys in the living room and went into the kitchen to make a pot of tea. Adrey was already up, having risen early to make what she called *kerststol*, which turned out to be some kind of fruit loaf traditionally eaten at Christmas for breakfast.

'Peter loves his new teddy,' Karen told her. 'It looks expensive. You really shouldn't have.'

Adrey turned with a smile. 'He's such a good little boy. I wanted to give him something nice for *Sinterklaas*.' She reached into the pocket of her dressing gown and produced a small, brightly wrapped parcel. 'I get this for you too. You and Simon have been so kind and welcoming.'

Karen was surprised. Opening the package, she found a tiny brooch in the shape of a Dutch clog, encrusted with crystals. 'Oh, Adrey, how sweet,' she said. 'It'll look great on my black dress. Thank you so much. There's a little something from Simon and me under the tree. We'll be opening those later.'

Putting the kettle on, she thought how pretty Adrey was. In her red dressing gown and with her fresh complexion and her long blonde hair hanging down her back in a thick plait, she looked like a Christmas angel. Karen turned and gave her a quick hug. 'I know you must be missing your family today,' she said. 'And you must feel free to telephone them.'

'Thank you, Karen. I would like to do that very much.'

The kitchen door opened to admit Simon in his old navy dressing gown. His hair tousled and his jaw dark with stubble, he still looked grumpy. Glancing at the two women he enquired, 'Any tea going?'

'I'm just making it,' Karen said, reaching for the teapot.

Adrey touched Karen's arm. 'I go now to make the telephone call to my family, if it is permitted?'

'Of course, help yourself — and take as long as you like,' Karen added.

'Thank you. Then I take Peter upstairs to wash and dress.'

Simon slumped at the table. 'Her family does live in Holland, you know,' he growled.

'I am aware of that.'

'Now you've given her carte blanche she'll probably be on the bloody phone all morning.'

'No she won't. She's not the type to take advantage.' Karen poured two cups of tea. 'Cut the poor girl some slack, Simon. This is her first Christmas away from home.'

Simon looked at the loaf, cooling on a wire rack on the worktop. 'What's that thing?'

'It's called *kerststol*. Adrey got up early specially to make it. It's a kind of fruit loaf. They eat it for breakfast in Holland at Christmas.'

Simon sniffed. 'Do they? Well, it smells OK anyway.'

'I'm going to put the turkey on in a minute. If you want, you can help with the vegetables.'

He snorted. 'No way. You know I'm all thumbs when it comes to domestic stuff.'

'All right, then, if Adrey is going to help me, you can take Peter to the park after breakfast.'

* * *

When everyone else was upstairs getting dressed, Karen took the telephone into the kitchen and dialled Susan's number.

'Mum — it's not too late to change your mind,' she said. 'There'll be plenty for all of us — including your friend.'

'That's perfectly all right,' Susan said. 'I have everything ready here. Ted and I are going to have a lovely day, thank you.'

'Oh, Mum, you're not still cross, are you? You know I'm only thinking of you.'

'I don't think that's quite true, Karen, but

87

please don't worry. Maybe I'll see you sometime in the New Year.'

'Please, Mum, don't be like that,' Karen begged. 'Look, why don't you come round for a drink tomorrow — bring Ted too. I could make a brunch with some of the leftovers.'

'I'll eat my own leftovers if it's all the same to you,' Susan said. 'I'm not cross, Karen, just a little disappointed by your attitude. But don't worry. I'm perfectly all right and looking forward to having someone to cook for again.'

'But, Mum . . . '

'No, I'm not being awkward. I mean it, Karen, I'm fine. Ted and I are going to have a really nice Christmas and I hope you do too. Goodbye, dear. Give my love to Simon and little Peter.'

'Oh — thank you for the presents, Mum.'

'I'm glad you liked them. Thank you for yours. The scarf will go beautifully with my new coat. Happy Christmas, dear.'

'Happy Christmas, Mum,' Karen said faintly. There was a lump in her throat as she switched the phone off. She hated falling out with her mother. Sometimes lately it seemed that she couldn't do right for doing wrong.

11

Ted arrived on the dot of twelve. Susan answered his ring on the entry-phone and pressed the button that released the main door to the flats. Ripping off her apron, she took a quick look in the hall mirror to check that her newly set hair was still in place.

When she opened the door she found him beaming outside, a huge bunch of chrysanthemums in one hand and a carrier bag containing a bottle of sherry and another of champagne in the other. He handed both to her. Susan blushed with pleasure.

'Oh, Ted, how thoughtful. But you really shouldn't have.'

'Not at all, my dear. It's so good of you to invite me.' He took off his overcoat and hung it on one of the pegs inside the door. Susan saw that he wore his best dark-grey suit with a pristine white shirt and tasteful blue tie. She thought he looked very handsome.

'Happy Christmas, Ted,' she said. 'Come through and make yourself comfortable. Everything's almost ready so we can have a drink and relax for half an hour.'

'Oh, but I thought I was going to help.'

Susan smiled. 'It's all right. I haven't been up since dawn. I did most of the preparation yesterday afternoon.'

Ted followed her through to the living room

and looked around appreciatively while Susan fetched glasses and poured the sherry. A cosy fire was burning in the hearth and in the centre of the room, the table was laid with her best glass and cutlery, set off by red napkins and crackers by each place setting. A Christmas tree stood in one corner, its coloured lights twinkling, and holly was draped around the mirror above the fireplace. There were red candles on the mantelpiece, their flickering flames reflected in the mirror.

'It all looks very festive,' he said, rubbing his hands and holding them out to the fire. 'Nice and warm too.' Susan handed him a glass of sherry.

'Here's to a happy Christmas,' she said.

★ ★ ★

Lunch was a great success. It was some years since Susan had cooked Christmas dinner for a man and she had loved every minute of it. Her reward was seeing him clear his plate with obvious relish.

'I'd forgotten how good home-cooked food tasted,' he said, pushing his chair back from the table and sighing. 'I don't think I'll need to eat again for at least a week!'

Susan laughed. 'I'm sure you will,' she said. 'I hope so anyway. I've got Christmas cake and mince pies lined up for later on.'

He smiled almost impishly. 'Oh well, I suppose I'll have to force them down.'

He insisted on helping her with the washing-up

and then they settled down to see the Queen's speech on TV. When it was over, Ted went out into the hall and came back with a small package which he handed to her.

'Just a little token of my appreciation,' he said almost shyly.

Susan blushed. 'Oh, Ted, you shouldn't have done this. I haven't got you anything.'

'Indeed you have,' he said stoutly. 'This is the best Christmas Day I've spent for years. All the work and the planning you've put into it makes my little offering look meagre. Please open it and see if you like it. If not, please feel free to change it.'

Somewhat flustered, Susan quickly unwrapped the gift. Inside a black velvet box she found a single crystal threaded onto a fine gold chain. In the light it glittered and flashed like a diamond. She took it out of the box and held it up.

'Oh, Ted. It's beautiful!' Standing in front of the mirror she held it out to him. 'Will you fasten it for me?'

He clipped the chain around her neck and the crystal lay winking in the light at the base of her throat. She looked up at him with shining eyes.

'Thank you,' she said. 'It's a long time since anyone gave me anything as nice.' She stood on tiptoe to kiss his cheek but his hands cupped her face, turning it gently to kiss her lips.

For a moment his eyes held hers then he said softly, 'I'm so happy that I found the courage to speak to you that day on the bus, Susan.'

She smiled. 'So am I, Ted. And this is the

nicest Christmas I've had for many a day too.'

'I can't wait for the next few weeks to pass so that we can start working on the allotments together.'

'Neither can I.'

They sat down side by side on the settee in front of the fire and Ted's hand found hers, squeezing it lightly. 'I can't remember when I've felt so happy,' he said.

'Neither can I.' For a moment they looked into the firelight together then Susan said, 'Tell me about your wife, Ted. Meg, wasn't it?'

His brow clouded. 'I'm afraid it wasn't the happiest of marriages,' he said. 'If you don't mind, I'd rather not talk about it at the moment. Let's not spoil a perfect day.' He smiled at her and squeezed her hand. 'What about you? All I know is that you have two daughters. I take it your marriage was happy.'

She nodded. 'Frank was a good man. Louise is my stepdaughter. Frank's wife walked out on them both when Louise was a toddler. When he and I married she was ten and she resented me dreadfully — thought I'd stolen her beloved dad away, which wasn't the case at all. I tried my best but nothing seemed to work and I'm afraid she still sees me as an outsider.'

'But you have your own daughter.'

'Yes. Karen made up for a lot, but she has her own family now and lately even she seems to be drifting away from me.'

She looked at him. 'I suppose we've always been what they call a dysfunctional family.'

'Sometimes I wonder if there's any other kind,'

Ted said with a wry smile. 'Do you know, I think it's time to open that bottle of champagne. I can't think of a better occasion.'

12

We were three days into the New Year when the rehearsal schedule arrived. I rang Mark as soon as I'd opened it and scanned through.

'It doesn't look very intensive,' I said. 'Only two rehearsals a week — and it seems we're still in that draughty old hall in Stoke Newington.'

'So I see,' Mark replied. 'Still, at least things are moving. In the enclosed letter, Paul mentions extra sessions for the music and some with a choreographer. How's your dancing?'

I laughed. 'I think I can hoof it with the best.'

'I'm sure you remember my galumphing efforts. Let's hope Wickham doesn't have anything too energetic to do.'

'I see the first one is the day after tomorrow,' I said, looking at the schedule. 'How are you getting on with the lines?'

'Not too bad, how about you?'

'Oh, OK.' I was remembering Di's cool response when I'd asked her to test me. She'd treated the request as though I were some tiresome kid rehearsing for the school play. No one would ever have thought she'd once longed to become an actress herself. It was more the kind of reaction I'd have expected from Karen.

'See you on Wednesday, then,' Mark was saying.

'What? Oh yes, fine.'

Since Di had returned from her Christmas break, she'd been a bit distant. Apparently the engagement party had gone well and she'd had a great time with her family, but I could tell there was something brewing.

To tell the truth I was a bit jealous of Di's happy family life. I'd had a card from Karen and Simon and one from Susan, but no presents and certainly no invitations to visit or enquiries about the new show. I know it was partly my own fault. The trick I played on Karen last time I was staying with her was pretty much over the top, but there is something about Karen that stirs up the devil in me. One look at that sanctimonious, smug little face and I can't help myself. I realize now that what I did could have had disastrous consequences. I just hadn't thought it through and she was right to be angry with me. Nevertheless it hurt to be so completely excluded, especially at Christmas. Now that Dad has gone, I feel I have no one who really gives a damn about me.

Inevitably my thoughts turned again to my mother. I wondered if she regretted what she'd done just as I did. Was she lonely? Maybe she had married again. I could have half-siblings I didn't know about; a whole new family! The thought excited me and I promised myself that I would look into ways of finding her again just as soon as the rehearsals had got underway.

I was right about Di having a bee in her bonnet. When she got in from work that evening,

I showed her the schedule that Paul had sent but as she set about unpacking her briefcase, I could see that there was something else on her mind. Eventually she stopped me in mid-sentence.

'Lou — look, can we just sit down a minute? There's something I need to tell you.'

My heart sank. I could tell from her face that whatever it was, it wasn't going to be to my advantage. 'OK, Di, what's on your mind?' I asked. 'I've been trying really hard to keep the place tidy and I'm not behind with my share of the rent, am I?'

'No, nothing like that.' She took a deep breath. 'It's just that — well, while I was at home this time I met up with an old flame of mine again. Mike and I used to go out together when we were teenagers but we drifted apart when I came up to London to drama school and he went off to study law. He married someone else during that time but they divorced last year.' She glanced at me. 'We found we still liked each other — quite a lot actually, the old spark was still there. Over the holiday we met a few times. Mike has just landed himself a fabulous job up here with a law firm. He said he was going to look me up when he started — ask me to help him find a place to live, so it was lucky our meeting again.' She glanced at me again. 'So — I thought — I said . . .'

'You told him not to bother looking because he could move in with you,' I completed the sentence for her. I laughed at her expression. 'Christ, Di, I thought you were never going to spit it out. You could have said it all in a few words: 'I've met an old boyfriend and we still turn each other on so we're going to move in together — oh, and by the way, I want you to move out.'

She had the grace to wince. 'You make me sound like a . . . '

'I make you sound like what you are,' I told her. 'A good friend who's put up with me for far too long. I know I've out-stayed my welcome by a mile. It's high time I was out of your hair. Good luck with the renewed relationship, Di. When do you want me to leave?'

She looked so relieved that I thought she might faint. 'It's very good of you to take it so well,' she said. 'There's really no hurry about leaving. Where will you go?'

'Oh, don't worry about me,' I said lightly. 'I've got some contacts. I'll be fine.' Secretly, I have to admit that I'd never have been so generous if it hadn't been for Mark. I felt confident that he'd be more than delighted to have me move into the apartment with him. As for me, I was thrilled. The sex was fantastic and I wouldn't have to pay any rent.

★ ★ ★

The first rehearsal was a bit of a shambles. Paul brought this guy along who he said was an experienced director. He introduced him as Marvin Nash. Neither Mark nor I had ever heard of him. Not that either of us was that clued up about West End directors but he was certainly no Cameron Mackintosh, anyone could see that. When we were finally dismissed, Mark and I went along to the Prince of Wales, the same pub we'd lunched at before, and sat down with stiff drinks to pool our opinions.

'I daresay it'll all come together once we get the music and choreography sorted,' Mark said optimistically.

I shrugged. 'I hope you're right. They're like a bunch of amateurs, and that Carla is the worst. God only knows what her singing voice is like.'

Mark grinned. 'Well, old Ma Bennet isn't exactly supposed to be a diva, is she?'

'She is as played by Carla bloody Dean.' I took a quick swig at my gin and tonic. 'And I can't wait to see her dance!' I put my glass down on the table and took a look at Mark's face. This seemed like a good moment to spring my proposition.

'Talking of movement, I've got something I want to run past you,' I said, looking at him from under my lashes in the way I knew turned him on.

'Oh?' He raised his eyebrows. 'Am I going to like it?'

'I hope so.' I toyed with the stem on my glass. 'Since Christmas I've been thinking a lot — about us. We had a great time, didn't we?'

He nodded enthusiastically. 'The best.'

'I was a fool to be so rotten to you all those years ago,' I said. 'We have so much in common and I just couldn't see it. We make each other laugh. We're really compatible in every way, aren't we?'

'I've always thought so, yes.' He leaned

98

towards me, his eyes twinkling. 'You're not trying to propose, are you? Because if you are I'm going to have to insist that you get down on one knee.'

'In your dreams!' I gave his shoulder a push. 'No, I'm not proposing — not marriage anyhow. What I am suggesting is that it might benefit both of us if I moved in with you. The lease on my flat is about to run out and my flatmate would like to take it over from me. Of course it would only be until we go on tour with the show and . . .'

'*Lou!*' He had grasped my hand so hard that the pressure made my eyes water and stopped the words in my throat. His grin spread from ear to ear. 'Bloody hell, that would be marvellous. Just fancy — home-cooked food every day!'

I kicked him under the table. 'On your bike! That was a Christmas one-off. We share the cooking and the chores or the deal is off.'

He gave me a mock salute. 'Yes, *ma'am*! Anything you say. When can you move in?'

'Well, I'll have to break the news to my friend that I'm leaving sooner than expected. I daresay she'll be a bit upset but she'll get over it.'

'Are you sure? I'd hate you to lose a friend because of me.'

I smiled at him. 'I'm sure. I'll find a way to make it up to her somehow.'

'OK — so when?'

'Give me a few days. I'll let you know at the next rehearsal.'

I started packing that night. I'd told Di that I'd found somewhere else to live and she seemed pleased. A bit too pleased to be flattering, actually. I overheard her talking to Mike on her mobile later and arranging for him to move in the week after next. She certainly didn't intend to waste any time. But it didn't matter, I told myself. Two weeks from now I'll be living in the lap of luxury in Mark's lush apartment.

★ ★ ★

The day of the next rehearsal was grey and wet; a typical January day. The walk from the bus stop seemed endless. My heels skidded on the greasy pavement and my umbrella blew inside out so many times that I eventually gave up and put it down. After that, the icy rain dripped relentlessly down the back of my collar all the way to St Mary's Hall. Pulling the heavy door closed behind me with relief, I took off my wet mac and shook as much of the water off it as I could. Mark was already there. He was standing with his back to one of the lukewarm radiators and I joined him.

'Brrr! Budge up and let the dog see the rabbit,' I said, giving him a playful shove. 'I've got good news. I can move in at the weekend if it's OK with you.'

He turned to me with an expression like a whipped puppy and my heart sank. I knew right then that it wasn't going to be my day.

He began haltingly, 'Lou, darling — I don't know how to tell you this but I'm very much afraid that our plans are going to have to be put on hold — for the time being at least.'

I stared at him. 'You *what*? Why? What's up?'

He took a deep breath and looked at the floor. 'Last night I got an email from Cathy, my sister in Australia. She and her husband have split up and she's flying home today.'

I frowned. 'Home?'

'To England — and to me as there's no one else.'

'She's landing herself on you? What a cheek.'

'Not just her but her two kids as well. I couldn't say no, could I, Lou? She's the only family I've got and she's going through a crisis.' He looked at my bemused face. 'I've only got the two bedrooms so it's going to be a bit of a squeeze.'

'Yes, but I'll be sharing yours.'

'I know, but . . . ' He looked uncomfortable. 'She'll want to talk. She's bound to need some advice and moral support.'

'So? I won't get in the way.'

He shook his head. 'I'm sorry, Lou. It just won't work; not with five of us in the apartment. It won't be forever,' he added hurriedly. 'I'm sure she'll want to find a place of her own quite soon. Obviously she'll need to find schools for the kids and settle them down into some kind of normality as soon as possible, poor little devils.'

'Oh, yes — *tough*!'

He reached for my hand but I pulled it away. 'I've already told Di that I'm moving out.'

'But she won't mind if you change your plans temporarily, will she? After all, it's your flat and it'll give her all the more time to find someone new to share with. And you said she'd be devastated that you were leaving.'

There, I'd done it again, I told myself. What's the phrase — hoist with my own petard? (What *is* a petard anyway?) Mark was looking at me, his face creased with concern.

'I'm so sorry, Lou. I was really looking forward to the two of us being together.'

'So disappointed that you let your sister call all the shots,' I said, shaking off his hand. 'She and her kids have to come first, I suppose. After all, who am I?'

'Please — don't be like that. I told you, it's only temporary.'

'Does she know you'll be going on tour with the show in a few weeks' time?'

'I did mention it, yes.'

'Then she's not going to be in any hurry looking for a place of her own, is she?' I gave a dry little laugh. 'You'll have the perfect flat-sitter. Just let's hope that you don't come back to find the kids have wrecked the place!'

'They're good kids actually,' he said.

I stared at him. 'How would you know? They live in Australia. How many times have you seen them?'

'Well, not many admittedly.'

'I just hope you know what you're letting yourself in for.'

Paul chose that moment to arrive with Marvin in tow and there was no more time to discuss our ruined plans. I poured my heart and soul into the rehearsal, putting special effort into my scenes with Darcy, who seemed delighted by my enthusiasm. Whilst close to him, I endorsed Mark's opinion that he wore a toupee. I also

102

discovered that he had terminal halitosis which didn't auger well for our love scenes. After the rehearsal, Marvin came up to me and congratulated me on my talent and the hard work I'd put in learning the lines. I felt it was no more than I deserved.

'Paul's done a good job of the casting,' he said. 'Especially in your case. Just wait till we get to the West End.' He grinned at me. 'Fancy your name in lights, do you?'

'I certainly do.'

'We'll have to get you a really good press agent,' he said. 'And a photographer. Some great pics for the magazines.' He looked at me, his head on one side and his eyes half closed. 'That wicked mixture of sexiness and innocence. I can see it now. You'll knock 'em dead, Louise.'

His comments made up a little for the day's disastrous start. I was slipping my arms into the sleeves of my still-damp mac when Mark sidled up. 'Shall we go to the Prince of Wales for lunch?'

I glanced round casually at him. 'Not today,' I told him. 'I'm not hungry — or in the mood.' I turned up my collar and picked up my bag. 'See you soon, Mark. Goodbye.' I noticed that Phil, the actor playing Darcy, was just about to leave. I called out to him.

'Oh, Phil! Wait for me. Do you fancy a drink?'

He looked surprised and delighted. 'Great! Yes, I'd love to.'

I turned to Mark, seeing with satisfaction his downcast expression. 'Have to rush. See you soon. Bye!'

★ ★ ★

'What do you mean, your plans have fallen through?' Di clearly wasn't pleased with my news. 'I've told Mike he can move in next week.'

'I can't help it,' I told her. 'The friend who was going to put me up has had a sudden family crisis.'

'Oh?' She failed to look sympathetic.

'I promise I'll keep out of your way,' I said. 'Presumably he'll be sharing your room and I'll keep to mine. It's only temporary anyway.'

'Actually we hadn't got as far as sharing a bed,' Di said stiffly. 'Mike thinks he's having my spare room.'

I couldn't disguise the little smile that lifted the corners of my mouth. '*Oh!* I thought you said you found the *old spark* was still there.'

'I didn't mean we'd jumped straight into bed together,' Di said icily. 'We're not all as promiscuous as you, you know.'

I laughed. I couldn't help it. '*Promiscuous!* Come off it, Di. How stuffy can you get?'

She bridled, and the red patch on her neck that always appeared when she was furious flared angrily above the neck of her sweater. 'Right, you can move all your stuff out of the spare room right now,' she said. 'And from next week on you'll be sleeping on the sofa.'

I picked up my bag, inwardly regretting the fact that I'd laughed at her.

'OK,' I said over my shoulder. 'As long as you realize that means I'll have nowhere to go to keep out of your way!'

104

I only slept on the sofa for three nights. I think it was partly the fact that I was always around playing gooseberry and partly the rekindling of that *old spark* they shared that had Mike moving in with Di so that I had my old room back again.

Mike and I disliked each other on sight. I thought he was a charmless weed and he made no bones about making me feel like a shameless scrounger. Personally, I couldn't see what she saw in him with his specs and his pedantic way of talking, but that was up to her. She always did have strange taste in blokes. I kept to my side of the bargain, spending my evenings shut away in my eight-by-ten bedroom while they canoodled on the sofa, recently vacated by me. But their audible lovemaking penetrated the thin walls into the small hours, making sleeping all but impossible for me, specially when I thought of what Mark and I could have been enjoying.

Rehearsals continued and we had one or two sessions with the choreographer and two more with Paul and the musical score. It wasn't going too badly. Mark and I were barely speaking. He told me that Cathy, his sister, and her two adorable angels had settled in happily. I don't know if that was supposed to make me feel better but I couldn't see why he expected me to work up any enthusiasm, seeing that this woman and her two brats had completely scuppered my plans. It seemed that I was doomed to be the outsider — the unwanted — surplus to everyone's requirements. Di had her beloved

Mike; Mark had his sister and her kids and as for my so-called family, they had each other and for all they cared, I could go to hell.

Lying awake as dawn was breaking one morning, I made my decision. I'd find somewhere else to live. After all, it would only be for a few weeks. I made up my mind about something else too: I'd start looking for my mother. Maybe she'd been waiting for me to find her all these years. We might strike up a good relationship together. Getting together again might be just what we had both been waiting for. Who knew? But if I didn't try I'd never find out, would I?

A couple of days later, after scouring the local paper I found myself a bedsit in Stoke Newington. It was pretty grim, shared bathroom and kitchen, and the occupants of the other rooms looked a weird lot. But it was cheap and close to the rehearsal venue. It was only temporary, I told myself, so I could stick it out for a few weeks. I told Mark that I'd found a really nice flat; Di too, and I think she believed me. I say believed but she didn't try very hard to conceal the fact that she didn't really care one way or another. I was about to leave her and Dream Lover Mike to share their little love nest in peace. I moved into the bedsit and later made that all-important call to the Sally Army. If I was going to find Mum it was better to do it before the tour started.

13

At the first signs of spring, Ted began to work on his allotment. Susan had applied to the local council before Christmas and to her delight, she heard soon after that she had been allotted the vacant plot next to his. She lost no time in donning the wellingtons she had thought she would never need again, and began to accompany Ted to the huge plot of allotments on the outskirts of town, the car boot loaded with their assorted gardening equipment.

As the weeks passed, Susan could feel herself growing fitter. Her skin took on a healthy glow and seeing the weeds vanish from the ground to be replaced by rows of tiny seedlings gave her immense satisfaction.

Her relationship with Ted had grown from friendship to a comfortable affection. Sometimes she thought they were like an old married couple, sharing their love of working with nature. On the days when they returned tired from several hours of gardening, Susan would go home with Ted and cook a meal for them both. As the weather grew warmer, Ted would drive them both to the coast on Sundays where they would treat themselves to a leisurely lunch then take a bracing walk along the sea front. For Susan it was a whole new life, and Ted confessed that it was the same for him.

The first time Ted had tentatively suggested

that Susan might stay the night after one of their outings she had reservations. It was a long time since she had shared her bed with a man. There had only been one man in her life and that of course was Frank. One of her uncertainties was that it would feel like a betrayal. But Frank had always urged her not to be alone when he had gone. *You're a woman who needs a man,* he had fondly told her once. *You need to be loved and cared for.* The fact was that Frank had never really known how strong she was. And maybe not letting him see that had been the secret of their happy marriage. But now there was Ted. She recognized that they had reached a milestone in their relationship and she was wise enough to know that the decision had to be mutual. Ted had insisted that it must be; he had urged her not to do anything she wasn't absolutely sure about but she felt that things would never be quite the same between them if she declined.

For a while she held back, thinking carefully about the difference intimacy might make to the pleasure they already had in each other's company. Ted did not pressure her and when at last she made up her mind, he asked her over and over if she was sure. By then she was.

So one Sunday in late March, she took an overnight bag with her when they drove to the coast and later, after they had spent a pleasant evening watching television, they retired to bed together as though they had been doing it for decades.

Ted was so sweet and gentle. He was kind and

loving, arousing in her feelings and sensations that she had expected never to experience again. By morning she knew that she had made the right decision. Their new-found intimacy had brought them even closer than before and she felt happy and contented.

As the weeks went by, it occurred to Susan that Ted might ask her to marry him. She searched her mind, asking herself what she really wanted from their relationship. She had always vowed that she would never marry again and really, why change that? she asked herself. Nowadays, no one seemed to mind people being together without the benefit of a marriage licence. They were happy as they were. But as the weeks continued to fly, a tiny doubt nagged at the back of her mind. Ted was a conventional kind of man. Surely he would want to put their relationship onto a more formal basis. Then, one Sunday evening as she was taking her overnight case from the car, something happened to answer her questions in a way that was to shatter her world.

Mrs Freeman was the elderly widow who lived in the bungalow next door to Ted's. She was often to be seen twitching her net curtains on the days when Susan visited Ted. They had even laughed about it. On this occasion, she was watering her front garden when they returned from one of their Sunday outings. Ted had already gone indoors to put the kettle on while Susan took her case out of the car boot. She slammed the lid down, only to see Mrs Freeman's sour face inches from hers on the other side of the fence.

Susan smiled. 'Good evening.'

The woman glared at her. 'Good evening *indeed!*' she grunted. 'You do know he's married, I suppose? Or are you the kind of woman who doesn't care about little details like that? I've seen you sneaking off first thing in the morning. Ought to be ashamed of yourself!'

Susan frowned. 'Mr Mumford is a widower,' she said. 'Not that it's any of your business.'

'Huh!' The old woman gave a mirthless laugh. '*Widowed!* Is that what he told you? Well, you can take it from me that he isn't. His wife's still alive. Shoved into a home and left to rot while he enjoys heaven knows what with loose women. I think you should know that the disgraceful way you two are behaving is getting this neighbourhood a bad name!' She looked Susan up and down. 'I'd have thought a woman of your age would have had a bit more decency about her! Downright depraved, that's what it is . . . .'

Susan didn't wait to hear any more. Picking up her case, she hurried in through the open front door of the bungalow and slammed it behind her.

In the kitchen Ted was humming happily, his back towards her as he waited for the kettle to boil.

'I'm ringing for a taxi,' Susan said, fishing her mobile out of her handbag. 'I'm going home, Ted.'

'Going home? Why . . . ' He turned to see Susan standing in the doorway. Her face was white and she was trembling. '*Susan!* Darling,

110

what's the matter?' He took a step towards her.

'You might well ask,' Susan said, holding out one arm to prevent him coming any closer. 'You should hear some of the things that woman next door just said to me. You lied to me, Ted. You told me your wife was dead and I believed you.'

'Susan, I never said any such thing. I . . . '

'I want to go home.' Her voice was shrill and trembling. 'I won't wait for a taxi. I'll walk!'

'No, please! You don't understand. What did she say? Was it Mrs Freeman?' Susan turned and walked down the hall without another word but he caught her up, grasping her arm. 'Don't go like this. Please — let me explain.'

She shook off his hand. 'There's nothing to explain. Goodbye, Ted. Please don't try to get in touch again.'

'Well, at least let me drive you. You're in no fit state . . . '

'No!' Trying not to look at his wounded expression she picked up her case and left.

Afterwards she didn't remember walking home. Once inside the flat, she gave way to the tears that had threatened all the way home, collapsing onto the bed to sob into the pillow. How could she have been taken in by him? They say there's no fool like an old fool and she'd been taken in good and proper. For days she didn't leave the flat. When the telephone rang she didn't answer it and she saw that there were several missed calls on her mobile, most of them from Ted. There were texts too but she deleted them all without reading them.

By the end of the week, she was obliged to

venture out to the supermarket. Donning a pair of sunglasses and tying a scarf over her head, she went during the lunch hour when she felt she was unlikely to run into anyone she knew but she was just rounding the end of the fruit and veg section when a voice hailed her.

'*Mum!*'

Her heart sank. She'd forgotten that Karen often popped into the local supermarket in her lunch break. There was no escape. She turned and forced a smile. 'Oh, hello, dear. How are you?'

'More to the point, how are *you*?' Karen looked cross. 'I've been trying to ring you for days on your mobile and your landline but no reply. I've been really worried. In fact, I was going to come round after school today to see if you were all right.'

Susan felt a pang of guilt. 'I'm so sorry, darling, I didn't think.'

'That's not like you, Mum.' Karen looked closer, narrowing her eyes. 'Are you really OK? Why are you wearing sunglasses in here?'

'My eyes felt a bit strained. The lights are very harsh in here.'

Karen laid a hand on her arm, her face concerned. 'What's wrong, Mum? You don't look well at all.'

Susan opened her mouth to speak but suddenly and without warning, her eyes filled with tears. She swallowed hard but she was totally powerless to stop the sobs escaping her. Just a few caring words and suddenly here she was, sobbing her heart out like an idiot, right

112

here in the middle of Tesco with everyone staring at her. Karen grasped her arm.

'*Mum!* What is it?' She glanced round at the curious customers trying to pretend they weren't looking. She took the handle of the trolley from Susan's hands. 'You can finish your shopping later. Come on, leave it for now. Come and have a coffee.'

There was no escape. Susan meekly allowed herself to be led by Karen to the cafeteria and deposited at a corner table, while she fetched the coffees. In a moment of wild panic, she contemplated making a run for it while Karen was otherwise occupied, but suddenly she found that she hadn't the strength, either of purpose or purely physically. Days of eating scratch meals, plus the shock of what had happened at the weekend, had sapped all her energy.

Karen returned to the table with a determined look on her face. She set down the tray and began to unload it. 'I've got you a sandwich too,' she announced. 'Prawn, you like prawns, don't you? You look to me as though you haven't been eating properly.'

The sight of the sandwich, mayonnaise oozing from between the slices, made Susan feel sick but she sipped the hot coffee gratefully.

'And for God's sake, take off those awful glasses and that headscarf,' Karen instructed. 'They make you look like Olga, the Russian spy!'

Susan obediently removed the sunglasses and scarf, smiling in spite of herself. Karen smiled back.

'That's better.' She reached out a hand. 'Oh,

113

Mum, your eyes are all red. You've been crying. Please tell me what's wrong.'

Susan pushed the plate containing the sandwich towards her daughter. 'I can't eat that. You have it.'

'No, I had lunch at school.' Karen took a paper napkin and wrapped the sandwich up. 'Put it in your bag, you can eat it when you get home.' She squeezed Susan's hand. 'Tell me what's wrong, Mum.'

Susan looked at her watch. 'Shouldn't you be getting back to school?'

'I've got a little while yet. Anyway, I'm not moving from here till you tell me what's wrong so if you don't want me to be late . . . Mum — you're not ill, are you? It isn't something — serious?'

'No, nothing like that.' Defeated, Susan leaned back in her chair. 'It — it's Ted,' she said. 'I thought he was a widower but it seems that his wife is still alive — and in a home.'

'Oh, dear.' Karen shook her head. 'I did warn you, Mum.'

Susan felt the blood rush to her face. 'I don't need you saying *I told you so*, Karen. Not now, if you don't mind. I know what you said and I know I didn't listen, but I don't need my nose rubbing in it, honestly.' She dabbed at her eyes. 'We had such a lovely Christmas together. I rented the allotment next to his and we've had such a wonderful time, gardening together. We had so much in common, Karen. We were going to sell some of our produce at the farmers' market in the summer. We've had some lovely

114

outings to the coast at weekends and — and . . . '

'And you've been sleeping together?' Karen said gently as she leaned across the table. 'I'm right, aren't I?'

Susan blushed furiously. 'You must think me a silly, gullible old woman,' she said, shredding the damp tissue in her hand.

'Not at all,' Karen said gently. 'And you're not an old woman, Mum. You're a very attractive *mature* woman, with feelings just like anyone else. You've been taken in, that's all.'

'I feel so ashamed.' Susan fumbled in her bag for a fresh tissue. 'You must think I've taken leave of my senses. It was his next-door neighbour who told me — last Sunday. It was almost as though she was waiting for us to get back. It was horrible, Karen. She was so nasty and spiteful. You should have heard what she said — that I was lowering the tone of the neighbourhood; that I was depraved and had no morals. She made me feel like — like some old trollop.' She blew her nose and dabbed at her cheeks.

'So what did Ted say when you told him what she'd said?'

'I didn't give him the chance. I walked out — came straight home.'

'And he hasn't tried to get in touch?'

'Oh, he's tried of course. He keeps on ringing and texting, but I don't reply. I don't want to hear his lame excuses. He lied to me.'

'He definitely told you his wife was dead?'

'Well . . . ' Susan took a deep breath. 'I've been thinking about that. I don't think he

115

actually used those words, but he did say he'd been on his own for some years.' She looked at Karen. 'Devious. That's what he was. He let me believe what I wanted to believe. He thought he could pull the wool over my eyes.'

'Well, I think he owes you an explanation,' Karen said. 'You deserve one.'

'I don't want any more to do with him,' Susan said firmly. 'You said he could be a conman and it turns out you were right.'

Karen looked at her watch. 'I'm sorry, Mum, but I'll have to go. Look, pay for your shopping and I'll run you home on my way back to school.'

'But it isn't on your way,' Susan protested as she got up and took the trolley handle.

Karen took her arm. 'I haven't time to argue with you. Just let's get to the checkout.'

★   ★   ★

In the car on the way home, Susan realized that they'd only talked about her problems and she felt slightly guilty. Turning to Karen she said, 'You must think I'm awful; full of my own woes. I haven't asked how things are going with you. How are Simon and little Peter? And how is that new au pair girl of yours fitting in?'

'Simon and Peter are fine,' Karen told her. 'As for Adrey, I'm letting her go home to Holland for Easter. Her father hasn't been well and she wants to see him and the rest of her family. Seems there are quite a few of them back in Amsterdam. I think she's been feeling a little bit homesick too.'

116

'Do you think she might want to stay, once she gets back?' Susan asked, but Karen shook her head.

'No. She's promised me she won't do that. She loves it here really and she adores Peter.' She glanced at her mother. 'Why don't you come and stay with us for a few days at Easter?'

Susan hesitated. 'Oh, I don't know.'

'Come on, Mum,' Karen urged. 'You don't want to be stuck in the flat over the holiday feeling sorry for yourself, do you?'

Susan bridled. 'I don't think I've ever been one to wallow in self-pity.'

Karen laughed. 'Come off it, Mum. You know what I mean. It's ages since we've had a real family Easter.'

So finally Susan had agreed.

★ ★ ★

Once Susan was back in the flat, she felt better. Whether it was Karen's sympathy or just the change of scene, she didn't know or care. She felt stronger; almost ready to try and forget Ted and his duplicity and start making fresh plans for the future. 'I'll be fine,' she told herself as she unpacked her shopping and put it away. 'Maybe that Dutch girl will want to stay at home in Holland once she gets there, then they'll want me to take care of Peter again. Ted Mumford can go and find some other gullible woman to tell his lies to.'

But later that afternoon, as she sat there alone watching afternoon TV, she thought longingly about the allotment. All her little seedlings would be ready for pricking out now. She thought about the little shed on Ted's plot and how they'd brew mugs of tea when they took a break. Often, she'd take homemade cake or scones and jam to eat with it. Ted had loved that. He had loved her home cooking. Her thoughts wandered to the muscles in his strong arms and how they had rippled as he loaded the car boot with their gardening implements — and although she tried hard not to remember — the same strong arms, warm around her later as they lay together in his bed.

She sighed. They could have been so happy together if only — if only . . .

14

'So I've asked her to come and spend Easter with us,' Karen said as she unpacked her briefcase.

'You've *what?*' Simon turned to look at her. 'You might have asked me first.'

Karen stared at him. 'Are you saying that I have to ask your permission to invite my own mother to stay for Easter?'

Simon gave an exasperated snort. 'Bloody hell, Karen! I'd planned for us to have some time to ourselves as Adrey is going home. I even thought we might slip away somewhere for a proper break.'

'I had to ask her, Simon. You should have seen her. She's absolutely devastated about this guy lying to her.'

He frowned. 'Well — she's only got herself to blame really, hasn't she? I mean, some old geezer who goes around picking up women on buses. I ask you!'

'She really liked him though,' Karen said. 'They'd been gardening together. Mum had even got herself an allotment. They'd been on weekend jaunts to the seaside and they had all sorts of plans.'

'You'll be telling me next they'd been sleeping together!' Simon laughed.

'Well — as a matter of fact . . .'

'*No!*' He stared at her incredulously. 'At their age? Well, well. He must be a right old dog. Good for him!'

'*Don't!*' Karen said. 'It's not funny. I shouldn't have told you. Don't you dare let on to her that you know.'

Simon pulled a face. 'As if! Right, so they've split up. What happened? Was he two-timing her with some other old . . . ' He caught the look on Karen's face and stopped. 'What did he lie about anyway?'

'She'd got the impression that he was a widower but it seems that his wife is still alive.'

'But they're not together so . . . ?'

'And in a care home,' Karen finished.

'Oh, I see. Well, I suppose that was pretty devious.'

'Exactly. So now perhaps you can see why she feels let down. She's humiliated and shamed.'

He shrugged. 'That's overreacting a bit, isn't it? It's not her fault. Anyway, I daresay it happens all the time.'

'Not to my mother, it doesn't. She's a different generation, Simon. In her day, that kind of thing was really scandalous. I still think it's a pretty rotten way to behave anyway. Morals have may have reached an all-time low but I'd have expected better from a man of his age.'

Simon smiled indulgently. 'I can see that some of Susan's indignation has rubbed off on you, my love.' He put his arms round her and pulled her close. 'Tell you what, if your mother is coming why don't we slip away, just the two of us and leave Peter with her?'

She pushed him away. 'We can't do that. She'll think I only invited her so that we can use her as a babysitter.'

He shook his head. 'Oh, you and your bloody conscience! OK, so we have to have your mum here and sit listening to her going on and on about her car crash of a love affair.'

'Oh, don't be ridiculous.' Karen sighed. 'You make having Mum for a couple of days sound like a boring chore.'

'Oh, heaven *forbid*!' Simon sneered.

'Why can't you cheerfully do something for someone else for a change? At least we're not going to be saddled with Louise this year.'

Simon turned in the doorway. 'Well, I suppose that's what you'd call a *small mercy*. Here's to a dreary Easter. I can hardly wait!'

15

As we were preparing to break for lunch, Mark sidled across to me.

'Lou, can we talk?'

I was chatting to Phil and I gave Mark my freeze-'em-dead look. 'Can't it wait? I'm busy.'

He looked at Phil. 'Sorry, mate but will you excuse us? It's important.'

To my annoyance Phil grinned and walked away. 'See you, Lou,' he muttered.

I stared at Mark. 'For your information, that was an important conversation. What can you possibly want to talk about?'

'Us.'

I raised an eyebrow. 'I wasn't aware that there was an 'us'.'

He ignored the remark. 'We can't go on like this,' he said. 'It's too ridiculous for words. All I'm doing is putting a roof over my sister's head for a few weeks and you're hardly speaking to me. Can't you see I had no choice?'

'That's not the point. You let me down, Mark. I'd already told Di — I mean, I'd already given my flat up.'

He frowned. 'But you've found another one. It was only for a few weeks anyway. We'll be going on tour soon.'

'As I just said, that's not the point.'

'Look, you say your flat is quite near, so can

we go there and talk? I want to put things right between us, Lou.'

I panicked, remembering the glorified description I'd given him of my so-called flat. I'd die if he saw that it was only a bedsit, and a grotty one at that. I shook my head. 'It's not convenient.'

'Well, the pub, then. It won't be as private but it'll do. Oh, come on, Lou. Get down off that high horse of yours.'

I have to admit that it was nice, being on good terms with Mark again and knowing that he really cared what I was feeling, though I wasn't about to let him think me a pushover. It was true that he'd let me down and he was going to have to work hard for forgiveness. In the end, he offered to treat me to lunch and I accepted. We were just studying the menu when my phone buzzed in my bag. I fished it out.

'Hello.'

'Hello. Is this Louise Delmar?'

'Speaking.'

'This is Daniel from the Salvation Army. I have good news for you.'

I felt my heartbeat quicken as I listened to what he had to say. When I'd spoken to him earlier, he'd laid out the way things worked. He'd warned me that if the person being sought was tracked down, their whereabouts would not be disclosed unless they'd agreed. That was a given and not up for negotiation. I'd explained to him who I was and briefly, the circumstances of losing touch with my mother. I also told him that I was an actress, about to star in a new musical in the West End. I thought that might sway things a little. Now he was on the other end of my phone, telling me that he had found my mother and that she was willing to meet me. I could hardly believe my luck.

'Where?' I asked him breathlessly. 'And when?'

'She suggested meeting in the coffee lounge at Selfridge's — possibly tomorrow afternoon — about three o'clock, but I can give you a telephone number and you can alter the arrangements if you need to. She has reverted to her maiden name by the way. Jean Sowerby.'

'Oh, really? Thanks. I will ring, just in case, so if you give me the number I'll make a note of it. Thank you so much, Daniel.' He gave me the number and I added it to my contacts. As I shoved my phone back in my bag, I looked up at Mark, who was staring at me enquiringly.

'That sounded intriguing,' he said. 'And from the way your eyes are shining, I'd guess it was good news.'

'The best!' I told him what the caller had said and the tentative arrangements that had been made. 'I'll ring her this afternoon,' I told him. 'I have to admit that I feel quite nervous now that it's really happening.'

'Do you want me to come with you?' Mark offered. 'I mean, I'd keep out of the way while you meet and talk, but I could be there for you just in case it doesn't work out.'

'Oh no, everything will be fine. I don't need any moral support,' I told him. Seeing his disappointed face I reached out and touched his arm. 'But thank you, Mark. It's kind of you to offer.' I really did feel touched at his thoughtfulness. I was sorry I'd been so mean to him; after all, I knew he really did care for me and he could be so useful in the months to come, once he got rid of that grasping sister of his.

Our food arrived and we tucked in. Mark told me that he intended to take the Ferrari down to Bournemouth when we opened on tour. 'It'll be much more convenient than catching trains,' he said. 'I was sort of hoping you'd join me. I'd appreciate your company.'

'That would be lovely,' I said, trying not to let him see how excited I was at the thought of being driven everywhere in Mark's glamorous car.

He looked at me with his puppy-dog eyes over his plate of pasta. 'Do I take it that I'm forgiven, then?'

After the exciting phone call I'd just had, I would have forgiven the Devil himself. I leaned across the table and kissed his cheek. 'Of course I forgive you,' I whispered in my sexiest voice. 'How could I not?'

★　★　★

Back at the bedsit I took out my phone and clicked in the number Daniel had given me, holding my breath. In just a few seconds I'd actually be speaking to the mother I'd lost all those years ago.

'Hello.'

I gasped at the sound of her voice. 'Oh — er — hello. Ms Sowerby?'

'Speaking. Who is this?'

'It's Louise. Your — your daughter.'

There was a pause at the other end, then she said, 'Hello, Louise. Fancy hearing from you. It was a real surprise when the chap from the Sally Army rang.'

'Yes, I expect it was.' I swallowed hard, my mouth suddenly dry. 'He said you'd suggested meeting tomorrow afternoon at Selfridge's.'

'That's right, but if it isn't convenient . . . '

'No! I mean, yes, it is. I'm busy with rehearsals but I'm free in the afternoon. Shall we say three o'clock?'

'That would be fine. See you there, then.'

'Wait! How will I recognize you?' I asked. 'And you me of course. I've grown a bit since you last saw me.'

'Oh yes, of course. Best if I wait for you in the coffee lounge,' she said. 'I'll be wearing a royal-blue coat.'

'I'll wear a black suit,' I told her. 'You used to have dark hair,' I went on tentatively. 'Is it still?'

'Blonde now,' she said quickly. 'You?'

'Blonde too.' I laughed shakily. 'See you at three, then . . . ' I found suddenly that I had no idea what to call her. I couldn't quite bring myself to call her 'Mum' after all these years.

'Yeah — see you.' She hung up.

I was there at five to three the next afternoon. I went up to the coffee lounge and looked around. She clearly hadn't arrived. I took a corner table and watched from a distance. For some reason, I wanted to see what she looked like before I made myself known to her. People came and went but so far no one in a royal-blue coat. I began to think she'd chickened out. Then at ten past three she arrived. I was shocked. She was nothing like the woman I remembered. She was short — shorter than I remembered her. She was quite plump too. Her hair was longish and bleached a brassy shade of blonde that spoke of home hair-dressing. She looked thoroughly down at heel. Could this really be my mother? But there was no one else around in a royal-blue coat. As I watched she stood looking round nervously. I hadn't the heart to keep her waiting any longer so I took a deep breath and stood up. Catching her eye, I smiled. She hurried towards me.

'Louise?'

I nodded. 'Good to see you. Please, sit down.'

Now that I was closer I could see that life had not been kind to her. Her face was very lined and her upper lip had the creased look of the heavy smoker. I ordered a pot of tea and cakes and when the waitress had gone, I smiled at her.

'Well — I hardly know where to begin.'

'I hear you're a big star,' she said enthusiastically. 'Who'd have thought it?'

I shook my head. 'I'm not quite a star yet but the show I'm about to take the leading part in is destined for success.'

'How wonderful.' She paused. 'How — how's your dad?'

I frowned. Of course, she wouldn't know. 'Dad died a few years ago,' I told her. 'He married again after your divorce. Her name is Susan and they have a daughter, Karen.'

She showed no emotion at all. 'I married again too,' she said. 'But it was a disaster.'

'You weren't happy?'

'Happy?' She gave a short laugh. 'Gotta be joking! He was bad through and through — treated me something rotten but eventually the law caught up with him. He was caught — aggravated burglary, the verdict was. He battered a poor bloke half to death in his own home and this time he went to prison. The only good thing to come out of it was my boy, Steven — Steve.'

I stared at her. 'So — I have a . . . ?'

'Half-brother,' she said. She looked at me. 'I suppose when your dad died, this Susan woman came in for everything, did she?'

'No. He left me the house and everything in it,' I told her. 'He left Susan and Karen provided for, of course, but I think I came in for the bulk of his estate because he felt I'd had a raw deal.'

Her eyes lowered. 'A raw deal, eh? Well, he would say that — and I suppose it was true in a way.' She looked up at me. 'But believe me, Louise, no one will ever know what it cost me to walk out and leave you behind. But I had no money and nowhere to go so I had no choice. Frank loved you and you had a comfortable home with him. You were better off where you were. I was only thinking of you.'

I shook my head. 'It's all water under the bridge now.'

'I didn't forget you,' she said. 'I sent you birthday cards for a few years but I never got no replies so I reckoned he didn't let you see them.

Oh, well . . . ' She applied herself to the cake on her plate. 'Well, now that you've found me, we must stay in touch,' she said at last.

'Tell me about Steve,' I prompted.

She looked away. 'Maybe I will, eventually. We'll see.' I was about to pursue the matter when she suddenly changed the subject. 'When does your show open — which theatre?'

'We're going on tour first so I can't tell you that yet,' I told her. 'At the moment we're still rehearsing at St Mary's Church Hall in Stoke Newington and I've taken a temporary flat nearby, but as soon as I know where we open, I'll send you tickets for the opening night.'

'Ooh!' She smiled. 'Fancy me being the mum of a big star.'

I watched her as she helped herself to another cake. 'Your husband — is he still alive?' I asked.

She shrugged. 'I s'pose so. I've divorced him since he's been banged up and reverted to my maiden name. I daresay he's spittin' blood about that. Still, there's not a lot he can do about it in there.'

I felt a stab of alarm. 'How long is he in for?'

She shrugged. 'He got a seven stretch but they only serve about half o'that, don't they? He'll be due for release in a few months' time, but my Steve'll see I don't come to no harm if he comes round lookin' for revenge.'

'Aren't you worried?'

'No. I'll soon get the police onto him again if he starts threatening me. He won't want to go down for another stretch, will he?' She helped herself to another cake and devoured it with relish. 'Those folks at the Sally Army are really clever, you know,' she remarked through a mouthful of cake. 'Tracking me down through three different names.'

By half past four, all the cakes had disappeared. She looked at me. 'I'm sorry but I'll have to go now, Louise,' she said. 'It's been lovely meeting you. Maybe we could do this again.'

'Perhaps I could come to your home next time,' I suggested.

'Yeah.' She looked flustered. 'Well, maybe sometime, we'll see.'

'I'll give you my mobile number.' I scribbled it down on the corner of a paper napkin and passed it across the table to her.

She took it from me. 'What about your address?' she asked.

'Well, as I said, it's only temporary at the moment. I had to give up my flat in Earl's Court,' I said. 'Do you know Stoke Newington?' To my relief she shook her head. 'Well, as I told you, we're off on the pre-West End tour soon so I took this room in Mason Street. It's not very nice but it's quite close to the rehearsal venue. I won't be there after next week though, but if you give me your address I'll keep in touch.'

She looked shifty. 'Oh — well, they've recently altered the postcode and I can't remember it at the moment but I'll ring and let you know.'

I paid the bill and we travelled down together on the escalator. 'Are you heading for the Undergound like me?' I asked as we stood in the store entrance. She shook her head.

'I've got a couple of things to do yet.' She

looked me in the eye. 'Louise, I suppose you couldn't lend me a few quid, could you, love? I'll pay you back next time I see you.'

I was taken aback. 'Oh! Yes, OK. How much?'

'A couple of hundred will do,' she said calmly.

I was stunned. I'd been expecting her to ask for a fiver — a tenner at most; something to tide her over till next pension day and I had to stop myself from gasping with shock. 'I don't carry that much money around with me,' I told her.

'A cheque will do.'

Once more her coolness shook me. I took out my cheque-book and managed to write a cheque balancing the book on my handbag. I tore it out and gave it to her. 'I hope I haven't given you the wrong impression,' I told her. 'Dad did leave me well provided for but I've had to put money into this production and it's left me quite short.'

She smiled derisively as though she didn't believe a word of it. 'Yeah, but no doubt you'll get it all back. You'll be quids in once the show opens in the West End, won't you?' She put the cheque away in her handbag and looked across the road. 'Oh, there's my bus. I'll have to run. See you soon, Louise — and thanks.'

I watched as she scuttled across the road. What was I to make of all that? The afternoon had turned out to be far from what I'd expected.

16

Karen picked her mother up in the car on the afternoon of Good Friday.

'Thank goodness we've got a couple of weeks off now,' she said as they drove. 'What with making Easter cards and decorating eggs, it's been pretty hectic these last couple of weeks.'

It didn't sound all that onerous to Susan, who sat beside her daughter quietly. She didn't feel much like talking after yesterday afternoon and she wished Karen would shut up for a minute. Her constant chatter was grating on her nerves like a steel file.

Sensing her mother's unease, Karen glanced at her. 'Everything all right, Mum?'

'Perfectly, thank you.'

'You seem a bit — well, not quite yourself.'

Susan turned to look at her daughter. 'We can't all be chatterboxes.'

'Oh! Is that how I seem? I'm sorry.'

Susan bit her lip. 'Oh, Karen, I'm sorry. I didn't mean that the way it came out.'

'What is it, Mum? I can tell something's upset you.'

Susan shook her head. 'It's nothing. I've got a bit of a headache, that's all.'

'Oh, well, a nice cup of tea and a couple of paracetamol will soon put that right. We're nearly home now.'

'Has your Dutch girl gone home?'

'Yes. She went yesterday. She's only away for a week. Simon's looking after Peter this afternoon.'

'I can't wait to see him. It seems ages.'

Karen flushed guiltily. It was true that she hadn't taken Peter to visit his grandmother for weeks. There just hadn't been the time. 'You always seemed to be so busy with Ted,' she said defensively.

Susan turned to look out of the window so that Karen wouldn't see the quick tears that sprang to her eyes. One spilled over to run down her cheek and she fumbled in her handbag for a tissue. Karen looked at her.

'I knew it! There *is* something wrong, isn't there, Mum?' She pulled the car over and switched off the engine. 'Tell me now, before we get home.'

Susan sniffed and put the tissue away. 'I'm just being silly really,' she muttered. 'It's just that yesterday I had a sudden urge to go and look at the allotment. All the seeds I planted would be needing attention and I . . . '

'You saw Ted?' Karen prompted.

Susan swallowed. 'I — came away before he saw me,' she said. 'I couldn't face speaking to him.'

'Oh, Mum. You should have stayed and had it out with him — cleared the air.'

Susan shrugged. 'Maybe.' She forced a smile and changed the subject. 'Let's not talk about it any more. Let's just look forward to Easter.'

Karen said nothing. She wondered what kind of reception Simon's idea of their taking a weekend break and leaving Susan to look after

Peter would get, especially as her mother was in this emotional state. She'd tried to talk him out of it but he insisted that they both needed a break and she had to admit that she was looking forward to it.

Susan sat staring out of the window. It had been a shock yesterday afternoon when she'd decided, after a lot of heart searching, to take a walk round to the allotments to see Ted. She'd expected to see him working away on his plot and envisaged his pleasure at seeing her. She'd even taken a couple of slices of newly baked raspberry sponge; his favourite. Over and over in her head she'd rehearsed what she would say and imagined his response. But when she got there, she found him working on what had been her allotment. And he wasn't alone. A woman was helping him. Aged, Susan guessed, in her forties, the woman was tall and slim with dark curly hair. Susan had certainly never seen her before. She could see that all the seedlings she had planted had been pricked out and were now in neat rows, coming along nicely. She watched from a distance as they worked together, hoeing the rows. The woman straightened up, one hand to her back. She said something and they laughed together and set off towards Ted's hut, no doubt to take a break for refreshment. Resentment tore at Susan's breast. It hadn't taken him long to find someone else! Was *she* aware of the situation? she wondered. Did he take *her* back to his bungalow? Had they — were they — more than friends? Unable to bear it any longer she had made a hasty retreat, returning

134

home with her mind in turmoil and wishing she had not given in to her impulse to try to see Ted that afternoon. He obviously wasn't missing her at all!

★ ★ ★

At they walked in through the front door Peter came running to meet her. 'Granny!' He threw himself into her arms and she lifted him up to hug him.

'Let's see what Granny has brought you,' she said, putting him down again. Opening her bag she produced a bar of chocolate. 'Only a little bit now,' she said. 'And save the rest for after tea.'

She fed Peter his tea and then asked to be allowed to bath him and put him to bed. She read him a story about his favourite Thomas the Tank Engine and came downstairs, savouring the smell of Karen's home-made lasagne. As the three of them sat down to eat, Simon looked across at his mother-in-law.

'Susan,' he said casually, tearing off a piece of his roll and buttering it. 'We were wondering if you would like to do us a little favour while you're here.' He carefully avoided Karen's grimace.

Susan looked up. 'Of course, what is it?'

'Well, we — Karen and I have both been working really hard and we thought — wondered how you would feel about our taking a little break while you're here to be with Peter?'

'Oh.' Susan's heart sank. 'Over Easter, you mean?'

135

'Well, yes, this weekend is our only chance.'

Susan glanced at Karen, whose eyes were on her plate. 'I don't see why not,' she said. 'It would give me time to spend with Peter — as long as he doesn't miss you too much.'

'Oh, he won't,' Simon said quickly. 'And even if he did it would only be for a couple of days.'

'Where were you thinking of going?' Susan asked.

'Paris actually,' Simon replied. 'It's a nice little hotel quite close to the Eiffel Tower.'

'Oh, I see. You've already booked it, then?' Susan couldn't keep the resentment out of her voice. It was only too clear now that they'd taken her for granted. She had only been invited so that she could babysit while they went away for a break.

Karen broke in. 'We booked before Adrey asked if she could go home,' she said. 'With her father being ill we could hardly refuse.'

'No, of course not,' Susan said, wondering why Karen hadn't mentioned it before. 'And of course I'll be happy to take care of Peter while you're away. It'll be a pleasure. When are you going?'

'Tomorrow,' Simon said, maintaining his casual manner. 'Our flight leaves at ten o'clock so we'll have to be away from here quite early.'

★ ★ ★

Susan got up early next morning to see Karen and Simon off for their break. She stood at the front door with Peter in her arms, waving as they drove away.

'Where Mummy and Daddy goin'?' Peter

136

asked, his little face bewildered.

'They're going for a little holiday,' Susan told him, giving him a hug. 'But it's only for two days and you and I are going to have such a lovely time while they're away, aren't we?'

The little boy nodded uncertainly. 'Brekspup?' he said hopefully.

Susan laughed. 'Yes, Nana and Peter are going to have breakfast together now. And afterwards we'll go to the park and feed the ducks. Would you like that?'

He smiled. 'Yes, please. Have poddidge now?'

'Yes, porridge coming up.'

After Susan had cleared away the breakfast things and washed up, she got Peter's buggy out from under the stairs. It was a lovely morning, although the wind was still keen, and she wrapped Peter up warmly before they set out. In the park, the snowdrops and crocuses were out and even a few early daffodils. They made her think of the allotment and her heart twisted, reminding her of how much she missed it.

Down at the lake, she broke up the bread they had brought into duck-sized pieces and Peter threw it to them, laughing as they squabbled and splashed, racing one another to get it first. When all the bread had gone they went for a walk, Susan pushing the buggy and holding Peter's hand as they made their way slowly around the lake. She was trying to persuade him to get back into the buggy again when she spotted Ted. Her heart quickened and she tried to hurry away in the opposite direction but Peter complained loudly.

'No — *this* way,' he cried loudly. 'Want to see birdies.'

She had promised him a visit to the aviary where there were peacocks and other rare birds. 'Tomorrow,' she said. 'Nana will take you tomorrow.'

'No! *Now!* Want to go now!'

Susan glanced up and saw to her dismay that Ted had heard Peter's cries and was hurrying towards them. She sighed. 'All right,' she said resignedly. 'We'll go now.'

Ted was breathless as he caught up with them. 'Hello there.' He bent down to Peter. 'Did I hear you say you wanted to see the birdies? Well, suppose I come with you?' he said. 'I was on my way there anyway. Now, are you going to sit in that comfy pushchair again? And will you let me push you?'

'Yes.' Peter obediently climbed back into his buggy and Ted took the handle from Susan.

'I've tried countless times to ring you,' he said quietly as they walked. 'You never get back to me.'

Susan couldn't look at him. 'There's a good reason for that,' she said.

'Maybe, in your eyes,' he replied. 'But you've never given me the chance to explain.'

'I don't want to listen to any more lies,' Susan said, looking straight ahead.

'You're being very unfair,' Ted said thickly. 'There's a very good reason for everything if only you'd stop and listen.'

They'd reached the aviaries and Peter had climbed out of his buggy to look at the birds.

Susan turned to Ted. 'Actually I came up to the allotments yesterday afternoon to see you,' she said.

His eyebrows rose. 'You did? I didn't see you.'

'No, you were too busy laughing with your new lady friend!' She took Peter's hand and bundled him, protesting, back into his buggy. 'We have to go now. Peter is due for his nap.' She set off at a smart pace while Ted gazed after her.

'Susan — wait,' he called. But Susan didn't look back.

★ ★ ★

When Karen and Simon arrived home, Susan sensed an atmosphere between them.

'Did you have a nice time?' she asked as Karen unpacked her case in the bedroom.

'Yes, thank you. It was lovely,' Karen replied without enthusiasm.

Susan sat down on the bed. 'So — what did you do? Did you go to the Louvre and the Moulin Rouge?'

'Oh yes, we did all the usual touristy things just as you'd expect.'

'You don't sound very enthusiastic.'

Karen sighed and looked at her mother. 'That's probably because we spent most of the time rowing.'

'Oh, no! That's a shame. What did you find to row about?'

Karen hung the last of her clothes in the wardrobe and sat down beside her mother. 'I broke it to him that I've agreed to be one of the teachers to go on the school trip to Spain during the spring break. He was furious.'

'But surely as head, decisions like that are up to him, aren't they?'

'Neil Harris, who takes RE. and games, is organizing this trip,' Karen explained. 'He's got carte blanche.'

'I see. So what is Simon's objection?'

Karen shook her head exasperatedly. 'You know how old-fashioned he is. He still hasn't really got his head round the idea of me going back to work. And leaving him and Peter for a whole week is completely beyond the pale.'

'Oh, dear.'

'But that's not all,' Karen said. 'Neil is a very friendly guy and Simon's got it into his head that he . . . ' She glanced up at her mother. 'That he fancies me and that he's only invited me on the trip for — well, for obvious reasons.'

'And is there any truth in it?' Susan enquired bluntly.

'*Mum!*' Karen looked scandalized. 'Of course there isn't.'

Susan shrugged. 'I only asked.'

'There's something else,' Karen said unhappily. 'Simon keeps on about us having another baby.'

'And you don't want one?'

'It's not that so much, Mum,' Karen said. 'It's just that I feel he's using it as a way to bring me to heel.'

Susan frowned. 'Bring you to heel? What on earth do you mean?'

'He never wanted me to be a working mother.

140

He obviously thinks that I'd be obliged to give up if I had another child.'

'Lots of people do work with more than one. And you have your au pair.'

Karen looked at her mother exasperatedly. 'You don't get it, do you, Mum? Simon wants to *control* me and it's not on. This is the twenty-first century and I'm not his property.'

Susan decided it wasn't up to her to express an opinion or take sides so she just shrugged. 'I'm afraid that's something you're going to have to work out for yourselves,' she said.

'But you do see my point, surely?' Karen pressed.

'It's really none of my business,' Susan said. 'For what it's worth, I think it's something you need to be in complete agreement on.'

'But we've reached stalemate. Simon won't change his mind.'

Susan patted her daughter's hand. 'Then maybe you'll have to come to some kind of compromise,' she advised. 'But don't stop discussing it. Keeping quiet only breeds resentment.' Susan looked at her daughter. 'And while we're on the subject, Karen, why didn't you tell me from the start that you wanted me to babysit Peter while you and Simon went to Paris?'

Karen coloured. 'I didn't know at the time.'

'You did, though. You told me yourself that the trip was already booked.'

'That was a fib, Mum. To begin with I asked you because I thought you needed a break. It was only after I told Simon I'd invited you that he said it would be a good idea for us to take a weekend away.'

'All right, but why didn't you say so? Why lie about it?'

Karen sighed. 'It's what I'm trying to tell you, Mum. He always expects to get his own way. It was never my intention to go away and leave you in charge. I thought it was an imposition but in the end I gave in. Then I had to lie to you to back him up.'

Susan shook her head. 'You're going to have to make up your mind what it is you do want,' she said. 'And then stick to it. It's the only way if you want your marriage to work equally.'

'I know you're right.' Karen sighed. 'I just wish it wasn't so hard, keeping everyone happy.'

17

When I got back to the bedsit, I thought a lot about my meeting with Mum. It couldn't have been further from what I'd hoped for. To begin with, I'd stupidly visualized her as looking exactly the same as the last time we'd set eyes on each other. That was more than thirty years ago and the truth of it was that we were strangers. If we'd passed each other in the street we'd have been none the wiser. Getting to know one another all over again was going to take time — a lot of time. The question was, after this disappointing meeting was I prepared to put in the necessary time and effort? I wasn't at all sure.

The fact that she'd asked me for money had definitely put me off. After all, it was our first meeting for more than three decades. Then there was the fact that she'd obviously sunk to the depths; married a criminal and divorced him while he was in prison. If he was as bad as she made out, there were bound to be repercussions. Surely he was going to be fuming when he came out of prison and would be looking for revenge. On the other hand, if she told him that the daughter from her previous marriage had plenty of money (even though I haven't any more) wouldn't that be an incentive for him to get me to share the spoils? I began to wish I hadn't told her so much or given her my telephone number — more, I wished I'd never bothered to look for her.

I was so disappointed and depressed. I'd had some stupid naïve vision of this sweet, gentle woman, overjoyed to find her long-lost daughter — of her being loving and supportive — proud of me even. I'd imagined her as having made good in spite of her difficulties. I'd even visualized her as glamorous. Instead, this shadowy figure from my past, returning to give me the special maternal love I'd missed out on for most of my life, had turned out to be nothing more than a conniving woman on the make.

★   ★   ★

When I saw Mark at rehearsals the next morning, he was eager to hear all about our meeting.

'Come on, then, how did it go?'

I forced a smile. 'Oh, very well really.'

'Is that all?' he asked looking disappointed. 'Are you seeing her again? Did you hit it off?'

'I couldn't make any arrangements,' I told him. 'I said I'd get back in touch after the tour.'

He pulled a face. 'You don't exactly sound euphoric about it.'

'We hadn't set eyes on each other for over thirty years,' I said. 'It's early days. One hour over tea and cakes isn't going to make up for all that time.' At the mention of cakes, I recalled the greedy way she'd scoffed every single one of them without even offering the plate to me. It was just another of her less than endearing qualities.

Mark was peering at me. 'Oh-oh, it didn't go

as well as you expected; you're disappointed?'

'Of course I'm not.'

'Did she fail to live up to your expectations?'

'No. She was — everything was absolutely fine.'

He grinned maddeningly. 'Ah — methinks the lady doth protest too much!'

I nudged him sharply in the ribs. 'Oh, shut up, Mark!'

I was relieved when Paul Fortune arrived at that moment and called for us all to gather round. 'This will be the last rehearsal for us here,' he announced. 'I'm giving you all next week off and then we're going down to Bournemouth where we'll have a week's rehearsal with the full orchestra. There'll be costume fittings as well and we open the following week.'

I felt a flutter of anticipation in my stomach, and Mark and I exchanged excited looks.

After the rehearsal was over, we went to the pub. As we sat down with our drinks I looked at Mark. 'So — we're really on our way!'

'Looks like it.' He took a long pull of his beer and set the glass down with a sigh of satisfaction. 'What are you going to do with your week's holiday?' he asked.

I shrugged. 'Not a lot. I'm practically out of money.'

He looked surprised. 'Really?'

I nodded. 'Down to my last few hundred and I don't suppose I'll be getting any refund on my investment for quite a while.'

'That's true.' He took another swig from his

glass and looked at me, one eyebrow raised. 'If you're struggling I can let you have a loan.'

'No, I'll be all right,' I protested. 'Just have to go easily, that's all.'

'There'll be digs to pay for on tour, don't forget,' he reminded me.

'I know. I think I can handle that OK.'

'Well, you know the help is there if you need it.'

I looked at him. Mark was such a good friend — but was he too good to be true? Could I really trust him? I didn't want him thinking he could start calling in favours and I'd no intention of dropping my guard. 'As a matter of fact, I thought I might go home for a few days,' I said. 'Not that it's really what you'd call home, but Karrie and Susan are all the family I've got.'

'I'm sure they'd be more than happy to see you,' Mark said heartily.

I nodded, doubting his optimism. 'How's your sister?' I asked, changing the subject.

'She's fine. She had an interview for a job last week and she heard this morning that she's got it. It's secretary at the local primary school which will fit in nicely with the kids' school holidays. She's seen a little house that she likes too.'

My heart lifted. 'Right, so you'll have the flat to yourself again when we come back from the tour.'

He smiled. 'Are you still interested in moving in?'

Something in me — the contrary side of my nature — resented his taking it for granted that I would jump at the chance. 'Well, we'll see,' I said. 'I might move back in with Di.'

To my satisfaction he looked crestfallen. 'Oh. I thought you'd given your flat up.'

'I did.' I searched my mind for a way out of the corner I'd backed myself into; trying to remember the last thing I told him. 'But Di took on the lease as I told you,' I said as inspiration struck. 'So it's still an option.' Sometimes I amazed myself by my quick thinking.

He drained his glass. 'Well, the offer's there if you change your mind. When are you going home?'

'I'll have to ring and ask when it's convenient,' I told him.

'Well, give me a ring when you get back and we'll arrange to drive down to Bournemouth together.'

Back at the bedsit, I rang Susan's number, but I got the answerphone. I left her a message to ring me and set about making myself a sandwich. I'd just put the kettle on for coffee when my phone rang. I picked it up.

'Hi, Susan, that was quick . . . '

'It's not Susan,' a male voice said.

'Oh, then who . . . '

'This is Steve Harris — your brother.'

My heart gave a jump. 'Oh — er — hello.'

'You don't sound very pleased to hear from me.' His voice was deep and coarse with a strong cockney accent. I had a feeling of foreboding.

'What can I do for you?' I asked stupidly.

He chuckled at the other end of the line. 'Now, there's an offer. I thought we could meet,' he said. 'I think it would be nice to get to know

147

one another, don't you?'

I bit my lip. This was something I had to nip in the bud. 'Forgive me but I can't really see the point,' I said.

'What? You're saying that you don't want to meet your little brother after all these years?' The voice held a mocking tone.

'Until yesterday I didn't even know you existed,' I told him. 'And you're not my brother — only a half-brother.'

'Blood's blood,' he said. 'We share the same mum. She thought you were a bit of all right,' he said. 'In fact it was her idea that you and I got together. She thought we'd have a lot in common.'

'I doubt it,' I told him. 'As a matter of fact, I'm going away tomorrow and after that I'll be away on tour so I can't really see an opportunity for us to meet.'

'Oh dear, that's a pity,' he said smoothly.

'Yes, but there, it can't be helped,' I said, thinking that by the time we came back to London he'd have given up, with any luck. 'Goodbye.' I ended the call quickly and switched my phone off so that he couldn't ring back. 'Damned cheek,' I muttered as I made myself a coffee. No doubt he thought he could get some money out of me. Well, he had another think coming.

★ ★ ★

Susan didn't ring me back and in the end, I decided to just turn up. Maybe she'd be annoyed but it was only for a few days and I really didn't fancy staying in the grotty bedsit for a whole week with nothing to do. I took the train next morning and arrived in Bridgehampton just before lunch.

Susan didn't look surprised when she opened the door and found me outside.

Her expression was more one of resignation. 'Louise — how nice. Come in.'

'I did ring you yesterday,' I told her as I walked in through the door. 'I left a message. Didn't you get it?'

She shook her head. 'I don't always check,' she said.

I didn't believe a word. 'Is it convenient for me to stay for a few days?' I asked.

She looked at me and then at the small bag I was carrying. 'A few?'

'Just until the weekend,' I said. 'We're off down to Bournemouth next Monday to begin our tour so I'll need time to pack and leave the flat tidy.'

She didn't even try to conceal her relief. 'Oh, well, that's fine then,' she said. 'I'm afraid it will have to be the sofa again.'

'Yes, that's fine.' I unzipped my bag and pulled out the bottle of rosé wine I'd brought as a sweetener. I handed it to her. 'I got you this, Susan,' I said with a smile. 'I know it's one of your favourites.'

She took it from me, looking a bit taken aback, and when she spoke, her voice had softened a little. 'Oh, that was thoughtful of you. I was just going to make a meal. We can have it with that.'

'Better still, why don't you let me take you out to lunch as a thank-you for having me at short notice?' I suggested.

She smiled. 'Oh, thank you, Louise. That would be lovely. I'll get my coat.'

Over lunch I heard all about Karrie and Simon clearing off to Paris at Easter and leaving her literally holding the baby. I thought it was a bit thick of them but I decided to play it cool.

'Well, I know how you love little Peter so I don't suppose you minded,' I said.

We'd drunk a bottle of wine between us and it had loosened her inhibitions somewhat. She frowned.

'Of course I didn't mind having him,' she said. 'We had a lovely time together, the two of us. What I did mind was that Karen felt she had to manipulate me into it. If she'd asked outright I'd still have said yes.'

'Oh well, no doubt she had her reasons,' I said tactfully. 'And what about you? What have you been up to since I was here last?'

Her face clouded. 'Well, to tell the truth, dear, I've had a bit of a disappointment.'

'Over what?'

She looked up at me. 'Over a man actually.'

I raised an eyebrow at her. 'A man, eh? Well, you dark old horse, Susan.' I looked at her, my head on one side. 'So — are you going to tell me about it?'

I got the whole story — about the duplicitous Ted and his double life; about the lovely time she'd enjoyed with him only to discover his deception. When she'd finished pouring it all out to me, she looked up.

'I expect you think I'm a foolish old woman.'

I reached across the table to pat her hand. 'Of course I don't. The truth is, Susan, we women never seem to learn, do we?'

She sighed. 'I suppose not. The truth is I only ever loved one man and that was your father. I'm not used to the kind of games people play nowadays.'

'I met someone I used to be at drama school with,' I told her. 'He's in the same show and I thought we'd get together again. We spent Christmas together and he even asked me to move in with him. Just when I'd decided to say yes, he announced that he'd moved his sister and her two kids in.'

'Oh dear, why was that?' Susan looked concerned.

I shrugged. 'Search me. At a guess, I suppose he regretted asking me and moved them in to make things impossible.'

Susan shook her head. 'How devious of him. And now you have to see him every day — work with him. How uncomfortable.'

'Oh, we're still friends,' I told her lightly. 'We have to be under the circumstances.'

★ ★ ★

The following morning, Susan went out to the supermarket. She'd asked me to go too but I fancied a lie-in, even though it was only on the sofa. Soon after she'd gone, I got up and made myself some toast and coffee. I was just about to get into the shower when the bell rang. I dragged on my dressing gown and went to answer it.

151

Outside stood a tall, elderly man carrying a large bouquet of flowers. I guessed him to be the notorious Ted.

'Good morning,' I said frostily. 'Can I help you?'

He looked a bit taken aback. 'Oh — is Susan — Mrs Davies in?'

'No, she isn't,' I said. 'I'm Louise, her stepdaughter. I take it you are Ted.'

He nodded. 'That's right.'

'Well, I can tell you for nothing that you're wasting your time,' I told him. 'I've heard all about you. She wants nothing more to do with you and your devious ways so you can take your flowers and give them to the next gullible woman you pick up on the bus!' And with that I slammed the door in his astonished face.

When Susan arrived home I told her about Ted's visit. Her cheeks coloured.

'Oh. What did he say?'

I shrugged. 'Not a lot. I sent him on his way — told him what he could do with his flowers.'

'Flowers?' she enquired weakly.

'Yes. He was carrying this enormous bunch of flowers. Daffodils and irises and those vulgar stripy pink things. I've always hated those, haven't you?'

'Tulips? No. I quite like them actually.' She was unpacking the shopping, her back to me. 'What else did he say?'

'Nothing. I didn't give him the chance,' I told her. 'I don't think he'll be bothering you again though. If he didn't get the message he must be thick!'

'I see.' She turned to me. 'I take it you were rude to him?'

'I only told him you didn't want any more to do with him.'

'Well, I wish you hadn't,' Susan said. 'I wish you'd told him I was out and left it at that.'

I stared at her. 'After what he did? You must be mad if you're even thinking of taking him back after that.'

'But it's my decision, isn't it?' To my astonishment, her eyes filled with tears and she fumbled in her sleeve for a handkerchief. 'What I told you was in confidence and in future, I'd be grateful if you'd mind your own business, Louise.'

'But you said — you were really upset and . . . ' But she'd disappeared into her bedroom and closed the door firmly behind her. I sighed. Really! There was no pleasing some people.

The atmosphere was distinctly frosty after Ted's visit. Susan was distant — hardly speaking to me, and the following afternoon, I decided to go and say hello to Karrie. When I announced my intention to Susan she seemed relieved.

'She should be home from school by four,' she said. 'But she usually picks up some shopping before coming home so I should give her another half-hour if I were you.'

I took myself off to the pictures after lunch, unable to stand Susan's glum face any longer. There was hardly anyone else in the multiplex and the film was mediocre. I came out feeling depressed. Maybe it hadn't been the best idea to

153

come home after all. Even a visit to my bourgeois sister was preferable to going home to Susan. I took the bus to Sunnyside Drive and arrived at Karrie's soon after half past four. I rang the front doorbell and waited but no one came. I rang again — still no reply. But Simon's car was in the drive so I knew that someone had to be at home. I walked round the side of the house and through the back gate. The kitchen looked out over the back garden and I took a peek through the window. What I saw gave me a start. There in the middle of the kitchen, Simon was embracing a blonde girl. She had her head on his shoulder and he was holding her close and murmuring in her ear. I jumped back before either of them spotted me. My God! Simon of all people. And that old cliché: the husband and the au pair! Poor Karrie! Did she even suspect? I tiptoed away as quietly as I could, closing the side gate behind me. Walking down the tree-lined avenue my head was in a whirl. Karrie and Simon. The perfect couple. Who'd have thought it?

I was almost at the end of the road when Karrie's little car came round the corner. She saw me at once and pulled into the kerbside, winding down the window.

'Louise. Mum said you were coming for a visit. Were you coming to see us?'

I opened the passenger door and climbed in. 'I've just been,' I told her. 'Karrie, I'm so sorry but I've got something to tell you.'

'To tell me?' She looked alarmed. 'What are you talking about? Is it Mum?'

'No, she's fine. Look, I don't quite know how

to tell you this, but I've just called at yours. No one answered the door so I went round to the back. Karrie — Simon was in the kitchen. He was *kissing* your au pair girl.'

The colour left her face. '*Louise!* What on earth are you talking about?' she said shakily. 'I don't believe you. If this is one of your sick jokes . . .'

'It's no joke. I tell you, I saw them with my own eyes,' I told her. 'Do you want me to come back with you? If he denies it, I'll tell him what I've told you.'

'No! Please go now, Louise. I'll handle this on my own. It's between Simon and me.'

'Are you sure?'

'More than sure.'

I was a bit disappointed. I'd been looking forward to seeing the perfect Simon get his comeuppance. 'Well, if you want me you know where I am.'

'I do.' Karen tapped the steering wheel impatiently. 'Please, Louise, if you don't mind.'

'OK, I'm going.' I got out and bent to speak to her through the car window. 'I'm here till the weekend so if you need . . .' Before I could finish the sentence, she was revving up the car and I had to leap back to avoid the car as it sped off. I stared after it. Well, that was gratitude for you!

★ ★ ★

Susan and I were having our evening meal when we heard a key grating in the front door. Susan looked up.

155

'That will be Karen,' she said. 'She's the only other person who has a key. I wonder what she's doing here at this time of the evening.' She got up from the table. 'I hope nothing's wrong.'

Your smug little lives have hit the skids this time, I said inwardly.

Karrie burst into the room before Susan could reach the door. Her face was crimson and she was breathing heavily.

'You *bitch*!' she yelled at me. 'You interfering, trouble-making *bitch*!'

I stared at her, spreading my hands. 'What am I supposed to have done?'

'You put two and two together and made a hundred and four,' she said. 'Can you imagine how I looked, bursting in and accusing Simon and Adrey of adultery?'

'It was no more than they deserved,' I said. I hadn't mentioned the occurrence to Susan and now she was looking from one to the other of us with a shocked expression, at a loss to know what was going on.

'Will someone please tell me what this is about?' she demanded.

Karen looked at her. '*She* . . . ' She pointed her finger at me. 'She stopped me on my way home this afternoon to tell me that she had seen Simon kissing Adrey in our kitchen.'

Susan gasped. 'Oh my God!'

'He wasn't *kissing* her,' Karen went on. 'He was comforting her because she was upset. She'd just received a telephone call from home to tell her that her father had died. Can you even *begin* to imagine how that made me feel?'

'And you believed him?' I said. 'A likely story if you ask me.'

'Well, I'm not asking you,' Karrie shouted. 'And it's true. She's packing to go home for the funeral as we speak.' She took a step towards me. 'Your trouble, Louise, is that you think everyone is as nasty and devious as you are. Every time you come home there are ructions. The last time you almost had me locked up and now this! It's going to take me a long time to put things right this time. Adrey has already said she won't be coming back and Simon won't even speak to me. And it's all down to you!'

Her hands were clenching and unclenching, and I thought for a moment she was going to hit me until Susan stepped forward and took her arm.

'Calm down, darling,' she said. 'I know you're upset but I'm sure Louise only meant it for the best . . . '

'*The best?*' Karrie screamed. 'Don't try to stand up for her, Mum. She causes chaos wherever she goes. She thrives on it — does it on purpose. If you take my advice you'll kick her out. I know one thing — I'll never speak to her again.' She shook off Susan's restraining hand. 'It's all right. I'm going now. Give me a ring when you've got rid of her. Goodnight, Mum.'

Susan went to the door to see Karrie out. When she came back, her face was grave. 'Why, Louise?' she asked.

I shrugged. 'I know what I saw.'

'And you actually *saw* them kissing?'

'He was holding her,' I hedged. 'She had her

face close to his. They were about to kiss. I'd lay odds on it.'

'So you didn't actually witness a kiss between them?'

I got up from the table. 'Why split hairs? It was obvious what was going on. If Karrie wants to bury her head in the sand; if she wants to let him get away with it, then it's her funeral. I should have . . . '

'You should have minded your own business,' Susan finished for me. She began to clear the table. 'I think it might be best if you left first thing in the morning, Louise,' she said quietly. 'Karen was right, unfortunately. There always seems to be trouble when you're around.'

'I'll do better than that,' I told her. 'If this is all the thanks I'm going to get for telling the truth then I'll go now. I can catch the last London train at ten o'clock and be back before midnight.'

Susan didn't argue. 'As you wish,' she said.

★ ★ ★

It was really late when I got back to Stoke Newington. I wasn't looking forward to going back to my dingy bedsit and as I climbed the stairs wearily, I told myself I'd be glad to be out of the place. I rummaged in my bag for my key but when I went to put it in the lock the door swung open. Inside I found chaos. I'd been burgled. I stood, staring around me in disbelief. The place had been well and truly turned over, drawers pulled out and the contents strewn

158

everywhere. The bed had been stripped; cupboards emptied. I pushed the door closed and it was only then that I saw that it had been forced. I couldn't even secure it for the night. I pulled the chest of drawers across to block the doorway, then sat down on the bed and surveyed the mess. What a horrible week it had been, and now to come back to this. Luckily, there had been nothing of any value in the room. Certainly no money, but the feeling that someone had been here — could possibly come back — gave me the horrors. My first thought was for Mark. I needed him — needed someone kind and sympathetic. I took out my phone and selected his number. After a few rings, a woman's sleepy voice answered.

'Hello, Mark Naylor's flat.'

'I need to speak to Mark,' I said. 'Tell him it's Louise.'

'Isn't it rather late to be ringing?' the voice enquired. 'It's almost one a.m. We were asleep.'

'I'm sorry, but this is an emergency. Who am I speaking to?'

'This is Cathy, Mark's sister,' she said. 'Mark isn't here, he's gone away for a few days. Is there anything I can do?'

My heart sank. 'No, not really. When will he be back?'

'Tomorrow evening. A friend invited him to go up to Scotland for a few days.'

'Oh dear.' I swallowed hard. 'The fact is, I've just come back from a few days away and I've been burgled. The place is in a terrible state and I don't know what to do.'

159

'Have you rung the police?'

'No. I can't see the point. We're off down to Bournemouth in a couple of days and I'd have to go through all that red tape. Besides, as far as I can see nothing's been stolen.'

'OK, I'll get Mark to come over to you as soon as he gets back. Does he have your address?'

'No. It's room three, fourteen Mason Street, Stoke Newington.'

'Right. I've got that.'

'Thanks.' I switched off my phone and lay down on the rumpled bed, feeling totally sick. I'd been fobbing Mark off about my so-called 'flat' for weeks and now he was going to see this horrible room. But I was past caring. Thank God we were off down to Bournemouth in a few days and leaving it all behind. This had been the worst week of my life. Why had everyone been so bloody awful to me? I'd only done what anyone else would have done under the circumstances, and anyway, it was time they were all jolted out of their little suburban heaven, damn them!

18

Karen had given Peter his tea early, bathed him and put him to bed. He'd just about worn her out today, whingeing and crying for Adrey all day. Simon had insisted that she stay at home to look after him. There had been a horrible scene about it last night when she got home from Susan's flat. Karen shuddered at the memory.

By the time she'd arrived home Adrey had gone. Simon had put Peter in his car seat and driven her to the station. He was waiting for her when she got back from her mother's. She found him sitting in the living room with a face like thunder and the moment she got in, he started.

'I hope you're proud of yourself!'

Karen began to take off her coat. 'Well, I'm sorry but Louise was certain you were kissing her,' she said. 'How was I to know . . . ?'

'You didn't wait to find out, did you,' Simon stormed. 'Just came steaming in, throwing accusations around like confetti. That poor girl! It was the last thing she needed, or deserved after the news she'd just had.'

Karen winced. 'I know that now and I'm really sorry.'

Simon snorted. 'Too little, too late. She won't be coming back, thanks to you!'

Karen hung up her coat and came back to sit down opposite Simon. 'Well, I'll write a letter of apology to her.'

'I'm sure that will be a big comfort to her but you still won't get her back,' he said sarcastically. 'She said she'd have to stay anyway, to support her mother.'

'Oh, then it isn't *all* my fault?'

'So — you think that makes it all right then, do you? Bursting in and accusing the poor girl of seducing your husband. And have you even given a thought to how humiliating it was for me?'

'I've said I'm sorry.'

'Have I ever given you any reason not to trust me?'

'No.'

'Then why start now at the worst time possible? And since when have you taken anything Louise said as gospel?'

Karen sighed. 'I don't know. I was tired, I suppose. Adrey is very pretty and just lately . . .'

'Just lately you've had no time for me or Peter. You're always too tired and preoccupied. You were suffering pangs of guilt, that's it, isn't it?' Karen's shoulders drooped and he went on: 'Incidentally, in case you're wondering, *I* put Peter to bed. You're so self-centred you haven't even enquired about your son!'

'Well, I guessed you'd put him to bed, obviously. And I told you, I'll write to Adrey and apologize. I suppose we'll have to get Peter into a nursery now,' she said, half to herself. 'Either that or ask Mum to — '

'Oh no! We'll do nothing of the sort,' Simon broke in. 'From tomorrow *you'll* be taking care of him.'

Her eyes widened. 'But that's not possible.

162

What about my class?'

'I'll get a supply teacher in until I can replace you. You're packing the job in right away, Karen; at least until Peter goes to school. I've had enough. You're a wife and mother. That should take priority.'

★ ★ ★

So here she was, stuck in the house all day with a fractious child and a whole heap of ironing that Adrey hadn't had time to do before she left. And all thanks to Louise. Karen ground her teeth at the thought of how much she'd like to wring her sister's neck. Why *had* she believed what she said? She had to admit that Simon had been right. If she faced up to the truth she knew it. She had been neglecting her home and family lately. Once home from school, she had been too tired to play with Peter — too tired to listen to Simon's news when he came home, and at bedtime, too tired to make love. It was weeks since she had shared any intimate moments with Simon and if he had strayed she knew that she would only have had herself to blame.

But to have to stay at home day after mind-numbing day felt like a punishment. Peter was adorable, of course, and she loved him to bits, but to be restricted to the conversation one could have with a two-year-old, or, worse, with the other mothers clustered round the swings in the park, obsessed with which supermarket was the cheapest or which were the best nappies, was enough to drive her mad. A wail from upstairs told her that Peter was awake and demand-ing attention again. She sighed. Maybe she'd put him in his buggy and walk round to her mother's. It would pass the afternoon and by the time she got home it would be Peter's teatime.

★ ★ ★

Susan was pleased to see them both and immediately put the kettle on for the inevitable cup of tea.

'What are you doing home at this time of day?' she asked as Karen took off Peter's coat.

'Simon has insisted that I give up my job now that Adrey has left,' Karen told her. 'She's not coming back. Thanks to Louise I made a complete fool of myself yesterday. That poor girl had just received a devastating telephone call and then I burst in with my accusation. Simon was absolutely incandescent with rage when I got back, and that was when he insisted that I give up the job at once and became a full-time mother.'

Susan smiled sympathetically. 'Well, I can't really say I blame him, dear,' she said. 'Peter needs his mum and you know, you never get these lovely baby years back again.'

Privately Karen thought it was just as well but she didn't say so. Like Simon, Susan held the old-fashioned notion that a woman's place was in the home. 'Peter is missing Adrey,' she told her mother. 'He's been really difficult all morning — nearly driven me barmy with his whingeing.'

Susan pulled the little boy onto her knee. 'Poor little chap,' she said, dropping a kiss on the toddler's blond head. 'At this age, stability and routine are important. I'm not surprised he's upset. If you want any help, Karen, you know I'm always willing to lend a hand, don't you?'

Karen smiled. 'Yes, I know you are, Mum, and I'm really grateful. I might take you up on that.'

'It's not as if I'll be doing anything else,' Susan said wistfully. 'Ted came round with a bouquet of flowers while Louise was here one morning. I was out and I'm afraid she told him where to go in no uncertain terms.'

'She had no right to do that,' Karen said. She looked up at her mother. 'Although you weren't going to think of starting the relationship up again, were you?'

Susan sighed. 'I don't know. I really miss him. Maybe I should have given him more of a chance to explain.'

Karen snorted. 'Huh! What's to explain?'

Susan sighed. 'Ah well, I'll never know now, will I?'

'Why can't Louise keep her meddling nose out of other people's business?'

'I think that's what they call the sixty-five thousand dollar question,' Susan said.

19

When there was a ring on my bell on Saturday morning, my heart jumped into my mouth. Ever since the break-in, I'd been really nervy and the landlord had refused to do anything about the broken door, saying that it was down to me to get it repaired.

I picked up the entry-phone. 'Who is it?' I called from behind the chest of drawers that had been securing it ever since the break-in.

'It's me — Mark.'

With huge relief, I buzzed him in and when I heard him outside, I pushed aside the chest and opened the door. He looked at me quizzically. 'What's with all the furniture removal?'

'Being burgled isn't something to joke about,' I told him. 'As I told your sister, I came back on Thursday night to find the place had been thoroughly gone over and the door still isn't fixed.'

He looked around. 'What are you doing in a dump like this anyway?'

'This is where I've been all the time,' I confessed. 'I didn't want you to see it.'

He laughed. 'I'm not surprised.' He looked around. 'Whoever broke in has certainly made a mess of the place.'

'Do you *mind*? I've tidied up since then. You should have seen it when I got back,' I told him.

'And you haven't notified the police?'

I shook my head. 'Nothing's been taken and I can do without the hassle.'

He sighed. 'Just as well we'll be out of here first thing Sunday morning. Are you packed?'

I pointed to the two suitcases standing by the door. 'You bet. I can't wait.'

Mark looked round. 'And you say they didn't get anything?'

I shook my head. 'There wasn't anything worth taking. Certainly no cash.' I looked at him. 'I can't help thinking I know who's behind this.'

'Really — who?'

'Just before I went away, I had a phone call from a guy who said he's my half-brother. He wanted us to meet. I didn't like the sound of him so I said no.'

'That's a bit of a long shot, isn't it? Presumably he doesn't even know where you live.'

I vaguely remembered giving Mum the name of the road. It wouldn't have been that difficult for him to find me. 'He might have found out,' I said.

Mark looked doubtful. 'Why did he want to meet anyway?'

'Said he wanted us to get to know one another.'

'So — is that bad?'

I shook my head. 'What would we have in common? I've never set eyes on the bloke. It seems my mother married again and had another child. His father was a violent man and she divorced him while he was in prison.' I looked at Mark. 'To tell you the truth, I'm beginning to wish I'd never set out to find her.'

He nodded. 'I got the feeling you were less than happy with the meeting.'

'That's not all. She borrowed money from me before we parted,' I told him.

'How much?'

'A couple of hundred.'

He whistled. 'Pheew! Maybe you told her too much about yourself. I have to agree that it doesn't augur well for re-forging your relationship with her.'

'Or *him*,' I reminded him. 'My so-called half-brother.'

He put his arms round me and gave me a hug 'Poor old sausage. Never mind, once we're out of here you'll have nothing to worry about.' He held me at arm's length and looked at me. 'Would you like to come back and spend the night at the flat?'

I shook my head. 'No. I'll be OK here. After all, it's only for one more night.'

'Well, let's go out for the day, then, spend our last day in London by celebrating.'

I laughed. 'Celebrating what — my burglary?'

'No, the start of our record-breaking success, of course.'

'You hope.'

'I don't hope — *I know*! I've got a really good feeling about *Oh Elizabeth*. We'll start with the London Eye, then lunch at a little place I know in Soho. How does that sound?'

We spent a lovely day in the West End and I felt much better when Mark dropped me off but for some unknown reason I had the nightmare

168

again that night. I hadn't had it for ages but this time it was different; this time *I* was the mother and the one doing the walking out. I couldn't make head or tail of it when I woke but it gave me a dark, disturbed feeling that lasted for ages. It was only when I came to enough to remember that this was the day we were travelling down to Bournemouth, one step nearer to my success as an actress, that I was able to clear my mind and set about getting ready.

Mark picked me up at eight o'clock in the Ferrari. I'd asked him to come early because I didn't want to encounter my landlord again. I'd paid the rent and the man in the room upstairs had fixed the door for me (after a fashion) but I hadn't given him the formal month's notice, and I didn't want an argument on my hands over the extra rent he was bound to demand.

We stopped off for lunch at a nice restaurant in Farnborough and arrived in Bournemouth late that afternoon. Mark did a tour of the town to get our bearings, then parked the car in a multi-storey car park and turned to look at me.

'Right, shall we go and find ourselves somewhere to stay?'

I nodded. 'Got any ideas? I don't know Bournemouth.'

His eyes twinkled. 'How about booking a room at the Royal Bath for a couple of nights? My treat,' he added. 'We can look around for somewhere cheaper once we begin rehearsals and get our bearings.'

We'd passed the Royal Bath on our tour and I'd been well impressed. My heart gave a leap.

'Oh, Mark, that sounds wonderful.'

We took our bags and checked in. A porter took our bags upstairs and ushered us into a wonderful room with a sea view. Once the man had gone, I turned to Mark.

'This is a real treat,' I said. 'I hope it's just a taste of things to come once we're famous.'

We went down to dinner and Mark ordered a bottle of bubbly to celebrate. He held his glass aloft.

'Here's to us,' he toasted. 'Us, the play, full houses and fame and fortune for my favourite leading lady.'

I sipped my champagne with relish. The future sparkled even more than the bubbles in my glass.

We hardly slept that night; partly because we were high on champagne and anticipation of the day to come and partly because our enthusiastic lovemaking kept us busy. Mark was so skilful and practiced that I was swept away on a cloud of sensual pleasure again and again. As I lay in his arms, my head on his chest, I asked him how he came to know so much about how to please a woman. He looked down at me.

'There's no secret,' he said. 'When you're as much in love as I am with you, it comes naturally.'

I didn't really believe him. It was always difficult to know when to take Mark seriously, but I didn't really care. After all, we were staying in the kind of luxurious hotel I'd always seen myself staying in and the future couldn't look brighter. He deserved my appreciation at the very least.

'Do you think you could ever love me back?' he whispered. 'Just a little bit?'

I snuggled closer. 'You are a silly old romantic, Mark Naylor,' I said, 'Stop getting carried away.'

'You make love as though you mean it,' he said softly.

'Of course I mean it,' I told him. 'You're so damned good at it I'd have to be made of stone not to.' I glanced at the bedside clock. 'Have you any idea what the time is? It's actually getting light. If we don't get some sleep we'll be good for nothing in the morning.'

★ ★ ★

We were due at the Pavilion Theatre at 10.30 so after a wonderful full English breakfast, Mark and I strolled across the road to the Pavilion. I stood in the forecourt looking up at it.

'Wow! It's so big.'

Mark nodded. 'Restaurants and a massive ballroom as well as a very large theatre. It's a wonderful place to be launching.'

I felt a thrill of excitement. At that moment, several other cast members joined us, led by Carla Dean. She looked at me with her usual disdain.

'Where did you two get to last night?' she asked. 'You weren't on the train.'

'We drove down in Mark's Ferrari,' I told her airily. 'And we're staying at the Royal Bath.'

To my great satisfaction her eyebrows shot up. '*Really?* Get you! Living it up as the leading lady already! Well, we'd better find the stage door, I suppose. Unless you want to stand here boasting all morning.'

We located the stage door and went inside. Carla was first to inspect the dressing rooms.

'Mmm, not bad,' she announced. 'But someone has left their stuff in this one.'

On inspection, the other dressing rooms seemed to be full of other people's belongings as well. Phil shook his head.

'It's too bad,' he said. 'The previous lot should have packed up on Saturday night. They should have moved out yesterday morning at the latest.'

At that moment, music could be heard coming from the direction of the stage above us. We stood speechlessly, staring at each other as a tenor could be heard singing 'The Music of the Night' from *Phantom of the Opera*. When the song came to an end, Carla made her opinion heard in no uncertain terms.

'What the bloody hell is going on?' Without another word, she stormed up the stairs to the stage, the rest of us straggling behind. I arrived just in time to see her striding onto the stage where a rehearsal was clearly in progress.

'Excuse me,' she said, her sonorous voice echoing round the stage. 'May I ask what is going on here?'

A man, presumably the director, stood up from his seat in the stalls and walked down to the stage. 'I might well ask the same question of you. Who are you, anyway?'

Carla swept her hand around in our direction. 'We are the cast of *Oh, Elizabeth*,' she said. 'We are supposed to be rehearsing here from this morning until our opening next week.'

The director looked puzzled. 'My company are opening here next week,' he announced. 'We are the number one tour of *Phantom of the Opera*. If you'd like to go up to the foyer, you'll see our posters and flyers. The forthcoming attractions posters are on display outside too. I'm surprised you didn't notice them.'

We stared at each other. I nudged Mark. 'Maybe we've got the wrong theatre,' I whispered. Mark cleared his throat and spoke up.

'Come along, Carla. We'll go and see the theatre management about it.' He nodded to the director. 'I apologize for the interruption. There's obviously some mistake.'

Appeased, the man nodded. 'That's quite all right. I hope you get it sorted out.'

Carla was furious and complained all the way back to the theatre foyer. 'What a cockeyed arrangement,' she complained. 'Just wait till Paul gets here. He's going to be hopping mad.'

The front-of-house manager knew nothing about us. We all crowded into his office and explained our predicament but he said he'd never heard of Paul Fortune or a show called *Oh Elizabeth*.

'There's another theatre across the road,' Phil pointed out. 'Do you think that's where we're supposed to be?'

We straggled across the road to the smaller Palace Court theatre, but there were billboards in the foyer advertising a thriller beginning next Monday. Defeated, we all repaired to a café further along the road to try to decide what to do.

'Well, I know what I'm going to do,' I said, getting out my phone. 'You go in. I'm going to ring my agent. I'll join you in a few minutes.' When they'd gone, I switched on my phone and clicked on Harry's number. His secretary answered.

'Sally, it's Louise Delmar,' I said. 'Can you put me through to Harry, please?'

'I'm sorry, Louise,' the girl said. 'But I'm afraid he's in a meeting with his solicitor at the moment. He's asked me not to put any calls through.'

'I can't help that. I must speak to him. He won't mind when you tell him it's me, calling from Bournemouth. Tell him it's really urgent, Sally.'

I waited, tapping my foot impatiently. When Harry came on he sounded upset. 'Louise. I think I know why you're ringing me.'

'It's not good enough, Harry,' I jumped straight in. 'We're all down here in Bournemouth and someone's made a hash of the bookings. There's another company rehearsing in the theatre.'

'I know — I know. Listen, Lou. I'm afraid I've got some rather bad news. There was never going to be a show. It was all a highly elaborate con. The truth is, Paul bloody Fortune has disappeared. He's gone, and taken all our money with him.'

I stood as though rooted to the ground, speechless; poleaxed; the blood freezing in my veins. All the work we'd put in. All those weeks of rehearsal! *All the money I'd invested!* It had to be some kind of horrible nightmare. It *couldn't* be true.

'What — what are you saying, Harry?' I said weakly. 'Paul's gone? Gone where?'

'Anyone's bloody guess! How much cash did you invest, Lou?'

When I told him he gasped. 'Christ! I invested too, but not as much as that. What about the others?'

'I don't know. Harry, look, we have to find him. Has anyone been to his flat?'

Harry laughed dryly at the other end of the line. 'Turned out it wasn't even his flat — borrowed while the owner was abroad. He cleared out of there days ago and no one has seen or heard from him since. He's had a good head start on us.'

'The police?' I suggested. 'Surely you've contacted the police.'

'Of course we have. D'you think we haven't been down every possible avenue? They've had roadblocks in place and they've had men at all the airports and ports. He's gone, Lou. As I said, he's had a week's head start on us. I doubt whether Fortune was even his real name anyway — appropriate though it was. He's probably counting his spoils in some luxury hotel in Monte Carlo as we speak.' He groaned. 'I can't believe I was taken in by him but he was so bloody plausible. I feel such a fool! And with all the years I've been in the business. This'll be the ruin of me when word gets around. God only knows what my other clients are going to say, not to mention the wife. I'm — '

'*Harry!*' I broke in sharply. 'Do you have any idea of the impossible position I'm in? Have you got any suggestions as to how I'm to break this news to the rest of the cast?' Stuff Harry's bloody wife! What about *me?* Here I was, trying to face the fact that all my dreams of fame were down the toilet, not to mention most of my inheritance, and all he was worried about was what his flaming *wife* would say.

'Look, Lou, I'm up to my neck in this as much as you are,' he said. 'I'm afraid you'll have to handle your end of it with your usual tact and diplomacy. I'm going to have to go now. I've got my solicitor here with me. I only hope he can come up with something that'll get us our money back but it doesn't look very hopeful at the moment.'

'I'll be in to see you when we get back, Harry,' I warned him. 'After this, I think you owe me, don't you?' Without waiting for his reply, I punched the red button and stood for a moment, trying to process the unbelievable disaster that was taking place. I'd never felt more like running away but I knew I had to go inside and tell the others. Gathering all my courage, I took a deep breath and pushed open the door of the café.

Inside, the rest of the cast were clustered round two large tables. As I walked in, all their faces turned towards me. I swallowed hard. It all felt so surreal. This had to be the worst day of my life.

'I'm afraid I've got bad news,' I began, my knees shaking. 'It looks as if we've all been taken for a ride. Paul Fortune has skipped the country with all our cash. There is no play. No West End run, no nothing — there never was. It was all a big scam.'

For a moment there was a shocked silence as they all looked helplessly at each other then, Carla sprang to her feet, incandescent with rage. 'Are you seriously telling me that bastard has fucked off with everything?' she shouted. 'That all these weeks he's had us on a bit of string like a bunch of bloody puppets, letting us believe we were going into the West End with his fictitious fucking play while stashing all the cash he'd conned us out of into some sodding Swiss bank?'

I nodded miserably. 'More than likely.'

'But what about those other guys — the choreographer, that useless bloody director?'

I shrugged. 'Either in it with him or being taken for a ride like the rest of us, I suppose. It's irrelevant now anyway, isn't it?'

Carla looked round at the others. 'Well, come on, you dozy lot!' she shouted. 'Are you going to sit there with your mouths open like a lot of fucking goldfish? Are we going to just sit back and let this happen?'

'It's no good, Carla,' I put in. 'He's long gone. Why do you think he gave us a week off?' I related everything that Harry had told me on the phone. When I'd finished, Carla slumped back in her seat.

'So we're all well and truly fucked!'

'Couldn't have put it better myself,' I said ironically. I looked at Mark. 'Shall we go and start packing?'

Mark nodded and got up from his seat. All this time he'd said nothing and his face gave away nothing of what he was feeling.

'It's all right for you two!' Carla accused, staring belligerently at us. 'You and him with his fucking Ferrari. You've obviously got enough cash between you not to worry about the odd fifty k. It might be peanuts to you but what about the rest of us? What are we supposed to do?'

Something in me snapped. I'd had just about enough of Carla. 'Oh, for God's sake, will you *shut up*, Carla!' I shouted. I'd always hated mouthy women who kicked off and threw their weight about. Carla had done it repeatedly all through rehearsals, arguing and turning the air blue with her crude outbursts. She wasn't all that good in her part and I'd often wondered how Paul and Mervyn kept their tempers. *Now I knew.*

'We're all in the same boat here. Some of us have put more than others into Paul Fortune's scam but we've all been well and truly conned, and there's nothing we can do but face it. We're going to have to chalk it up to experience.' I grabbed Mark's arm and left the café with him in tow.

It was only a short walk to the hotel and neither of us spoke until we were in our room. I kicked off my shoes and sank onto the bed, bitter tears of disappointment, anger and frustration streaming down my cheeks. Mark came and sat beside me. He didn't speak, just slipped an arm around my shoulders and pulled my head onto his shoulder, pushing his handkerchief into my hand.

Once I could trust myself to speak again I

looked up at him. 'I can't believe it, Mark,' I said. 'How could anyone be so evil?'

He gave me his lopsided, rueful grin. 'The thought of all that money, that's how,' he said. 'I reckon if all the cast members invested even half of what we did he must be the richer by at least half a million.'

I blew my nose. 'I still can't understand it. Why did he need to do it? He's a talented musician — and the play — '

'Face it, Lou. The music wasn't bad but the play was rubbish.' He kissed my forehead. 'He knew how to play a bunch of failed actors, darling, and he pulled us all in like a net full of little fishes. He played on our vanity — our dreams of success. In a way it serves us all right.'

'How can you say that?' I stared at hm. 'And what do you mean — *failed actors*? It's OK for you. You probably won't even miss the money you invested, whilst I — I put most of what I had into this — this disaster.' The tears began again. 'I was going to be a star. It was my last chance and now — now . . . '

'I know.' He pulled me close. 'Hey, for what it's worth, you'll always be a star to me.'

I sniffed and shook my head. 'All my money — I can't believe it's gone.'

'I know,' he said. 'It's awful — for you and for most of the others too. I happen to know that some of the poor devils put their life savings into the project, but we should all have known better. Didn't you ever wonder how he thought he was going to hit the headlines in the West End with no big names in the leading roles? We all had our heads in the sand — me as much as anyone. All we saw were our names up in lights. He held out that tempting bait and we fell for it.'

'And now it's all over,' I said bleakly. 'So I suppose there's nothing for it but to go home with our tails between our legs.'

He hugged me. 'Tell you what, why don't we stay on down here for another few days? Have a little holiday.'

I stared at him. 'A holiday! I've got to get back to London. I've got to go and see Harry and he's got to find me some work. He owes me that much after this fiasco. I'm broke, Mark. I'm homeless too. How could I laze about here and enjoy myself?'

He sighed. 'OK, I see your point. We'll go back this afternoon. And you must come and stay at the flat.'

Relief flooded through me. Thank goodness for Mark.

★   ★   ★

It was quite late in the evening when Mark drove into the underground car park and hauled our cases out of the boot. My two held all my worldly goods as I'd moved out of the bedsit. We travelled up in the lift and Mark took out his key and let us into the flat. Cathy, his sister, came out of the kitchen. She was small and dark with glasses, not at all as I'd imagined her. She stared at us both in surprise.

'Mark! I wasn't expecting you back again so soon.'

180

Mark sighed. 'It's a long story. Cathy, this is Louise, by the way. She'll be staying here for a while.'

'Oh?' she said shortly, looking me up and down. She looked at Mark enquiringly. 'So — why are you here? What happened?'

'It's all fallen through, Cath,' he said. 'There's no show after all. We've all been taken for a ride but I'll tell you more later.'

She gave a cynical little laugh. 'Well, I can't say I'm surprised.' She glanced at me. 'If you will play at being the thespian and mix with a bunch of dodgy theatricals, can you wonder? You should know by now that you can't trust them. I always said it would end in tears.' She looked at me again with undisguised distaste. 'I expect you'd like to freshen up,' she said, inferring that I was dishevelled and sweaty. 'And I'd be glad if you'd both keep your voices down. The children are asleep.' She sighed resignedly as she turned back towards the kitchen. 'I suppose I'd better put the kettle on.'

Mark looked at me. 'Put your things in my room. We can sort everything out later.'

In Mark's room I unpacked my overnight things. It was all too clear that Cathy didn't welcome the prospect of having me to stay. I 'freshened up', as she put it, in the en suite and then went back out into the hallway. Outside the half-open kitchen door I hesitated. Mark and his sister were clearly having a disagreement.

'Why are you with her?' she demanded. 'Don't you remember how she messed with your head all those years ago? You never stopped weeping on

181

my shoulder about how badly she treated you.'

'We were just kids back then,' Mark said. 'We're both different people now.'

'Her kind of leopard doesn't change her spots, believe me, Mark. I know her sort. She's got her eye on your money now.'

'Of course she hasn't.'

'Anyway, I can't have her sharing your room.'

'Why not?'

'I'd have thought it was obvious. What kind of example would that be to set Kevin and Sharon?'

'Where else do you expect her to sleep, then?'

'Well, the sofa's available as long as it's just for one night, or do you expect me to wake the children and turn them out for her?'

'Don't be absurd, Cathy.'

'What do you see in her anyway?' Cathy went on. 'What happened to that nice girl you were engaged to — what was her name — Felicity?'

'Francesca.'

'That's right. Your letters were full of her for months. You even sent photos of the two of you together. You were completely besotted, then all at once she was out of the picture.'

I didn't wait to hear any more. Back in Mark's bedroom I waited for him. When he appeared a few minutes later he looked sheepish.

'Lou, darling, there's a slight problem. Cathy . . . '

'I heard,' I said. 'I was coming to find you — and I heard.'

He winced. 'I'm so sorry. It's just that Cathy thinks . . . '

'Cathy obviously thinks I'm a trollop,' I

interrupted. 'I must say I'm surprised at you, Mark. It's *your* flat and your life so why does she think she can call all the shots? Anyway, I thought you said she was moving out.'

'She hasn't exchanged contracts on the house yet.'

'I see, so in the meantime she expects to have all the say in what you do?'

'She's just thinking of the children.'

'Well, *obviously* she and her kids have to come first! I'll stay for tonight,' I told him. 'Unfortunately I don't have a choice. I've nowhere else to go, but don't worry, I'll be out of your way first thing in the morning. I wouldn't want to be an evil influence on innocent children.'

'Don't take it like that.'

'How do you expect me to take it? Your sister obviously thinks I'm not good enough for you — not like the saintly Francesca.'

Mark turned pale. 'She didn't say that.'

'No? What do you call it, then? She even accused me of being after your money.'

He sighed. 'She gets a bit resentful sometimes about my inheritance.'

'Did your uncle leave her out of his will?'

He nodded. 'I told you; he didn't leave a will.' He reached for my hand. 'Let me take you out to dinner. We'll go somewhere nice to make up for everything.'

'No.' I snatched my hand away. I couldn't believe he'd stand there and let his upstart of a sister insult me without a word in my defence. 'I obviously count for very little as far as you're concerned. Anyway, I'm too tired and too disappointed. This has been the day from hell and I just want it to be over.'

I couldn't sleep. Not that the sofa was uncomfortable. Cathy had grudgingly supplied me with a duvet and pillow, but she hadn't offered either Mark or me anything to eat and my stomach wouldn't stop rumbling. I couldn't get Paul Fortune's massive con trick out of my head. My dreamed-of chance of success. All I had ever worked and prayed for, not to mention Dad's legacy — all gone in a puff of smoke. It hurt like a knife twisting in my heart. And as if that wasn't enough, there was Mark's betrayal. If he really loved me, why hadn't he put me first and told his bossy sister where to get off?

At last, in spite of the hunger pains and the disbelief of what was happening to me, I dozed off into a restless sleep in the early hours, only to be rudely awakened by two boisterous children jumping on me.

'*Who are you? What are you doing in our flat? What's your name?*' They shrieked questions at me, whilst bouncing all over the sofa. I sat up and gathered the duvet round me, fleeing in the direction of Mark's room. In the hallway I was stopped by Cathy.

'Where are you going?'

'I need to shower and get dressed,' I told her.

'Not in Mark's room,' she instructed. 'You can use the bathroom.'

'But my clothes — my luggage is in there.'

She sniffed. 'I'll get it for you.' She went into Mark's room and emerged a minute later, holding out my suitcases as though they were something she was putting out with the bins.

'Is Mark awake?' I asked.

She shook her head. 'No, and I'd be obliged if you'd allow him to sleep.' The two brats joined her and she slipped an arm round each of them. The girl put her tongue out at me. 'I'll be taking the children to school by the time you're finished.'

'Really?' I looked at them with distaste. 'Well, let's hope they learn some manners there. They certainly haven't been taught any by you!' I picked up my cases and walked towards the bathroom.

She aimed her final shot at my retreating back. 'I'd quite like you to have gone by the time I get back.'

'With pleasure. I can't *wait* to get away from here!' I slammed the bathroom door and sat on the edge of the bath, despondency sweeping over me afresh. Were things ever going to get better?

★　★　★

I took a cab to Charing Cross Road and climbed the stairs to Harry's office, leaving my suitcases in the lobby. Sally ushered me in and Harry began speaking the moment I walked in.

'Louise — I can't tell you how sorry I am about all this.'

'Not nearly as sorry as I am,' I interrupted. 'We've all been well and truly stuffed and there's nothing we can do about it now, but I'm not here for a post-mortem, Harry. I'm broke. I need a job and I need it *now*.'

He winced. 'I know, love, but look at it from my point of view. It's the end of May. All the summer shows are booked — about to open any day now.'

'Then find me something else,' I demanded. A touring play — anything. You know how versatile I am.' I leaned towards him. 'You owe me, Harry. You owe me big-time.'

'I know, love, and I feel for you, honestly.' He assumed a pleading expression and spread his hands. 'But I can't work miracles, can I?'

'Well you'd just better *try*,' I told him. 'You're supposed to be my agent and you've lost me a shed-load of cash and landed me in an unholy mess. If I don't hear from you in twenty-four hours, I'll make sure that everyone in the business knows about this scam you were involved in. And I still haven't made up my mind whether to sue you or not. *Right?*' I got up from my chair and stood glaring at him.

He shrugged resignedly. 'OK — OK.'

I was lugging my suitcases back into the street when my phone rang. I put the cases down and fished it out of my handbag. It was Mark. I switched the phone off in disgust.

★   ★   ★

Back in Stoke Newington, I tapped on my ex-landlord's door. No, I couldn't have my old room back. He'd already let it. But he did have one on the floor above (sloping ceilings and a dormer window). Only problem was, it wasn't available till the week after next! Did I want it? Its only advantage was that it was cheaper than the one I'd vacated. An offer I was in no position to refuse.

'By the way, you owe me a couple of weeks' rent,' he reminded me with a smile. 'Oh, and I nearly forgot. You had a visitor yesterday,' he added. 'She said she was your mum.'

20

As Susan put her key in the lock, she heard the telephone ringing. Dumping her shopping on the floor, she rushed to answer it.

'Hello, Susan Davies speaking.'

'Mum, it's me, Karen. I wondered if you could have Peter for me this afternoon?'

'Of course, love. Are you all right?'

'Yes, fine. It's just that I've got an interview.'

'I see. Well, just bring him round when you're ready.'

'Thanks, Mum. You're a lifesaver.' She paused. 'Mum — I had a text from Louise this morning. She had the cheek to ask if she could come and stay for a few days. I told her absolutely no, not after last time. If she rings you — '

'She asked to come home?' Susan interrupted. 'But I thought she was down in Bournemouth, about to open this musical.'

'Well, she's obviously not,' Karen said. 'She didn't go into any details. Anyway it's irrelevant to me. All I care about is that she stays away from us. So, Mum, if she rings you, don't be an old softie again and say yes.'

'I wonder what's gone wrong,' Susan mused.

'Mum! Are you listening? You won't let her come and walk all over you again, will you?'

'What? No — oh, I don't know, Karen. I'm making no promises. We're all she's got and . . .'

'Yes, and she plays on the fact that you're a

pushover! Promise me, Mum.'

'What time did you say you'd bring Peter round?'

'About two. Did you hear what I said?'

'Two o'clock. Right, I'll be ready. We'll go to the park. He always loves that. See you at two, then, dear. Bye for now.' Susan replaced the receiver firmly. She wouldn't have Karen dictating to her. If and when Louise got in touch, she'd make up her own mind about what to do.

She didn't have long to wait. She was washing up after her lunch when the phone rang. She dried her hands and went to answer it. 'Hello, Susan Davies here.'

'Susan, it's me, Louise.'

'Louise. How are you?'

'Not good, I'm afraid. I'm throwing myself on your mercy, Susan,' Louise said. 'Things are not well with the show and I'm back in London. I gave up my flat to go on tour. I have got another in view but the trouble is, it won't be available till the week after next. I know there were a few hiccups last time I was there and I can't apologize enough for the — misunderstanding, but could you possibly bear to put up with me for a few days? I've nowhere else to go and I'm throwing myself on your mercy.'

'Well, I suppose it's all right,' Susan said. 'But what about that nice friend of yours; Dianne, isn't it?'

'She's moved her boyfriend in.'

'I see, but she's got two bedrooms, hasn't she? And as you said, it's only for a few days.'

There was a slight hesitation at the other end

of the line then Louise said, 'There was a bit of a problem when I left last time. We parted on — well, not the best of terms.'

Susan sighed. Clearly Louise had upset her friend. When would she ever learn? 'Well, in that case you'd better come to me,' she said resignedly. 'When do you want to come?'

'Today, if that's all right.'

'Today! When? I'll be out for most of the afternoon but I'll be back about four.'

'OK. Susan — thanks. I do appreciate this. I know last time things got a bit fraught and I'm sorry, but it was all a misunderstanding.'

'Never mind that now,' Susan said. 'I'll see you later.' As she replaced the receiver she sighed. God only knew what Karen would say. Maybe she needn't find out, she told herself; after all, it was only for a few days. Oh well, she'd just have to deal with that when and if it happened.

★ ★ ★

Karen arrived dead on the stroke of two and refused Susan's offer of a cup of tea.

'I've left Peter's buggy in the hallway downstairs,' she said, handing over the bulging bag containing all his toys and accessories.

'What is this interview you mentioned?' Susan asked.

Karen hesitated. 'Mum, I'm going mad, staying at home with Peter all day. I love him to bits of course and I wouldn't be without him, but I never visualized being a full-time mum. I saw this advert for teachers willing to do some

190

tutoring. It's an agency.'

'And that's where you're going this afternoon?'

'Yes. I telephoned them and I've got an interview this afternoon.'

'Is Simon all right with this?'

'He doesn't know — yet.' When she saw her mother shaking her head Karen went on defensively, 'Well, it might all come to nothing so what's the point of telling him?'

'And if it does — come to something, I mean?'

'I'll cross that bridge when I come to it.' Karen looked at her watch. 'Look, I'll have to go or I'll miss the interview. Sure you're all right with Peter?'

'Yes, of course. You get off. What time will you be back?'

'I don't really know. By four, I hope.' She bent to kiss Peter. 'See you soon, darling. Be a good boy for Granny. Bye, Mum.' And she whisked out of the door.

★　★　★

Peter loved his outing to the park. They fed the ducks with corn that Susan bought at the park kiosk along with ice cream, and finished up in the children's play area. Peter played happily in the sandpit and then begged to go on the swings. Susan hesitated. He was still very little for the swings. Peter sensed the reason for her anxiety.

'Mummy lets me go on the fwings,' he assured her. 'She pushes me up to the sky.' He raised one chubby arm as high as it would go, treating his

191

grandmother to his most beguiling smile.

'All right,' Susan said. She lifted him and began to ease his fat little legs into the baby swing but he screwed up his face and struggled.

'Not baby fwing,' he protested. 'Big-boy fwing.'

'No, you might fall and hurt yourself.'

'No! Won't — *won't!*' He began to cry and Susan could see that he was going to have a tantrum. Since Adrey had left, she had noticed that he was more prone to them than before.

'All right, then, don't cry,' she said. 'But you must hold on very tightly and not let go.'

Having got his own way, Peter smiled again and allowed himself to be extricated from the barred swing. The next minute he was seated on the swing next door.

'Push, Granny. *Push,*' he shouted as Susan gently moved the swing.

Very tentatively, she pushed him a little higher but it wasn't enough for Peter. He twisted round to shout at her again and the next moment he had let go and slipped from the seat. He let out a loud wail as he hit the ground.

Heart in mouth, Susan picked him up and surveyed the damage. His knees were grazed and bleeding. The moment Peter saw this he let out a scream of fear.

'It hurts! Want Mummy!'

Susan lifted him into her arms and put him into the buggy. There was a little first aid hut not far from the play area with a St John's nurse on duty. Taking him there would be quicker than going home. She glanced at her watch as she hurried along, and was concerned to see that it

192

was a quarter past four. She'd better let Karen know she'd be a bit late getting back. Pausing to take out her mobile phone, she pressed in Karen's number but her phone was switched off. With a sigh of frustration she hurried into the first aid hut, hoping it wouldn't take long.

The kindly middle-aged nurse bathed the grazed knees with antiseptic and applied a couple of plasters. 'There,' she said soothingly. 'You're a very brave boy, aren't you? And now you've got two lovely plasters to show off.' She slipped a chocolate button into Peter's mouth. 'There, no harm done,' she said to Susan. 'Might be as well to put him in the baby swing next time,' she said. 'He's very little to go on the big ones yet.'

'He said his mummy lets him go on the big ones,' Susan said, feeling feeble. The nurse smiled.

'They can be very manipulative, even at this age,' she said. 'Still, no real damage this time.'

When she got back to the flat, Susan found an irate Karen waiting outside the door. 'Oh, Mum, there you are. Where have you been and . . . ' She spotted the plasters on Peter's knees. 'What's happened?'

Susan was puffing a little as she put a struggling Peter down. 'It's nothing, he fell and grazed his knees,' she said. 'I took him to the first aid hut in the park. That's why we're late.'

'I got p'asters,' Peter announced proudly. 'I went on the big-boy fwing and I falled off.'

Karen stared at her mother in horror. 'Mum! Why didn't you put him in the baby swing?

Haven't you got any sense at all?'

'He wouldn't go,' Susan said wearily. 'He said you let him go on the big ones.'

'Of course I don't! He's only three, Mum. What were you thinking?'

'I tried to ring you,' Susan said as she put her key in the door, 'but your phone was switched off.'

'Well, of course it was,' Karen snapped. 'I wouldn't leave it on when I was in an interview, would I?'

'Well, Peter's all right, Karen, and please stop shouting at me for all the neighbours to hear.' Inside the door she turned to her daughter. 'After all that, did you get the job?'

Karen's expression brightened a little. 'As a matter of fact, it does look hopeful but they said they'd let me know.' As Susan went into the kitchen to fill the kettle she called out, 'No tea for me, Mum. I'd better get going. Simon will be home soon.'

She was gathering up Peter's things ready to leave when there was a ring at the bell. She called out, 'Are you expecting anyone?'

Suddenly Susan remembered Louise and her heart sank. Before she could say anything Karen was calling, 'It's OK, Mum. I'll get it.'

In the kitchen Susan held her breath — then Karen's outraged voice confirmed her worst fear — Louise had arrived.

'What the *hell* are you doing here? Your bloody nerve after last time! You're not welcome here, Louise, so you can turn right round and get back to where . . . '

'It's all right. I said she could stay,' Susan put in calmly, standing behind Karen at the door. 'Let her in, Karen. It's only for a few days.'

Karen stared at her mother. 'You *have* to be joking! Well, on your own head be it!' She stood aside and allowed Louise to walk into the flat. 'What new drama has she cooked up this time?' she asked. 'What tale of woe has she conned you with now, Mum? Well, don't expect any further help from me.'

Susan bridled. 'If you get that job, Karen, I daresay it'll be you, wanting help from *me*.'

Karen opened her mouth to say something then closed it again. Bending down, she picked up Peter and his bag and headed for the door, but as she opened it an irate Simon stood outside, about to ring the bell.

'Oh, so *there* you are!' he said, his voice deep with anger.

'Simon!' Karen looked deflated. 'You'd better come in.'

Simon stepped inside and closed the door behind him. 'You might be interested to hear that you've *got the job*!' he growled. 'The job you applied for behind my back. I'd just got in when they rang on the landline — said they'd been trying your mobile but it was switched off.'

Karen put Peter down. 'I didn't want to tell you until I was sure I'd got it,' she said.

'Can you imagine what a fool I felt, not knowing what they were talking about? And just what do you propose to do with our son while you're doing this job?' he demanded. 'I understand from the agency that you've announced that you're

195

free to work daytimes, as well as out of hours. Did you even *tell* them that you have a child?'

Karen threw a look of appeal towards her mother. 'Mum said she'd babysit.'

'As she's done today, I suppose. So you're in on this too, Susan?'

Susan shook her head. 'Like you, I knew nothing about it until today.'

For the first time Simon looked down at his son. 'Look at him. He's filthy — and what's wrong with his legs?' he demanded.

'He tumbled and grazed his knees,' Karen said defensively. 'You know he's always doing it.'

'Granny let me go on the big-boy fwing.' Peter said proudly. 'I fell off an' I got p'asters!'

Glaring at his wife Simon said, 'What are you thinking about, Karen? You know she's past it. Something always happens when she has him. And here you are, willing to risk our son's safety for some two-bit cramming job. My God! What kind of mother are you?' Suddenly he noticed Louise, who had made herself at home on the sofa. He pointed at her. 'What is *she* doing here?' he demanded. He looked at Karen, who was close to tears. 'Can't you see now what a fool your mother is, letting that devious cow back again after the trouble she always causes?' He picked Peter up. 'I'm out of here!' he shouted. 'You'd better come too, Karen — if you put any value at all on your son and our marriage, which I doubt!'

When they'd gone, the flat suddenly felt to Susan as though all the air had been sucked out of it. She sighed and sank down onto the sofa next to Louise.

'Oh, dear.'

Louise, who had enjoyed every minute of the little drama played out before her, smiled sympathetically at her stepmother. 'Wow! He was in a right strop, wasn't he?'

'He wants Karen to be a full-time mother until Peter goes to school. It's not much to ask really, is it? Although she shouldn't have gone behind his back like that.'

'Personally, I'm on Karrie's side.'

Susan glanced at her. 'Well, you would be, wouldn't you?'

'I can't believe you can be so charitable about Simon after what he said about you!'

'He was angry,' Susan said. 'We all say things we don't mean when we lose our tempers. He's probably regretting it already.'

Louise shrugged. 'Generous of you to be so understanding. He needs dragging into the twenty-first century if you ask me. Other women go back to work after having a child so why should he think his wife is above all that? You wouldn't catch me putting up with that kind of bullying.'

'No, I daresay.' Susan looked at her step-daughter for the first time since her arrival. 'What brings you here, Louise? You didn't go into details on the phone, except to say that it was something to do with the show.'

Louise had done a lot of thinking on the train coming up. There was no way she could admit to Susan that she'd been conned out of her father's legacy and she had no intention of losing face about her career rise either. 'Just a hitch with the bookings,' she lied. 'There would have been a long gap between the tour and the West End opening so we're taking a bit of time out now instead.'

'Oh, well, that's nice,' Susan said. 'I'm afraid it will have to be the sofa again.'

'That's OK.' *I'm getting used to sofas*, she thought. She looked at Susan. 'I'm sorry I put my foot in it with your — chap,' she said. 'But I expect you've kissed and made up by now, eh?'

Susan shook her head. 'Ted? No. I couldn't keep seeing a man who could be so deceitful.' She glanced at Louise. 'What about you? Are you seeing anyone special at the moment?'

Louise was reminded sharply of Mark and his betrayal. Had he been seeing this other woman all the time and stringing her along? She winced, remembering the previous night and Cathy's obvious loathing of her. She couldn't help thinking that Mark must have been talking to his sister about her — complaining about the way she'd treated him all those years ago when they were at drama school. Surely she must realize that they'd all grown up since then?

'Louise!' Susan prompted. 'Are you all right?'

'Yes, of course I am.' Louise quickly pushed her negative thoughts away. 'You asked if I was seeing anyone. I was, but like your Ted, he turned out to be devious and two-timing.'

'I'm sorry to hear that. Was it the young chap you were at drama school with?'

Louise remembered now that she'd told Susan about Mark the last time she was here.

'No,' she lied. 'Someone new.'

198

'Oh dear, you don't have much luck with men, do you? Were you in love with him?'

The question threw Louise slightly. 'No, not really,' she said. 'Whatever love is.'

Susan patted her hand. 'Well, you'll soon be busy with your exciting new play. Once you're away on tour, you'll soon forget him.'

Louise cringed inwardly. If only that were true. She turned to look at her stepmother. 'All that business with Karen and Simon last time I was here. It really was a misunderstanding, you know. I didn't intend to make trouble between them.'

'Well, it's all water under the bridge now,' Susan said. She got up from the sofa. 'I daresay you're hungry and I haven't even offered you a cup of tea. I'll make one now. The kettle has boiled.'

'So — am I forgiven?' Louise asked. 'For Ted, I mean.'

Susan sighed. 'As I said — it's over and done with but I can't say I don't miss him, as I expect you miss your boyfriend too. Come and help me start supper and you can tell me all about this wonderful musical you're going to star in.'

Louise got up and followed her into the kitchen. For the first time she realized that she was going to miss Mark. Underneath the anger she already did — a lot. Did that mean that her feelings for him went deeper than she'd meant them to? *Were you in love?* She'd always considered love to be a myth — something for films and books. Certainly an emotion she'd never experienced. Lust, maybe — infatuation, but love? No, surely not. She watched Susan bustling around, making tea and getting out the biscuit tin. If only her life could be as uncomplicated as hers.

★ ★ ★

The rest of the week was difficult for Susan. She'd telephoned Karen early the morning after Louise's arrival to ask if she and Simon had made up their quarrel and come to any kind of compromise.

'No, we haven't,' Karen snapped. 'Simon is adamant that I turn down the job and stay at home with Peter until he's five. That's another *two whole years* of sheer drudgery and boredom. If it wasn't for Louise, we'd still have Adrey and I'd still be teaching. And if you hadn't been so careless and stupid yesterday, I'd have been home long before Simon and I'd have dealt with things in the way I'd planned.'

'Please don't speak to me like that, Karen. I am neither stupid nor careless and if you want to know, I think it's a mistake, going behind Simon's back like that.'

'Well, when I want your opinion, Mum, I'll ask for it and I'm sorry but I'm afraid I do think you're careless, putting Peter in danger like that. And as for letting Louise come and stay again after all she's done — well, words fail me!'

'I think there have been times when you've been quite happy to forget my so-called careless stupidity,' Susan said.

'Yes? Well, thanks for rubbing it in! You can

safely believe that those days are over,' Karen snapped. 'I won't be asking for your help any more!' And there was an ear-splitting crash as she slammed the receiver down.

She'd only just replaced the receiver when the phone rang. It was Simon.

'Susan — I'm ringing to apologize for the scene I made at your flat yesterday.'

'It's all right, Simon. I understand. You were upset and I do sympathize — with both of you.'

'That's your trouble, Susan,' he replied. 'You're far too understanding. But as I said, I'm sorry. I just lost it and I shouldn't have said what I did.'

'Well, as you've brought the subject up, Simon, you didn't mind leaving Peter with me while you and Karen went to Paris.'

'No, I know and I'm deeply ashamed of letting my temper get the better of me.' There was a pause then he said, 'Look, Susan, don't think I'm interfering but you really shouldn't have allowed Louise back after what happened last time. She is at the root of all this mess we're in now.'

'I know but I couldn't see her without a roof to her head, could I?'

'Well, it's your decision, of course. Anyway, I'm sure you know that I didn't mean any of those things I said and I hope you'll accept my apology.'

'Of course, it's already forgotten. Thank you for ringing, Simon.' She put down the phone with a heavy heart. She'd tried to please every-body and finished up pleasing no one and landing

201

herself in the middle of a row.

In the days that followed, Karen would have nothing to do with her. Every time Susan tried to ring her she'd refused to pick up. As for Louise, she was as untidy and disorganized as ever. Susan gave up trying to tidy up or do any housework. She was a little disturbed by the nightmares that Louise obviously had. On several occasions, she had been awakened in the early hours by her stepdaughter's loud sleep-talking. She wondered if it had anything to do with her broken romance, which she'd already guessed had upset Louise more than she would admit. She'd had a lot of calls on her mobile during the week, but she hadn't taken any of them. Had they been from the disloyal boyfriend? she wondered. Clearly she was upset about something.

★   ★   ★

It was the night before Louise's visit was over and she and Susan were sitting together in the living room, when Louise suddenly turned to her stepmother. 'Susan — there's something I need to tell you.'

'Yes, dear?' Susan looked up from the little sweater she was knitting for Peter. 'What's that?'

'I found my mother.'

Susan's glasses slipped to the end of her nose as she looked up in surprise. 'You found her — how?'

'The Salvation Army found her for me actually. They arranged a meeting and we met for tea at one of the big stores in London. She told me that she'd married again after she and Dad split up and they had another child; a boy — well, man now. He's called Steven.'

'So you have a half-brother. That's interesting. Is she happy?'

'No. Her husband was — *is* a criminal. He's in prison and she's divorced him. I was disappointed, Susan. Frankly, I didn't like her. I didn't like her son either. He telephoned me and I found his manner quite nasty — almost menacing.'

Susan dropped the knitting into her lap and took off her glasses. 'Oh, Louise!'

'The trouble is that I told her too much. She asked about Dad and when she knew he'd died, she wanted to know what was in his will.'

'And you told her?'

'I got a bit carried away at seeing her again after all the years.' She hesitated. 'I told her about the play too — and my big breakthrough. She obviously got the impression that I'm rolling in cash because before we parted, she asked me for money.'

'Oh dear. I'm afraid you've rushed things a bit too much.'

'You can say that again! The thing is, will she let it go at that or is she going to be constantly on my case? What can I do?'

Susan considered for a moment. Privately, she wondered if all that had been the cause of Louise's troubled dreams. 'Well, you'll be away on tour for some time, won't you? After that, maybe she'll have forgotten.'

Louise sighed. If only it were as simple as that.

Susan didn't know the half of it. And because she'd been economical with the truth, she couldn't press it any further.

She left the following morning. Susan saw her off gratefully, longing to get her hands on the hoover and dusters. How could one person make such a shambles of the place?

'Don't forget that I intend to be there on your opening night,' she called as Louise ran down to her waiting taxi. 'I'm going to try to persuade Karen to come too, but I'll be there even if she isn't. Good luck, Louise!'

'Thanks, Susan. Goodbye — and thanks for having me.' Louise forced a smile that vanished as soon as she climbed into the taxi. They'd all have to know about her catastrophe before too long and how would she face them all then?

'Where to, missus?' the taxi driver enquired.

She sighed, recognizing that she didn't even qualify for 'miss' any more.

'To the train station, please,' she told him.

She settled back in her seat. Back to a grotty bedsit in the East End, she reminded herself with a sigh. Back to God only knew what!

21

The bedsit under the eaves looked more depressing than ever after the cosiness of Susan's flat. The weather had suddenly warmed up and when I unlocked the door, the stuffiness and odours left by the previous tenant hit me like a wave; a mixture of stale sweat, unwashed clothes and several dozen takeaway meals. By the stench that still hung about the room like a fog, most of them had been curries. I hurriedly crossed the room and threw the window open wide, making a mental note to buy a can of air freshener next time I went to the shops.

It was only when I turned back to close the door that I saw the note that had obviously been pushed under the door. I slipped a finger under the envelope flap and pulled out a single sheet of lined paper, obviously torn from a cheap notebook. My heart plummeted. It clearly wasn't from Mark, not that I expected it, after refusing all his calls. He'd surely have to give up soon.

There was no address on the note and the handwriting was barely readable. The spelling was atrocious too but the message was only too plain.

Deer Louise. Sorry you an me coodnt meet up. Yor landlord sais you are cumin bak so Ill giv you a bell soon. Yor luvvin bruther, Steve.

I ran downstairs and tapped on the landlord's door. He answered it looking as though he'd only just got up. He wore jeans and a grubby singlet and his greasy hair was tied back in a ponytail. He blinked at me blearily. 'Yeah?'

I held out the envelope. 'How did this come to be pushed under my door?' I asked him. 'I've been away so how did he manage to get in?'

He peered at the envelope. 'Oh, yeah,' he said. 'That was a couple of days ago. When he couldn't get you, he rang my bell and asked me to give you that.'

'Right. Well, if he turns up here again don't let him in, OK?' How on earth had he found out where I lived? My stomach lurched with apprehension as I turned back towards the staircase.

'That's all right,' he called after me. 'Don't *thank* me, will you. I'm not your bleedin' butler — snotty cow!'

I carried on up the stairs without a backward glance. What did he do for the rent he charged anyway?

I hardly slept at all that night. The bed was lumpy and lopsided and the sun burning down on the roof all day had made the heat and the overpowering smells unbearable. The thought that Steve Harris had tracked me down kept me awake too. If only I hadn't chosen to stay on at the same address!

I was up early, down the street to the supermarket to stock up with food and air freshener. By the time I got back I reckoned that Harry would be in his office so I took out my phone and clicked on his number. To my surprise he answered himself.

206

'Harry Clay Theatrical Agency.'

'Harry, it's Louise. I've just got back from a week away. I've been expecting a call from you. What have you got for me?'

At the other end of the line I heard him sigh. 'I've tried, Lou, but I told you, there's nothing going in your line at the moment. The summer shows are all booked and there's nothing else suitable.'

'So what do you suggest I do? I'm sure I don't have to remind you that I've been conned out of a job and most of my money. You owe it to me to find me something, Harry.'

'Look, Lou, I'll be frank with you. I'm winding the agency up. I'm past retiring age and I've had enough. I've already let Sally go.'

'I see, so the rat is leaving the sinking ship, is he?' I snapped. 'I've a bloody good mind to sue you.'

'Go ahead,' he said wearily. 'You can't get blood out of a stone. I'm sure I don't have to remind you that I'm in the same position as you. Look, I know it's tough but my blood pressure has gone sky high and my doctor says I'm heading for a heart attack. My wife has put her foot down. This business with Fortune has just about finished me. It's time to pack it in and that's what I'm doing.'

'It's all right for you, Harry, but — ' Before I could complete the sentence he'd hung up, leaving me listening to the dialling tone. I hit the red button in disgust. What the hell was I going to do now? I'd soon get through the little money I had left. I had to earn some cash somehow. I clicked on my list of contacts. There was only one name on the list that would sympathize. I highlighted Mark's number but my pride refused to let me press the call button.

For a long time I sat on the bed, despair washing over me like an all-engulfing tide. Why couldn't something go right for me? What had I done to deserve all this bad luck? I got up eventually and opened the suitcase containing most of my clothes, as yet unpacked. It was hardly an haute couture collection. It made me angry to think of the lovely things I could have bought, if only I hadn't blown all my inheritance on Paul bloody Fortune and his godforsaken play. I hung everything up and examined each garment critically. Nothing looked fashionable or smart. I had to admit that even the Chanel suit was beginning to look a bit shabby as I pulled at a loose button. Suddenly I made up my mind. If I was going to get myself a new agent, I was going to have to look a bit less down at heel. I'd go up west today and buy myself a few nice things to wear with some of the cash I'd got left. They wouldn't be designer but I'd always had a good eye and the summer sales were just beginning. I might find some bargains. I'd get my hair done too. It would be a good investment.

First, I trawled my list of agents. As I'd expected, none of them would see me there and then, so I left a copy of my photos and profile along with my mobile number, then I took the Tube to Oxford Street. I bought a classic suit, a casual skirt, a jacket and three tops. I also found some really elegant shoes and a handbag, all at reduced prices, then I sat in the best hairdresser's I could afford for most of the afternoon, having my roots done and my hair cut and blow-dried.

It was while I was walking to the Tube station that I passed a bridal shop and a tiny card in the corner of the window caught my eye.

Assistant wanted.

I stood looking into the window at the beautiful designer bridal gown displayed for some time. It was unusual for a shop of this calibre to advertise in this way. I was intrigued. Eventually, I pushed the door and was immediately surprised by the tinny notes of Mendelssohn's Wedding March. As I walked into the shop I was trying not to laugh. A stylishly dressed woman of about fifty approached me.

'Can I help you?'

I took a deep breath. 'I've just noticed your advertisement in the window,' I said. 'It so happens that I'm looking for work.'

She looked me up and down critically. 'Do you have retail experience?'

I treated her to my best smile. 'I'm actually an actress,' I told her. 'But I have often taken retail work when I've been between engagements as I am now.' It wasn't strictly true of course but I hoped she'd swallow it.

'In that case you'll have references.'

Trying not to look taken aback, I shook my head. 'All the jobs were temporary, of course. But they were all in the fashion trade,' I added quickly. 'I do have quite a flair for fashion; being an actress it's all part of the training.'

'This is a designer boutique,' she said. 'I design most of the gowns, although I do stock a few low-budget dresses.' She appraised me again. 'As it happens, I only need temporary help at the moment, so this might very well suit us both.' She eyed my outfit doubtfully. 'I take it you own a smart black dress or suit?'

'Naturally.' I made a mental note to give the Chanel suit a good sponge and press and get the loose button firmly sewn on. I looked at her. 'What salary are you offering?'

She named a figure that was ludicrous. I shook my head. 'I'm afraid I'd need twice that,' I told her. 'London rents don't come cheap and if you want me to look smart . . . '

'All right, I agree,' she said, throwing me completely. 'When can you start?'

'Well — tomorrow if you like.'

She nodded. 'As you can see, I'm on my own here at the moment so I really do need help — and quickly,' she said. 'Which is why I put the notice in the window. Normally I'd advertise in the usual way.'

'That would suit me. What time would you like me to be here?' I asked.

'Be here at eight, then I'll be able to show you around and explain our routine.'

I walked out of the shop feeling really cheered up. I'd get back onto my feet in no time, I told myself.

But on the Tube on the way back to the horrible bedsit, the spectre of Steve Harris and his threat to get back in touch reared its ugly head. I couldn't stay on in that room like a sitting duck, just waiting for him to come and find me again. Besides, Stoke Newington was an awfully long way from the new job. A sudden thought hit me and I took out my phone and called Dianne. She'd be home from work by now. She could always say no.

She answered the call almost immediately. Clearly she'd deleted my number from her phone because she didn't know who was calling.

'Hello?'

'Di, it's me, Lou,' I said. 'Long time no see. How are you?'

'I'm fine — and you?'

She sounded a tiny bit frosty so I turned on the charm. 'I've really missed you, Di,' I said. 'I hated the way we parted company last time. Any chance I could pop in and see you some time soon?'

She hesitated. 'Aren't you busy with the new play? I'd have thought you'd be on tour by now.'

'It's a long story,' I told her. 'Actually it all fell through in quite a spectacular way. I'd love to tell you all about it. Look, I'm working in the West End at the moment. Any chance I could come and see you after work tomorrow?'

'Yes, OK then,' she said. I knew I'd have aroused her curiosity. 'Though I won't be able to make an evening of it. I have to go out later.'

'That's all right.' I paused. 'How is Mike?'

'Fine — I suppose.' There was a long pause at the other end then she said, 'I'll tell you all my news when we meet. Around six, OK?'

'Fine, look forward to it.'

I returned to the dreadful bedsit that evening,

211

feeling much better. I was just tucking into my microwave meal for one when my phone rang. It was an unfamiliar number. Could it be a call from one of the agents already? Full of optimism, I clicked the green button.

'Hello. Louise Delmar speaking.'

'Hello, darlin'. Little brother Steve here. How are you — all right?'

'Leave me alone,' I snapped, my good mood evaporating instantly. 'Look, there's no point in you ringing me. I don't want to meet you, so please don't ring me or write any more notes.'

'Oh, now is that nice?'

'Frankly, I don't care whether you think it's nice or not,' I said. 'Just go away!'

'I only want to meet you, sis,' he said smoothly. 'I only want to get to know you. After all, blood's thicker than water.'

'I told you. If you don't piss off, I'm calling the police,' I told him. 'This is harassment.'

There was a short pause and then he asked, 'Louise — have you seen last week's edition of *The Stage*?'

'No, why?' My stomach lurched. What did he know that I didn't?

'It was Mum who spotted it,' he said. 'She's so proud of you, our mum. She bought the magazine to see if there was anything in it about you. Imagine how upset she was when she saw an article with the headline: The Show That Never Was. She's really upset for you, Louise.'

My blood ran cold. I'd no idea that the news was buzzing around the business already, but at least it was only the trade paper. 'I don't know what you're talking about,' I bluffed.

'Oh, I think you do,' he said softly. 'I bet your family in Bridgehampton are pissed off for you. Or maybe you ain't broke the news to them yet, eh?'

I caught my breath. 'Look, just leave my family out of it,' I said. 'If you were thinking of blackmailing me, forget it. I've got no money left, and after tomorrow I won't be here so don't bother trying to ring again.'

I cut him off before he could reply and switched off my phone. Something about that voice of his chilled me to the marrow. Maybe I should buy another mobile and throw this one away. I only hoped I'd be able to persuade Di to take pity on me tomorrow. I looked at the remains of my meal, congealing in its plastic tray, and tossed it into the bin, my stomach churning. For the second night I hardly slept, tossing and turning as I tried to think of ways to stop the man who called himself my 'brother' from persecuting me.

* * *

The bridal boutique was called Camilla and I soon discovered that it was the name of the boutique owner and designer. I arrived bright and early and she looked me up and down.

'It's a nice suit,' she said.

I nodded. 'It's Chanel.'

'Mmm.' She pursed her lips. 'The best thing about Chanel is that their suits keep their shape — however old they are.'

That was me told! She showed me around, drawing back the velvet curtains on the rails. The gowns were beautiful but some of the price tags took my breath away — anything from a 'humble' two grand as she put it, to over £5,000. Camilla, as she asked me to call her, caught my expression and smiled.

'You get what you pay for, I always say,' she said smoothly. 'All the highest-priced dresses are unique — one-off, so the bride who wears them can be sure that no one else can upstage her.' She fingered the material. 'Nothing but the best fabrics, French lace and silk from manufacturers in Belgium where I have a standing order. Here, feel for yourself.'

I touched the material reverently, feeling that it might mark if I as much as looked at it. 'It's lovely,' I said. 'And you design them all yourself?'

'All the best ones, yes. In my studio upstairs.'

'And do you do the actual sewing?'

'No. I have four expert out-workers,' she told me. 'And two embroiderers, one of them a young man.' She turned away. 'Follow me and I'll show you the staffroom where you can take your breaks.'

After the showroom and the luxurious fitting rooms with their mirror-lined walls and little gilt chairs, I was surprised at the so-called staffroom. It consisted of a sink unit with a kettle and toaster, a Formica-topped table and two wooden chairs. The floor was covered in cracked vinyl. I looked at her. 'Isn't there a microwave?'

She looked down her nose. 'No. If you want a hot lunch, you could always go out. I'm told there's a McDonald's in one of the side streets. Personally, I like to watch my figure.'

My first customer arrived when Camilla had popped out to the bank. A very pretty young girl and her mother stood looking around them self-consciously as I approached.

'Good morning. Can I help you?'

The mother spoke first. 'We're looking for a wedding dress,' she said.

'I love the one in the window,' the girl said. 'But there isn't a price tag on it and we . . . ' She looked at her mother uncertainly and I guessed that Camilla's prices were going to frighten the pants off them.

'That one is very expensive,' I told them. 'Camilla herself designs all the expensive dresses and they cost a lot because they are unique. Would you like to try something on?'

The young girl's cheeks flushed. 'Oh, could I?'

'How much *is* the one in the window?' the mother insisted. She cast a warning glance in her daughter's direction. 'Before we get too carried away.'

'I'll just check.' I drew aside the curtain at the back of the window and peered at the price label, concealed inside the back of the neck. Holding my breath, I stepped out again and turned to look at them. 'It's £3,500,' I told them. 'But of course, as I said, it is . . . '

'I think we'll leave it, thank you.' The mother grasped her daughter's arm and began to hustle her towards the door.

'That is one of our most expensive dresses,' I said quickly. 'We do have some lower-priced

215

gowns, if you'd like to come this way.'

At the back of the showroom were two rails of what Camilla called 'budget dresses'. I drew one or two out and the faces of mother and daughter relaxed a little. The girl picked out a couple to try on and eventually chose one. As I packed it carefully in tissue paper and one of the distinctive black and pink *Camilla* boxes, I was thrilled to think I'd made a sale and when Camilla returned, I couldn't wait to tell her. She looked pleased until I told her which dress it was.

'I told you to push the *designer* gowns,' she said, looking cross.

'I did but they were obviously out of their price range.'

'What does that matter? You'll find that if you push in the right way they usually give in. After all, they can always economize on something else.'

'How do you mean, push in the right way?'

Camilla sighed. 'Flatter them, of course. Tell them the dress was made for them — that they have the perfect figure for it. Point out that they'll regret it for the rest of their lives if they don't get the very best — that sort of thing.' She glared at me. 'Use your two and a half brain cells for once, *dear*!'

I opened my mouth to give her both barrels but I bit my tongue just in time. For two pins, I could have walked out there and then but like it or not I needed this job and after all, she was paying me what I asked. But as she turned away, I promised myself that the minute one of the agents I'd contacted came up with a half-decent job, I'd be out of here in a flash.

As the day went by and more customers came in, I observed Camilla's sales technique. She really did go over the top with her flattery and oiliness. The amazing thing was that it seemed to work. I wondered how much mark-up there was on a dress designed by her and reckoned it couldn't be far off eighty per cent. No wonder she pushed so hard. After each sale she was impossible; so conceited and overconfident that I longed to bring her down a peg.

★ ★ ★

Di had only just got in from work when I arrived at the flat. She looked tired and took a bottle of wine out of the fridge and poured us both a glass. I'd had nothing to eat since breakfast and I secretly hoped she'd ask me to stay for supper.

'So . . . ' she said as she handed me my glass. 'Tell me your news. What's this West End job you've landed?'

'Not what you think.' Perched on one of her kitchen stools at the breakfast bar, I told her about Paul Fortune's treachery. I went on to describe my first day as sales assistant at Camilla's. As the wine relaxed me I found myself camping it up a bit — imitating Camilla's voice and mannerisms — and soon Di was in fits of laughter.

'Oh, Lou, you are priceless,' she said. 'I'd love to have been a fly on the wall. Looks as if you've met your match in the formidable Camilla.'

217

I wasn't sure what she meant by that. Somehow it didn't feel like a compliment, but I decided to let it go. 'Look, Di, I might as well cut to the chase and tell you why I'm here,' I said. 'I've got this horrific bedsit in Stoke Newington. It takes ages to get up to the West End in the rush hour and I wondered . . . '

'If I could put you up,' she finished for me.

'It would only be temporary,' I assured her. 'I'm expecting an offer from my new agent any day now.'

'Your new agent? What about Harry Clay?'

'He's decided to retire,' I told her. 'He put money into the show too and it's just about finished him. Of course, if Mike isn't happy with the situation, I'd look elsewhere. I don't want to ruin your relationship.'

'Mike and I aren't together any more,' Di said.

I'd suspected as much but I feigned surprise. 'Oh, Di — I'm sorry to hear that.'

'I found out that he was only using me and my flat as a stop-gap until he found somewhere else to live,' she said with more than a hint of bitterness. 'Plus the fact that he met someone else.' She shook her head. 'I won't go into details but it wasn't the happiest of partings. It'll be a long time before I trust another man!'

'Well — I know the feeling.' I left a respectful gap in the conversation then I said tentatively, 'Does that mean you'd be willing to put up with me for a week or two?'

She sighed. 'OK, I suppose so, as long as you pay your way, Lou. I can't afford to let you stay rent free.'

'Of course, I wouldn't dream of putting on you.'

'And as long as you try to keep the place tidy,' she went on. 'No dirty laundry hanging around the place. And you take your turns with the shopping and the chores.'

'But of course.' I frowned. 'Didn't I always?'

'Not always, no.'

'You make me sound like a slut.'

'Precisely,' she said, looking me straight in the eye.

For a moment we stared at each other, then we both burst out laughing.

'Oh, Lou,' Di said at last. 'Slut or no slut, it's good to have you back again.' She looked thoughtful. 'You know, from what you've told me about this Paul Fortune crook, I'm surprised you haven't thought of selling your story to one of the tabloids.'

Her words hit me like a ton of bricks. *What a brilliant idea!* Why hadn't I thought of that? But had the thought crossed the minds of any of the other members of the cast? Had I missed the boat? It was certainly worth finding out.

'Dianne,' I said. 'You are a genius!'

Using Di's computer and at her suggestion, I emailed three of the most popular tabloids there and then while she rustled up a quick supper.

'I'll text you if there are any replies,' she promised. We arranged that I'd move in with all my worldly goods the following week and by the time I got back to the bedsit that night I was feeling a lot more optimistic.

It was a couple of days later at Camilla's that it

happened. It was halfway through the morning and business had been slow. I was in the grotty little staffroom making coffee when I heard the shop doorbell chime out its naff ringtone. Camilla rushed into the showroom like she had a wasp in her knickers.

'Good morning. Welcome to Camilla's. How can I help you?'

Hearing her dulcet Estuary English tones, I peeked through the curtain and got the shock of my life. There in the centre of the shop was Cathy, Mark's stroppy sister. She wasn't alone though, the woman she had with her was about thirty, very pretty and quite well dressed. I eavesdropped shamelessly. Cathy's friend was getting married and wanted a wedding dress immediately.

'My fiancé wants us to be married as quickly as possible,' she explained. 'He's given me *carte blanche* on the dress and I want to look spectacular.'

'I'm sure you'd look that, dear, even without the help of one of my creations,' Camilla oiled. She must be feeling as though all her birthdays had come at once as she reached for her most expensive creations.

'This would be perfect for you,' she simpered. 'This style is just right for your lovely figure.' I turned back to my coffee, a wave of nausea washing over me, then I heard something that stopped the breath in my throat and I almost choked as Cathy said, 'Oh, yes. Do try it on, Franny. I'm sure you'll look lovely in it.'

Franny! Surely that was short for Francesca

— Mark's ex? Was he going to marry this girl he'd been engaged to after all? My first thought was that he must be on the rebound. Then another thought occurred to me: had I been the one on the rebound after her? Had he never really loved me? Had I lost him for good? I held my breath as Franny disappeared into one of the changing rooms, hoping against hope that the dress wouldn't require any alterations. If it did, Camilla would be sure to ask me to help her with the pinning. The thought of facing Cathy made my stomach churn. I couldn't bear the thought of her taking the news of my humiliation triumphantly back to Mark, and them laughing about it together.

Luckily, the dress fitted perfectly and Franny decided to buy it. She paid the exorbitant sum with her credit card and she and Cathy went off together in high spirits, chattering away excitedly. Camilla came back into the staffroom, flushed with the pleasure of success, only to glower at me as she tasted her coffee.

'Stone cold!' She pushed the cup at me. 'Make me another. And please do not peep round the curtain in that vulgar way. Don't think I didn't see you. If you want to learn how to conduct yourself, just come into the shop and help me as any sensible person would do.'

'I was on my break,' I pointed out to her.

'Business comes before breaks in my establishment, as you'll soon learn,' she said.

Who the hell did she think she was, speaking to me like that? I was a mature woman, not some spotty teenager. I longed to pour the cooling coffee over her elegant coiffeur but I controlled myself. My turn would come, I promised myself with gritted teeth. At the first sniff of a job, I'd be out of here like a rat up a drainpipe.

Whilst Camilla was out at lunch, I switched on my phone. There were three missed texts from Di. I went into 'messages' and read them. They all said the same.

Editor of the Daily Sphere *wants you to get in touch ASAP. Good luck, Di.* A phone number followed.

Praying that no customers would come in, I tapped in the number and waited with bated breath, hoping he wasn't out at lunch. His secretary put me through at once. Yes, he'd heard rumours about Paul Fortune's scam, and yes, he was certainly interested in my story. I tentatively asked what the paper would pay, pointing out that I'd lost my entire savings. He was sympathetic. Could I go in and talk about it?

Yes, I could!

This afternoon?

That threw me for a moment. Camilla would never agree to letting me have the afternoon off so I'd have to wangle something. One thing was for sure — I wasn't going to pass up a chance like this, whatever it took.

'Is that a problem for you?' he asked.

'No! Not at all,' I assured him. 'Just say a time and I'll be there.'

The meeting was scheduled for four o'clock so I was going to have to think quickly. As it happened the fates were with me. The answer dropped into my lap minutes before Camilla returned from lunch and I saw at once that this was my chance. Two people came into the shop, one young, the other, I guessed, around fifty-something. Mother and daughter, I guessed, but it soon emerged that the customer was not the daughter but the mother.

'I'm getting married for the second time,' she simpered. 'My first wedding was a rushed affair in a register office so I want this one to make up for what I missed the first time round. I'm planning the full works.'

I looked at her. She was short and on the tubby side, with a figure that I guessed owed much to pies and cakes. She wore too much badly applied make-up and her hair was an unlikely auburn with magenta highlights. I drew out one of Camilla's most expensive gowns.

'Oh, that's lovely but it's a bit plain and . . . ' She took one look at the price tag and gasped.

'Good God! I wasn't thinking of paying that kind of money,' she said. I saw the daughter flinch.

'Mum — you wouldn't wear a dress like that anyway, would you?'

The mother bridled. 'Why not?'

'Isn't it a bit — well — *young*?'

'Everyone says I look *years* younger than I am!'

'We do have a budget range,' I put in. 'Shall we see if there's anything there that you'd like?'

She cheered up at once — just as Camilla walked in. Seeing that I had a customer, she went to the back of the shop and disappeared into the staffroom, where I guessed she had her ear to the gap in the curtain, if not her eye. In the rail of budget dresses was one particularly hideous dress. I'd spotted it on my first day and asked Camilla about it. She told me it had been foisted on her by a sales rep. In return for taking it off his hands, he'd given her a good deal on six other dresses. It was a gypsy-style gown in fuchsia pink with a ruched skirt and the lowest neckline I'd ever seen. It was generously decorated with black lace and diamante and as I'd guessed she would, the woman fell in love with it on sight.

'Oh! I *do* like that!'

I saw her daughter wince but ignored it. Adopting my best Camilla manner I went into my act. 'This would look *perfect* on you,' I gushed. 'You have just the right figure for it. When your groom turns and sees you coming down the aisle in this, he's going to go weak at the knees.'

'He's eighty so he's weak at the knees already,' the daughter muttered. I tried hard not to laugh.

'Try it on,' I invited. 'And just you see if I'm not right.'

The woman emerged a few minutes later, flushed with delight. The dress was too tight for her. She'd obviously had trouble with the zip and her bosom was spilling over in the most alarming way, but at least she had it on. She looked at herself in one of the full-length mirrors, smiling as she turned this way and that. 'Ooh, I have to have this,' she said. Once again the daughter winced.

Casting me an apologetic look she said, 'Mum!

224

You look like something out of a pantomime.'

Her mother rounded on her. 'Shut up, Norma! You've got no fashion sense and anyway, you're just jealous!' She turned to me. 'Every bloke she gets dumps her after a fortnight,' she said nastily. The daughter flounced out of the shop. I could almost feel Camilla's eyes burning into the back of my neck and a few moments later, she emerged from the staffroom, a false smile plastered onto her face.

'I'm sure we can do better than that for you, madam,' she said.

The woman shook her head. 'Oh no, I've set my heart on this one,' she said. 'And don't you worry: I shall recommend your shop to all my friends.'

She changed back into her own clothes as I packed up the hideous dress, feeling Camilla's fury just waiting to erupt the moment the customer left the shop.

As the tinkling notes of the 'Wedding March' door chime died, she started spitting venom.

'What on *earth* did you think you were doing?' she stormed. 'That — that awful woman will tell everyone she bought the dress here. My reputation will be ruined!'

I raised my eyebrows. 'Well, it *was* for sale. And she was a very satisfied customer.'

'Do you honestly think I want *her* kind of customer?' Her eyes flashed. 'If I'd been here I would have put her off. I was going to take that wretched thing home tonight,' she said. 'I wish I'd done it weeks ago. I should have *burnt it*!'

'Well, you didn't, and now it's sold and you've

got the money for it,' I told her blandly.

Her eyes narrowed. 'You did it on purpose, didn't you?'

I smiled at her. 'Well, you did ask for it,' I said. 'You and your high-handed ways. If you think you can speak to me as though I'm your inferior and get away with it, you've got another think coming!'

'How *dare* you!' Her face turned a peculiar shade of puce and as she spoke, flecks of spit landed on my jacket. 'Get out of my shop this minute. You're dismissed! Do you hear me? *Get out!*'

'Not until you've paid me,' I said, standing my ground. 'If you refuse, I shall take it further and we don't want to ruin your reputation even more, do we?'

Practically fizzing with anger, she went behind the desk and opened the till, snatching a handful of notes she almost threw at me. She was flexing her fingers as she glared at me, and I looked at the long scarlet talons and decided that it was time to make my exit before she scratched my eyes out. As I left the shop I glanced at my watch. If I caught a bus now I'd be right on time for my date with the *Daily Sphere*.

The meeting was more than successful. I made the most of Paul Fortune's scam and the mess he'd landed me and everyone else in. The editor was enthusiastic and offered me a full page spread in the Sunday edition, complete with photograph. It meant that everyone I knew would get to hear of my humiliation but the fee I managed to negotiate more than made up for that. When I got back to the bedsit, I texted Di.

Thanks to your brill idea I'm on the up again. See you soon — Lou.

After I'd pressed 'send' I sat looking at my list of contacts then, on impulse, I highlighted Mark's number. He'd given up trying to contact me and now I knew why.

Congratulations, Mark! I tapped in. *Love, Lou.*

At least he'd know I was still thinking of him.

22

Susan was washing up her breakfast things on Sunday morning when the phone rang. She pulled off her rubber gloves and went into the living room to answer it.

'Hi, Mum, it's me, Karen. Have you seen the paper this morning?'

'No, I haven't been up very long. I'm still in my dressing gown. Why?'

'You do have the *Sphere*, don't you?'

'On Sundays, yes, I have to confess that I like the sensational stories they publish.'

'Well, there's none as sensational as the one on page three,' Karen went on. She sounded excited. 'Just go and get it, Mum. Have a look now while I'm on the phone.'

Mystified, Susan picked up the paper from the coffee table and unfolded it. Spreading it out, she turned the pages. There, on page three, the face of her stepdaughter smiled up at her. *Louise*! But what . . . ? She scanned the headline and the story beneath and gasped.

'Well — have you found it?' Karen sounded impatient at the other end of the line.

'Yes, I've found it. It says that the show she was supposed to be opening in turned out to be a huge confidence trick.' Susan was still running one forefinger down the page. 'Oh my God! It also says that she put — it says here — her life savings into the project and that she's lost the lot!'

'Have you been holding out on us, Mum? Did she tell you any of this last time she was with you?'

'No. Just that there was a problem and that there'd be a delay with the opening.'

'She's such a liar, Mum.'

Susan was shaking her head. 'It must mean that she's lost everything that her father left her. She wouldn't want to admit it, would she? Poor Louise. What a terrible blow for her.'

'Mum! You can't be serious. She richly deserved this. She's a nightmare. You know she is.'

'I know she has an unfortunate habit of upsetting people but you have to admit that this is something you wouldn't wish on your worst enemy.'

'Want to bet?' Karen said, half to herself. 'Well, I just hope that she isn't going to descend on you again, taking advantage of your good nature. Promise me you'll say no if she rings and asks you to take her in again.'

Susan bridled. 'I'm promising you nothing of the sort, Karen. I shall do as I think fair and right when and if it arises.'

'Well, on your own head be it. Don't say you haven't been warned, Mum.'

'I won't.' Susan waited a moment then asked, 'Is everything all right there — with you and Simon, I mean?'

'Of course. Why do you ask?'

'Don't be naïve, Karen. You know perfectly well why I'm asking. Have you resigned yourself to staying at home with Peter?'

'No, not completely. I've said I'll do the odd spot of tutoring. Not full-time, of course. Just when they're stuck for someone.'

'And is Simon all right with that?'

'Mum — I'm not a slave. Simon is my husband, not my keeper. I do wish you'd update to twenty-first century thinking.'

'Perhaps it's not me you need to convince,' Susan said. 'Anyway, thanks for ringing, Karen. I hope you feel that Louise's stroke of disastrous bad luck has vindicated you in some way. I'll have to go now, I need to get dressed.'

Susan sat thinking for a few minutes after hanging up. Louise had been so convinced that this play was her big breakthrough. She must be devastated. On impulse, she lifted the receiver again and dialled Louise's mobile number. After a few minutes Louise answered.

'Hi, Susan.'

'I've just seen the article in the *Sunday Sphere*,' Susan said. 'How awful for you and all the rest of the cast. You must be so upset and disappointed. Did you know about this when you visited last time?'

'Well, yes, I did actually.'

'And you never said a thing. How are you managing, dear? Did you lose all your money?'

'Quite a lot of it, yes, but don't worry, Susan. I had a temporary job and the paper paid me well for the article. Of course, everyone will know now that I ended up with the proverbial egg on my face, but never mind.'

'Have they caught this man — this Fortune person?'

'No and I'm not holding my breath that they will. He's left the country and covered his tracks pretty well.'

'Do you have a place to stay? Will you be able to find another job?'

'I'm staying with Dianne at the moment. We've made up our little quarrel. My agent, Harry, put money into the show too and it's put him out of business so I have to find a new agent.'

Susan sighed. 'Oh dear, what a disaster for you all! Louise — have you heard any more from your birth mother?'

'No and I don't want to. That's a closed chapter as far as I'm concerned. Anyway, if she's read the article, she will have lost interest in me by now. Thanks for ringing, Susan. I appreciate your concern.'

'Not at all. You know where I am, don't you, if you need me?'

'Yes, and thanks again. It's nice to know there's someone on my side.'

'What about your young man — the one you told me about? He was in the show too, wasn't he?'

'Yes, he was, but that's all over, Susan.'

'Oh. I'm sorry to hear that, dear.'

Susan hung up with a sigh. Whatever Louise had done in the past, it was certainly catching up with her now. She thought briefly of the rebellious child she had taken on all those years ago when she married Frank. Louise hadn't been easy to bring up, especially once she reached puberty. There was a time when it seemed that she would never have a normal life, but somehow she'd put all the distress she had suffered in her youth aside and made a life for herself. It was true that she'd become a difficult and unpredictable woman, but she'd suffered so much in her young life that Susan tried to make allowances. Maybe the trauma and the underlying sense of loss would never leave her.

★ ★ ★

It was two days later that Karen rang again.

'Mum — can you do me the most amazing favour?' She rattled on before Susan had time to reply. 'The things is, this agency, you know the one that offered me the job, need me to do some work for them today.'

'And you have no one to babysit?'

'Not at such short notice. It would only be for the morning, Mum. I'd be so grateful.'

'Does Simon know?'

'What's that got to do with anything?'

'I'll take that as a no, then.'

'What he doesn't know can't hurt him. I really haven't got time to discuss it now. Can you have Peter or can't you, Mum?'

'I suppose so. When and where do you want me?'

'I'll pop him round to you on my way. Have to go now. See you soon.'

Karen's visit was swift and brief. She handed a bewildered-looking Peter over unceremoniously. 'I've left the buggy downstairs by the front entrance,' she said breathlessly. 'It's a lovely morning so if you take him to the park I'll meet you there — say, by the café at one o'clock. OK?' And before Susan could confirm that this was convenient for her Karen was already halfway down the stairs.

Peter popped his thumb into his mouth and looked up at his grandmother. 'Mummy gone.'

Susan bent to pick him up. 'Yes, darling. Mummy's gone but she'll be back again soon. Have you had any breakfast?'

His little face brightened. 'Poddidge?'

'Yes, Granny'll make you some porridge and then we'll go to the park, shall we?'

As Karen had said, it was a lovely morning and Susan let Peter walk beside the buggy down to the lake. She'd brought stale bread and they bought a bag of corn which Peter delightedly threw to the ducks. They went to the playground and Peter went on a swing — a baby one this time — and sat on Susan's lap for a gentle ride on the roundabout. At the café they each had an ice cream, after which Peter began to look decidedly sleepy. Susan put him into the buggy and tucked his blanket round him, and by the time they had walked across the park to the bowling green, he was fast asleep. Grateful for five minutes' respite, she sat down on one of the benches to watch the elderly men playing their sedate game. The warm sunshine made her drowsy too and her eyelids had closed when suddenly she heard someone say her name.

'Susan.'

She opened her eyes to find Ted standing in front of her.

'Good morning, sleepyhead.'

Her heart leapt and she felt the warm colour stain her cheeks. 'I wasn't asleep,' she said. 'It's just the sun. It's very warm and — and dazzling.'

'Of course it is.' He chuckled and sat down beside her. 'Young Peter looks cosy.'

'Yes.' She sat up straight. 'I — we were just going, as a matter of fact.'

'Back to the flat? Mind if I walk with you?'

Susan glanced surreptitiously at her watch and sighed. It was almost half past twelve. Karen would be here in half an hour. She couldn't go now. 'No, not back to the flat,' she told him. 'Karen is picking Peter up at the café at one o'clock. I was going to walk across there in a minute.'

'Then I'll come with you.' He looked at her searchingly. 'That is if you've no objections.'

'There's really no need,' she said stiffly.

He laid a hand on her arm. 'Susan, please. Surely at our age there's no need for us to keep up this . . . ' He shook his head. 'Whatever you want to call it.'

'No — well.'

'I've missed you very much these last weeks.'

She turned to look at him. 'I — thought you'd found a new — companion.'

He smiled. 'The lady you saw helping me on the allotment was a fellow gardener's wife,' he explained. 'They saw me struggling to keep your plot going as well as mine and offered to help.'

Susan bit her lip. 'Oh. I see.'

'There's a lot you don't see, my dear,' he said. 'And that's all down to me. I should have been more upfront with you. My only excuse is that I

234

didn't want to frighten you away. If you'll just let me . . . '

'How did you know I'd be here today?' she asked him.

'I didn't.' He smiled. 'Believe it or not, I come here every day in the hope of running into you.'

Susan stood up. 'I'm sorry, Ted, but the time's getting on. I have to go. Karen will be waiting.'

He stood and faced her. 'Then may I?'

'I suppose so — if you must.'

'Oh yes, I must,' he said with a smile. 'I *really* must. If you only knew how much courage it took to speak to you just now.'

Susan said nothing as she rose and began to push the buggy, but she was slightly mollified by Ted's humility as he walked silently beside her.

Karen was already waiting. Her cheeks were glowing and she looked happy.

'Thanks so much, Mum,' she said as she took the buggy's handle. 'I've enjoyed this morning so much. Tutoring is so rewarding. They've asked me to continue. It's for a boy who's broken his leg in an accident and as he's taking his GCSEs next year, they don't want him to fall behind.' She kissed her mother and hurried off. Ted had been standing to one side and now, Susan felt him looking at her. He touched her arm.

'Lunch? Please say yes, Susan.'

She relented. 'Well — I normally only have a sandwich. They do quite nice ones here at the café.'

He nodded. 'Then a sandwich it shall be — for both of us. You pick a table out here in the sunshine and I'll go and get them.'

He returned with an assortment of sandwiches and coffee for them both. She looked at him.

'I never thanked you for the flowers you brought me,' she said. 'And I owe you an apology for my stepdaughter's outspoken remarks.'

He shook his head. 'Don't give it another thought.' For a few minutes they ate in silence then he said, 'Susan, I owe you an explanation and I'm determined that you shall hear it. It's all a bit convoluted and you'll have to bear with me but — '

'You owe me nothing, Ted,' she interrupted.

'Oh, but I do,' he insisted. 'There are things I have to tell you, if only for my own peace of mind.'

'All right.' She looked around. The tables were filling up now and two elderly women at the next table were clearly listening to their conversation with interest. 'But let's finish our lunch first and find a quiet spot.'

They finished their sandwiches in silence, then got up and walked slowly down to the lake. She waited for him to begin and it was obvious that he was nervous and hesitant.

'First, I must confess that it's true that I'm still married,' he said at last.

She stiffened. 'You gave me the impression that you were a widower.'

He looked at her. 'I'm sure I never actually said so.'

'Maybe not, but . . . '

'Meg and I have been married for more than forty years. We were both very young when we married, especially Meg, and I'm sorry to say that she cheated on me from very early on in the marriage. She had an endless stream of affairs, none of which lasted for long, and like a fool I always forgave her and took her back. But eventually she met someone and fell seriously in love. They ran off together — went to live abroad. I filed for divorce when it became clear that she had no intention of coming back to me but for some reason she refused to cooperate. I thought it must be because she was still unsure about her new relationship, but eventually that thought petered out and I began to pick up the pieces and make a new life for myself. I thought that eventually she'd want to marry her new partner and agree to a divorce, but the years went by and it never happened.'

'Do you know where she is now?' Susan asked.

He gave her a wry smile. 'Oh yes. I know where she is. Four years ago, Meg's partner got in touch with me quite out of the blue. He told me that she had developed dementia and he could no longer have — as he put it — the *responsibility* of her. He informed me that as I was still her husband that duty now fell to me.'

'*Oh no!*' Susan stared at him, appalled. 'But — how many years had you been apart?'

'Almost thirty.'

'But surely, isn't there something about a marriage being null and void after a certain period of desertion?'

'Desertion is grounds for divorce, yes, but I never applied to divorce her on those grounds.' He shook his head. 'And I could hardly do so at that stage.'

Susan shook her head. 'So what happened?'

'Her new partner brought her back to me and just left. He handed her over like an unwanted pet and disappeared over the horizon. Naturally, she didn't understand. She didn't even remember who I was. Life was sheer hell — not only for me but for her as well. Eventually, my only alternative was to get her into a care home. I chose the best I could afford and she's still there.'

Susan felt chastened. 'Do you visit her?'

He shrugged. 'Occasionally, though she doesn't recognize me.'

'Oh, Ted! How awful. I'm so sorry.'

'The woman next door knows some of this but not all. She had no right to speak to you as she did.'

For a while, Susan was silent as she tried to take in all that Ted had told her. At last she looked at him. 'I wish you'd told me this in the beginning.'

He smiled wryly. 'I wish I had too, but it isn't a happy story and it doesn't make me much of a prospect, does it? Apart from that, you might have thought I was to blame.'

'How could you be to blame?'

'For all you knew I might have driven her away. I might have been a bad husband — might have been violent or abusive.'

'Knowing you, I'm certain none of those things applied to you.'

'But back then you *didn't* know me. I would have told you eventually, Susan. I had no intention of keeping you in the dark. But when we first met I knew at once that you were going to be someone special and I couldn't risk losing you.' He sighed. 'Unfortunately Mrs Freeman forestalled me.'

'I should never have listened to her,' Susan said. 'I should have given you the chance to explain.'

He shook his head. 'It was understandable that you felt shocked and let down, believed that I'd misled you.' He looked at her. 'Under the circumstances I'll understand if you don't want to see me again. I just wanted you to know the truth. I couldn't bear the thought of you thinking me a liar and a — philanderer.'

Very tentatively Susan reached for his hand. 'Oh, Ted, what a sad life you've had,' she said. 'Now that I know all this how could you imagine that I would want to end our friendship? I've missed you too — so much.'

His eyes lit up. 'Are you saying you'd be happy for us to start seeing each other again?'

'Of course, though it might be better for us to meet at my flat in future.'

'Whatever you say.' Ted stood up and held out his hand to her. 'Shall we walk back to the café? I don't know about you but I could murder a cup of tea.'

Susan laughed and took his hand. 'Me too.'

Walking back through the park in the sunshine with Ted, Susan's heart lifted. Although she felt desperately sorry for the poor woman in the care home she felt that Ted deserved some happiness and contentment at last for all that he had suffered. As for her, she couldn't remember a time when she'd felt so happy.

23

I couldn't believe it. The very next day after the article had appeared in the *Sunday Sphere*, I had a call from one of the agents I'd left my details with. I called at once and an interview was arranged for the following day.

Di was thrilled. 'There! What did I tell you?' she said. 'I knew it was a good idea to put yourself out there.'

I pulled a face at her. 'Making myself look like a gullible idiot, you mean,' I said. 'Maybe they're just looking for a cleaning woman.'

'Get away with you,' Di said. 'This could be the making of you.'

Dressed in the Chanel suit, carefully sponged and pressed, I made my way to the agent's office at the appointed time and sat nervously in reception. Looking around the room, I was impressed by the signed photographs of many well-known celebrities displayed on the walls.

The door opened and a man came out. A moment after he left, the receptionist's phone rang. She listened briefly, then replaced the receiver and looked across at me. 'Mr Jason will see you now.'

He was middle-aged with silver-grey hair and an attractive, warm smile. He rose and offered his hand. 'Good morning, Miss Delmar. I'm Patrick Jason. Please have a seat.' When we faced each other across his desk he said, 'I read the article in the *Sunday Sphere* about your bad experience. The name rang a bell and I looked in my in-tray and found the details you left at the office a few days ago.' He looked up at me. 'Surely you had an agent before all this?'

I nodded. 'Yes, Harry Clay. Unfortunately he put money into the project too and it has put him out of business.'

'I see. I had heard he was retiring, but I had no idea that he was another victim of this terrible business.' He looked at me speculatively. 'This Fortune man fooled us all. It was brave of you to go to the national press with your story,' he said.

'I don't know about that.' I smiled. 'It might well turn out to be the end of my career, but frankly it was a case of desperation. I needed the money. It was as simple as that.' I looked at him and decided I might as well lay my cards on the table. 'I couldn't believe my luck when I got the leading role in this new musical. It seemed like the big break I'd been longing for, and when I was asked to put money into it I was only too eager. I was supposed to get my money back, plus generous interest once the show was up and running.'

'I can't begin to imagine how you all felt when you found yourselves stranded high and dry in Bournemouth.'

I gave him a wry smile. 'It was a blow to say the least. Then when Harry told me he was closing the agency, it looked as if I was going to be out of work for some time. I had to do something.'

He shook his head. 'So you decided to go public?'

'Yes.' I sighed. 'The price I paid being that now everyone will know how vain and gullible I was.'

'So, you've had no work since?'

'Not in the business. I did have a job at a West End wedding-dress boutique,' I told him. 'It only lasted a few days though. The owner was a twenty-four-carat cow.'

He laughed. 'I liked the sound of you in the article,' he said. 'It showed me that you have character, the ability to laugh at yourself.'

I decided to ask him point blank where all this was going. 'So — why did you ask me to come in? Are you offering to represent me?'

He pursed his lips. 'I do have one or two things in mind that might suit you.' He looked at me. 'Meantime, would you be willing to do some commercial TV?'

'Anything to keep the wolf from the door.'

'Right.' He made a note on his pad. 'Have you done any TV work before?'

I opened my mouth to tell him I had and then closed it again. The time had come to be honest. If I lied about this he'd be bound to find out and that could ruin any future chances I might have. 'No,' I said. 'But it's always been an ambition of mine.'

'OK. If anything comes up I'll give you a ring.' He leaned back in his chair and eyed me for a moment. 'I've just had a thought. One of the TV soaps is auditioning next week,' he said at last. 'Have you done character?'

I shook my head, remembering my decision to be truthful. 'Not really, though I admit I'm getting close to that age. What's the part?'

'A middle-aged motherly type,' he said. 'The kind of sympathetic woman everyone turns to in times of trouble. Do you watch *King's Reach*?'

I nodded. I'd seen it a few times when I was staying with Susan. *Susan!* She was just the kind of woman he'd just described to me. I knew Susan well enough to use her as a role model. 'I quite like the sound of that,' I told him.

'You wouldn't mind playing older than your age?'

'Not at all.' At that particular moment I wasn't at all sure about playing older but beggars certainly couldn't be choosers. And I reminded myself that some of those soap stars had been playing the same part for years. A guaranteed income sounded pretty good to me, playing older or not.

He opened a file on his desk and took out a sheet of paper. 'Here's the character description. She's called Amy Armstrong. Take it home and have a read. The audition is next Thursday. I'll text you the address of the venue when they let me have it. Meanwhile, I'll ring you if a commercial opportunity comes along.' He paused. 'Are you still at the address you left me?'

'Oh, no. What a good job you thought to ask. I'll be staying with a friend for the foreseeable future.' I scribbled down Di's address and passed it to him. 'But you can always get me on my mobile.' I stood up. 'Thank you so much for seeing me, Mr Jason.'

He smiled. 'Patrick, please. Let's hope it all works out for you.'

The following morning I had two calls; the first was from Patrick Jason, giving me the address of the audition venue. I was so excited when I clicked the call off that I went to the fridge and poured myself a celebratory glass of wine. I wished Di could have been with me to share the excitement. I was sipping my wine and studying the character description once more when my phone rang again.

'Hello.'

'Hello, Louise.'

I recognized the voice at once and my heart plummeted. 'What do you want?' I asked bluntly.

'Oh, come on Louise,' my mother said. 'I'm just ringing to say how sorry I was to read about your disappointment. It was such a lovely photo in the paper too.'

'So now you and your son will realize that I'm actually broke,' I said. 'If you think I'm rolling in cash and a soft touch, you're going to have to think again.'

'You're very suspicious, Louise. I can't think where you get that from.' Her voice had a hard note to it now.

'Neither can I. So we might as well call it a day now,' I told her. 'I'll be frank. I don't want a relationship with you. It's too late and I don't think we have anything in common anyway.'

'I'm sorry to hear that you think that, Louise,' she said. 'But before we part company, there's something you should know about yourself. Something important that no one knows about but me.'

'I don't think you know anything that I don't.' I held my finger over the 'end call' button but what she said next stopped me.

'Don't hang up, Louise! This is something you really should know — for your own sake. I'm not joking.'

There was something chilling about her tone and I began to be apprehensive. 'Then tell me now.'

'Not on the phone,' she said. 'It's not trivial, Louise, and I'm not kidding. We really have to meet for me to tell you — even if it is for the last time.'

She'd got me now. In spite of myself I was curious. 'All right,' I said. 'Where and when?'

'King's Cross Station,' she said. 'In the café — Thursday, at one o'clock.'

'Thursday?' It was the day of the audition. 'Can you make it any other day?'

'Thursday would be best.'

I thought about it. I should be able to make it by one o'clock. If not she'd have to wait. But why meet at a railway station?

'King's Cross? Why there?' I asked.

'I'm meeting someone off a train at two. It's convenient.'

'All right, I'll try to be there.'

'It's to your advantage to be there, Louise. See you on Thursday, then.'

After the call, I sat there for a long time, my excitement about the audition temporarily forgotten as I wondered what she was about to tell me about myself. Could it be that I was a carrier for some horrible disease? Or was it just some devious trick? I decided not to think about it for the moment. Concentrating on the audition was my priority.

★ ★ ★

I arrived at the studio in good time and was dismayed to find about twelve other actresses waiting, not least of which was none other but Carla Dean. To my dismay she soon spotted me and came across.

'Fancy seeing *you* here, darling,' she said. 'I saw the article all about you in the *Sunday Sphere*. Anyone would think you were the only one to be cheated.' She sniffed. 'A very flattering photograph, I thought. When was that taken — ten years ago?'

'It was taken by the paper's own photographer,' I told her.

'Then they must have airbrushed it,' she said. 'So how did you hear about this?'

'My new agent, Patrick Jason.'

Her finely plucked eyebrows rose. 'Jason, eh? Personally I was tipped off by a friend and it seemed like the sort of thing that would suit me down to the ground.' She smiled smugly. 'I know a couple of the production crew actually. Just between you and me the rest of you might as well go home now. I think it's pretty much a foregone conclusion.'

'Well, good luck, then.'

We were called in one by one. When it was my turn I pulled out all the stops, reading the test piece with Susan very much in mind. When everyone had auditioned, the production assistant came out and told us we'd be notified in a few days' time. Carla looked at me. 'Coming for a drink?'

I shook my head. 'No. I have another appointment,' I said. No way was I going to sit in some wine bar being bombarded with personal questions by Carla. We parted company in the street outside and she wandered off. I looked at my watch. It was a quarter to one. If I was going to make King's Cross on time I was going to have to hail a taxi.

* * *

I knew there was more than one café or coffee shop at King's Cross station and my 'mother' hadn't said which one, but I soon spotted her, sitting at one of the tables outside. She saw me and waved me over.

'You're late. I began to think you weren't coming.'

I hoisted myself onto the high stool opposite her. 'The traffic was bad.'

'Oh well, you're here now. Do you want to go and get a coffee?'

'No. I just want you to get to the point,' I said. 'What is this you need to tell me?'

She took a leisurely sip of her own coffee, looking at me speculatively over the rim of the mug. 'Do you remember the night I left?' she asked. 'Or were you too young at the time?'

'I remember it as though it was yesterday,' I told her. 'In fact, I've been having nightmares

247

about it ever since.'

She snorted disbelievingly. 'Well now, aren't you the drama queen!'

'So — it's something about the night you left,' I said. 'I thought you said it was about me.'

'It is.' She picked up her spoon and began to swirl what was left of her coffee. 'Did your dad ever tell you what we rowed about?'

'Of course not. Look . . . ' I was fast losing patience with her. 'Just get to the point. How does this concern me?'

She looked up at me with a hint of triumph in her eyes. 'Your dad and I rowed because I told him he wasn't your father.'

I stared at her. 'You *what?*'

'I told him the truth: that he wasn't the father of my child!'

It was as though a chill hand clutched my heart. 'I don't believe you.'

She smiled maddeningly. 'What do you want — a DNA test? It's a bit late for that!'

My mouth dried. Suddenly I had trouble breathing. 'But — he kept me — brought me up. He was my dad and I loved him. If what you say is true, why didn't you take me with you?'

She shrugged. 'I was young. I wanted to be free.'

I winced. 'If Frank Davies wasn't my father, then who was?'

'Could be one of several,' she said casually. 'I was a good-time girl back then. I played the field, as they say.'

I felt sick. Getting down from my stool, I took one last look at the woman who had given birth to me. '*You bitch!*' I said. 'I hope I never have to see you again.'

'Likewise, I'm sure,' she said with a laugh. 'You and your boasting about being the big wealthy star. You're nothing but a small-time extra — *if that!*' As I walked away she called after me, '*You'll never amount to anything — you're bloody useless — just like that fool you called Dad!*'

I made a beeline for the ladies' and locked myself in a cubicle where I was wretchedly sick. My heart was thumping and the tears ran unchecked down my cheeks. I came out of the cubicle feeling weak and stood shakily, clutching one of the wash-basins. A concerned-looking woman asked me if I was all right. I shook my head.

'I'll be fine in a minute,' I said. 'It's a stomach upset — something I ate.' I dashed some water on my face and hurriedly made my escape.

As luck would have it, Di was out all evening. One of her colleagues was having a hen night. I made myself a sandwich but it was like sawdust in my mouth and eventually I threw it in the bin and took myself off to bed. I heard Di come in around midnight but she was quiet and I didn't call out to her. I fell at last into a fitful sleep but the dream seemed to begin almost at once. A crowd of people were laughing derisively at me and in the centre of them was my mother, her face a mask of hate as she pointed and jeered. When I looked down I held a baby in my arms. In deep shock, I threw the baby from me and heard it scream as it fell. The screams and the scornful laughter grew louder and louder until they became unbearable. I put my hands over my ears and I heard myself shouting, '*Stop it! Stop it!*'

'Lou — Lou! Wake up!'

I opened my eyes to see Di's concerned face looking down at me. Still shaking, I hoisted myself into a sitting position, my heart thudding. 'Was — was I talking in my sleep?'

'Shouting more like,' she said. 'It must have been a horrible dream. Do you want to tell me about it?'

Suddenly everything crowded in on me. I was overwhelmed by a terrible feeling of grief and I burst into tears. Di put her arms round me and held me close.

'What is it? I've never seen you cry before.'

'I — I had some bad news,' I stammered, swallowing hard.

'What was it, Lou — the audition?'

The audition! I could almost have laughed. It seemed like a million years ago. So trivial that I'd completely forgotten about it. I shook my head. 'No. That was OK, they're letting us know. There were dozens of applicants so I don't suppose I've got a chance.' I looked at her. 'Afterwards I went to meet my mother — birth mother, I mean.'

'So you found her? You didn't tell me.'

I shook my head. 'It was some time ago and it wasn't what you'd call a roaring success. In fact it was a disaster. She was nothing like I'd imagined her. She was only interested in meeting me because she thought I was going to be a star and have lots of cash. Then I made the mistake of telling her I'd inherited Dad's money. She asked me for cash the first time we met but when she realized I wasn't going to be a never-ending source of easy money, she didn't want to know.'

'So why did you meet her again today?'

'She rang me to say she had some important information about me — something I really should know.'

'And did she?'

'Yes.' I bit my lip to stop myself from getting emotional again. 'She told me that Dad wasn't my real father. Worse — she'd cheated on him several times and she didn't really know who my father was.'

Di looked shocked. 'Oh, Lou. But is it true, do you think? Was she just being spiteful?'

'I don't know. I've been thinking — the one person who might know is Susan. I'll have to go and see her.'

Di squeezed my hand. 'I'm so sorry, love.'

'Me too.' I looked at her. 'Can you imagine, Di, how it feels, not knowing who you really are?'

'But you're *you* — Louise Davies. You're your own person.'

I sighed. 'I even dropped Dad's name. It's ironic, isn't it? I know I haven't been a nice person. I treated poor Mark horrendously when we were at drama school. No wonder his sister hates me. I've taken advantage of people — you included. I thought the world and everyone in it owed me when really I was just a pain in the backside. I'm a mess, Di. Maybe I take after my father — whoever he might be. Now there's no way I'll ever know.'

Di patted my shoulder. 'My advice is to get on a train first thing tomorrow; go and see Susan and have a good talk. She probably knows more than you realize.'

24

'Mum! You can't be serious. It's no time at all since Louise came to stay with you. What's her excuse this time?'

'She says she needs to talk,' Susan said. 'She's somehow managed to locate her birth mother and she seemed so upset on the phone. I couldn't say no to her.'

'But you can say no to me!' Karen protested. 'You know it'll all be some trivial nonsense she's dreamed up.'

'I don't think so. She . . . '

'So you're saying no to having Peter for me?'

'I'm afraid I can't,' Susan said firmly. 'Not this time. Anyway, Simon's at home now for the holidays. Can't he . . . ' She paused. 'I take it you have told him — about the tutoring?'

'Not exactly.'

'Well, don't you think you should?'

'I told him I had to be out for the morning and he's gone off somewhere in a huff so I can't; at least not at the moment.'

'Well, you know my feelings on that matter. You should start talking to Simon,' Susan said. 'Just be honest. No marriage can survive all this subterfuge. And I don't want to be a party to it either, Karen.'

Karen slammed the telephone down so hard that Susan was almost deafened. She hung up with a sigh. If Karen wasn't careful she'd ruin everything between herself and Simon. She was just making a shopping list ready for Louise's visit when there was a ring at her bell. She opened the door to find Simon standing outside.

'Can I come in, Susan?'

'Of course. Is something wrong? Can I get you a drink — coffee?'

He ran a hand through his hair. 'Have you got anything stronger?'

'I think there might be some whisky left over from Christmas,' she said. 'Will that do?'

'Yes, fine, thanks.'

Susan fetched the whisky and a glass and watched as he threw the drink back in one gulp. 'I think you'd better tell me what's wrong,' she said as he put the glass down.

'It's Karen,' he said. 'I don't know what she's up to, forever going off somewhere. I'm beginning to think she's — that there's someone else. I know she's lying to me and I'm really not happy about the way things are between us at the moment.'

Susan sighed. Things were getting to a ridiculously complicated stage between those two. Maybe it was time she put Simon straight. At the risk of being classed as an interfering mother-in-law, she took a deep breath and said, 'It's nothing like that, Simon. She's doing a bit of private tutoring, that's all. She didn't want to tell you because she thought you'd be angry.'

He sighed. 'Oh, for God's sake! Not that again.'

'She's a bright girl, Simon, and she hates wasting her education and ability. Surely a little part-time tutoring can't hurt? And I'm happy to have Peter when I can.'

He sprang to his feet. 'What does she take me for — some kind of ogre? I asked her outright this morning when she was making some excuse about being out again tomorrow morning but she always hedges.' He glared at her. 'And you knew about it all along!'

'You must admit you've been rather inflexible in the past.'

'Surely a man has the right to say what he wants in his own house!'

Susan smiled. 'Simon, can you hear yourself? You sound like some Victorian patriarch. Times have changed. Young women are no longer satisfied with a life of undiluted domesticity. Why can't you cut her some slack?'

'It was only going to be till Peter goes to school.' He sat down again, slightly calmer. 'She only had to ask.'

'*Ask?*'

He frowned. 'You know what I mean. We could have discussed it.'

'I remember the last time you *discussed* it,' she said. 'Right here in my living room. Look, why don't you go home now and try to be more reasonable with her? Offer to stay with Peter tomorrow while she does her tutoring. What she's doing is important to that family. It's very worthwhile.'

He shrugged. 'I suppose so.' He looked at her. 'Has she asked you to have Peter tomorrow?'

'Yes, but I had to refuse because Louise is coming to stay for a couple of days.'

He stared at her. 'Louise! *Again?* You have to be joking! After the trouble she always causes. You must be mad, Susan!'

She stood up. 'Never mind whether I'm mad or not, Simon. Just take care of your own problems and let me take care of mine. Go home and get it over with. Make things right between you.'

★ ★ ★

Louise arrived just after eleven. When Susan opened the door to her, she was shocked by her appearance. She looked pale and drawn.

'Come in, dear,' she said. 'You're looking tired. I'll put the kettle on.'

Louise came in. She had a small bag with her, Susan noticed. Only an overnight case, so she obviously didn't intend to stay long. Susan bustled about the kitchen, putting cups on a tray and getting out the biscuit tin.

'Did you have a good journey?' she called out. 'You must have made an early start. Have you had any breakfast?' Louise didn't reply so she gave up in the end and when she carried the tray through to the living room, she found her sitting on the sofa looking miserable. She sat down beside her. 'What's wrong, dear? You said on the telephone that you wanted to talk to me. Has something happened?'

'Yes.' Louise took the cup that Susan handed her and took a long drink. 'Thanks. I needed that. Yes, Susan, something has happened and I might as well come straight to the point. You know I told you I'd found my mother?'

'I do. And you were worried that she might not leave you alone.'

'After the newspaper article about the collapse of the play, there wasn't much fear of that. She got the message at last that there was no money.' Louise looked at her stepmother. 'I'm sure you saw the article too.' Susan nodded. 'So now you realize what a damned liar I am — if you didn't already know.'

Susan looked up in alarm. 'Louise!'

'Oh, I'm well aware of what a pain I've been to you all,' Louise said. 'There's no need to pretend. The thing is, she, my — the woman who gave birth to me — asked to see me one more time. She said she had something to tell me about myself and it was vitally important.'

'So you met her again?' Susan said cautiously.

'Yes. And what she gleefully told me was that Frank Davies wasn't my father. That was what they rowed about on the night she walked out. She didn't take me with her because she didn't want me and Frank wasn't my real father.' She looked at Susan, her eyes full of pain. 'Can you imagine how that made me feel?'

Susan laid a hand on her arm. 'Oh my dear, of course I can. How horrible for you.'

'So — the reason I'm here, Susan, is to ask you if you knew about it.'

Susan leaned back in her seat with a sigh. 'Yes, I have to confess that I did know. Frank told me when we were first married. Not that he ever really believed it. He always insisted that you were his daughter and nothing would dissuade

257

him from that belief.'

'I'll never ever think of him as anything else,' Louise said.

'He loved you very dearly,' Susan said. 'But being abandoned by your mother like that at such an early age had a very profound impact on you. It damaged something deep inside you and although maybe I shouldn't say it, it made you a very difficult child to handle.'

'I know. I remember how awful I was to you.'

'In your early teens things got worse. You rebelled — stayed out late — mixed with a crowd of young people that were — well, a disastrous influence on you.'

Louise frowned. 'I don't remember much about that.'

'No, you wouldn't. You ended up getting into real trouble and having a kind of breakdown. You spent quite a long time in hospital.'

Louise looked at her. 'Is that a nice way of saying I got mixed up with drugs and had to go into rehab?'

Susan sighed. 'I'm afraid it is. But you got better, that's the main thing. It took some time but you got better and you came home with very little memory of what had happened. I think that may have had something to do with the treatment. The psychiatrist warned us about that.'

Louise's eyes widened. 'Psychiatrist! I was *that* sick?'

'I'm afraid so. When you came home you had this deep desire — almost an obsession — to go to drama school and become an actress. I was doubtful at the time. I wondered how you would cope, being away from home, but Frank was only too pleased that you had something you really wanted to do — a goal in life. He was happy to make the necessary sacrifices to pay for you to go.'

'I never knew that.' Louise's eyes filled with tears. 'You both stuck by me — and look how I repaid you.'

Susan patted her hand. 'Never mind that now. It's all water under the bridge. Frank always loved you unconditionally. As for whether he was your true father or not, we'll probably never know for sure, but one thing I can tell you and that is that he was a father to you in every possible way he could be: a father to be proud of.'

'I know, and I am proud of him. And of you too, Susan.'

'Louise . . . ' Susan paused and took a breath. 'There's something else you should know,' she said. 'And I hope this is the right time for me to tell you. But you must prepare yourself for a shock.'

★　★　★

'Why couldn't you be straight with me, for God's sake?'

Simon and Karen were standing in the kitchen. Karen was wiping down the worktops, her back to him. Now she spun round to face him. 'Because you're always so bloody unreasonable if you must know.'

'Don't swear at me.' He looked round. 'Where's Peter?'

'He's fine. He's playing in the front garden.'

'So — about this tutoring. How did you think you could manage to do it in the holidays without me knowing?'

'I was going to tell you.'

'Oh yes — when?'

Karen threw the dishcloth she'd been using into the sink with a splash. 'When I could work up the courage. I knew you'd say I'd have to give it up. You're so controlling — always making me out to be a bad mother and wife. Do you have any idea how that makes me feel?'

He sighed. 'All I ask is that you stay at home with our son till he's old enough for school,' he said exasperatedly. 'He's three now so that's only another couple of years. Can't you even wait that long to shake off the shackles of motherhood?'

Karen snorted. 'Oh, will you *listen* to yourself? *The shackles of motherhood!* You sound like a character out of a Victorian novel. I ask you — how can it hurt for me to be away from him for a couple of hours a week?'

Simon seethed. For the second time that morning he'd been accused of being 'Victorian'. He'd always considered himself to be a forward-thinking man. In favour of female equality at home and in the workplace. But surely when a woman had a child . . .

'The poor kid's a bundle of nerves,' he lashed out. 'When you're not here he's constantly asking for you. You're damaging him — making him into an anxious, neurotic little wreck!'

Karen laughed. 'I've never heard of anything so ridiculous. Peter's a very well-adjusted child.

Every . . . ' Suddenly, through the open front door came the sound of squealing brakes, a bang and a loud shout. They stared at each other for a stunned second, then made a dash for the door.

'*Peter!*'

The front gate was open and a car stood at the kerb; the driver was kneeling over a tiny prone body in the road in front of his car. He looked up, white-faced, as Karen and Simon came running out.

'Christ! I'm so sorry,' he said. 'He ran out. I couldn't stop in time — didn't have a chance!'

Karen screamed, a hand over her mouth. Simon rushed to kneel by the lifeless child. He felt for a pulse and turned to Karen. 'He's alive. Quick, ring for an ambulance!'

★　★　★

'You were fourteen when you went off the rails and started getting into trouble,' Susan said. 'Your dad and I were already worried but the final blow fell when we discovered you were pregnant. We never found out who was responsible. It was soon after that you had your breakdown.'

Louise was staring at her stepmother, open-mouthed. 'I had a — baby? But what happened? Why don't I remember any of it?'

'You were very ill. The doctors thought you might lose the child or that it might be affected by the drugs. They kept you in hospital throughout the pregnancy.'

'And the — baby?'

'Thankfully the baby was fine — taken straight

261

from you at birth for adoption.'

'Without my consent?'

'You were in no fit state to know what you wanted — you never asked once about the baby and afterwards you seemed to have blanked it completely from your mind.' Susan laid a hand on her arm. 'Louise — we — your dad and I adopted her.'

'*You* did?' Louise took in the implication of what she had just heard. She stared at Susan. 'You don't — you *can't* mean . . . ?'

'Yes. Karen is yours. She was four months old when you came out of hospital and we thought at first that seeing her would trigger your memory, but it didn't. You never took any interest in her at all. So we decided to let sleeping dogs lie and bring Karen up as our own. You went back to school — a new school, then later to drama school.'

Louise was deeply shocked. It seemed bizarre. It was all so hard to take in. Then she remembered the dreams — about her mother leaving, then later, about rejecting a baby. Somewhere, deep in her subconscious she'd buried it all. She looked at Susan.

'I'm so glad you told me,' she said. 'I take it that Karrie doesn't know?'

Susan shook her head. 'She still thinks of Frank and me as her parents, although we did tell her a long time ago that she was adopted.' She looked appealingly at Louise. 'I really think that after all this time it's probably better to leave it at that.'

Louise was silent for a moment then she

slowly nodded. 'I'm sure you're right.'

Susan took her hand and squeezed it. 'It's not too late to have a child of your own,' she said, but Louise shook her head.

'I've never been the maternal type. Karen was lucky to have you and Dad. Better not to stir things up now.' She looked at Susan. 'I owe you so much, Susan; far more than I ever dreamed. I'll never be able to make it all up to you.'

Susan smiled. 'No need, my dear. I'm so sorry about your disappointment over the play. I only wish things could work out for you.'

The telephone began to ring and Susan got up to answer it. Louise watched as her stepmother's face suddenly drained of colour.

'Oh my God!' she cried. 'Yes. We'll get there as soon as we can. Thank you for ringing me, Simon. Goodbye.'

★   ★   ★

In the family room at the hospital, Susan and Louise found a shocked-looking Karen and Simon sitting silently together. Simon was holding Karen's hand. Susan sat down beside Karen.

'Any news?'

'Not yet.' It was Simon who spoke. Karen wept silently into Susan's shoulder.

'It was my fault,' she sobbed. 'If only we hadn't been rowing . . . '

Simon squeezed her hand. 'Don't. It was my fault as much as anyone's. I think it's time we got our priorities straight.'

Louise reached out to touch Karen's shoulder.

263

'Karrie — darling, I'm so sorry.' When Karen did not respond, Louise looked at Susan. 'Shall I go and get some coffees?'

Susan nodded. 'That sounds like a good idea.'

When she'd left the room Simon looked up angrily. 'Why on earth did you bring *her* with you? She's the last person we want with us at a time like this.'

'Something quite monumental has just happened in her life,' Susan said. 'I think you'll find she's going to be very different from now on.'

Simon grunted. 'Huh! I'll believe that when I see it.'

Louise returned with the coffees on a tray and they sat in silence as they drank them. When the door opened and a tall young man walked in, all four looked up expectantly. He introduced himself.

'Good morning. I'm Paul Grainger, senior paediatrician here at St Mary's and I've been looking after your small son.'

Karen was on her feet. 'How is he?'

'He has a hairline fracture of the skull but apart from a few bumps and bruises, that's all.'

'A skull fracture!' Karen cried, leaping to her feet. 'But that's serious, isn't it?'

'A hairline fracture in a child of his age heals very quickly,' the consultant told them. 'We'll keep him in for a couple of days just to be on the safe side.' He looked at Karen. 'You can stay here with him if you like. After that there's no reason why you can't take him home.'

Simon stood up and put his arms round Karen, who was weeping with relief. He looked at the consultant. 'Thank you so much.'

'Not at all.' On his way out the consultant said, 'By the way, the driver of the car is in the waiting room. I think he'd appreciate some reassurance.'

'I'll go in a minute.' Simon kissed the top of Karen's head. 'Don't cry, darling. Everything's going to be all right.'

'It's my fault,' she sobbed. 'If we hadn't been arguing about my wanting to work, it would never have happened.'

'Never mind that now.'

Susan gestured to Louise that they should give them some time alone and they quietly left the room.

As they made their way back to Susan's flat Louise said, 'Maybe I should go back to London. You'll be wanting to help Karrie and Simon and I'll just be in the way.'

Susan smiled. 'It's considerate of you to suggest that but don't go tonight. Leave it at least till the morning.' She looked at her watch. 'I must ring Ted and let him know what's happened.'

'Ted?' Louise looked at her. 'You're back together, then?'

Susan smiled. 'We met and he explained everything. I'll tell you about it over supper.'

25

I let myself into the empty flat and stood for a moment in the silence. In spite of Susan's revelations and what had happened over the last few days, I felt more estranged from my family now than ever before. They didn't need me. I was Karen's mother and Susan's stepdaughter. Another thought hit me: I was Peter's *grandmother*, for heaven's sake! And yet none of them needed or wanted me; in fact quite the opposite. Susan was kind and good. She always had been and no doubt she always would be. But could I ever begin to mend all the fences I'd ridden roughshod over in the past? They had all put up with so much from me. Perhaps now it was time to give them all a much deserved rest; to stand on my own feet and try to turn over a new leaf. It was a really strange feeling. It could be an end and yet if I really made up my mind to it, it could be a beginning — a fresh start. This could be make-or-break time and I realized that the outcome was up to me.

I put my case in my room and went into the kitchen to put the kettle on. As I waited for it to boil, my thoughts turned to Mark! Dear, patient Mark. I'd been so horrible to him, yet he'd given me nothing but love and consideration. But now it was over. He'd given up trying to contact me and he was about to marry someone else. I'd lost him. Anyhow, I'd never be able to face him now.

He'd be sure to see me differently when he knew the truth. I knew I owed him that but I shied away from telling him about my past — seeing the look of disgust and disillusionment on his face.

I found cold meat and salad in the fridge and as I set about putting a snack lunch together, it occurred to me that in the past I'd have taken Di's food without a thought. Now I promised myself that I'd go out later and replace what I'd taken. When I'd eaten, I went out to the supermarket and it was as I was letting myself back into the flat that my phone began to ring. I put down the bags of shopping and fished my phone out of my bag.

'Hello.'

'Louise. It's Patrick Jason. I've got some good news,' he said.

'Oh yes?'

'The audition you did — for the soap, *King's Reach* — I'm delighted to tell you that you've got the part. Congratulations!'

I stared speechlessly at the phone. Had he just said what I thought he'd said?

'Louise — are you there?'

'Yes — yes. Are you sure?' I asked, my knees trembling.

He laughed. 'Of course I'm sure. You start rehearsing next week, so if you'd like to come into the office tomorrow and sign the contract . . .'

'Oh, yes of course,' I said quickly. 'I'm still trying to take it in. I can't thank you enough, Patrick. What time would you like me there?'

'Ten would be fine,' he said. 'I'm glad you're pleased.'

'*Pleased!* I'm over the moon,' I told him. 'It couldn't have come at a better time. See you in the morning, then.'

As I unpacked the shopping, my hands shook so much that I kept dropping things. As soon as I'd put the last item away I went straight back out again — to the off-licence on the corner to buy a bottle of champagne.

★ ★ ★

Di was late getting home and I kept looking at the clock. I couldn't wait to tell her my news. She looked tired when she got in. I'd already cooked and dinner was waiting in the oven — the champagne chilling in the fridge.

She seemed pleased to see me. 'Hi. How was your home visit?'

'Traumatic,' I told her. 'Peter, my little nephew, was involved in an accident and rushed to hospital.'

'Oh no! Is he OK?'

'He's got a hairline skull fracture but apart from that he's all right. The doctor said that skull fractures in young children are fairly quick to heal.'

Di hung up her coat. 'How did it happen?'

'Seems that Karrie and Simon were having a row about Karrie working. No one was watching Peter. He was playing in the front garden and he got out onto the road and ran in front of a car.'

'They must feel so guilty.'

'I think they do. Maybe they'll realize now that they have to come to some kind of compromise over Karrie's work.'

'So what else happened?'

'Quite a bit. Susan and I had a long talk. But something happened after I got back and I can't wait to tell you that first.'

She smiled. 'I knew there was something. I can feel you fizzing from here!'

'Di — I got the part,' I told her. 'The part I auditioned for, in *King's Reach*.'

Her face lit up and she reached out to hug me. 'Wow! That's fantastic! I'm so happy for you.'

'I've got champagne and I've cooked us a special meal,' I said excitedly. 'Shall I open the bottle now?'

'What do you think?'

The cork popped and we toasted each other. I served the meal I'd cooked and we chatted excitedly. Di wanted to hear all the details. We were having coffee when she asked, 'So what about Susan? Was she able to throw any light on what your mother told you?'

'She knew about it of course — said that my dad never accepted that I wasn't his. It was something they didn't talk about.' I put my cup down, suddenly serious as I came down to earth. 'She told me a lot about my childhood, Di. I must have been a nightmare for them. Apparently I went off the rails big-time in my early teens — drugs. I ended up in rehab and later I had a bad breakdown.'

'Oh, Lou.'

I didn't tell her I'd given birth to a daughter

and that Susan and Frank had adopted her. I'd already decided to keep it to myself in case somehow it got back to Karrie. Di was looking at me aghast.

'I've just had a thought — those nightmares!'

'I know. It all makes sense now. It says a lot about the kind of person I became too,' I added. 'Somewhere at the back of my mind I felt I needed to pay someone or something back. God knows why. Susan and Dad were wonderful to me. I've been so lucky and I've got a hell of a lot of making-up to do. One thing I do know, and that is that I wish I'd never tried to get in touch with my mother. If I'd known all this sooner there's no way I would have wanted to know her.'

'My advice is to put it all behind you,' Di said. 'It's in the past and there's nothing you can do about it. Just concentrate on this new challenge and look forward to a fresh start.'

I smiled. 'Yes, I will. I can't wait to begin.'

'And what about Mark — surely you want to ring him with your news?'

'I don't think he'll be interested. I'm afraid I've blown it with him.'

'Why do you say that?'

'I think he's finally written me off. Anyway he's getting married.'

'Married! Who to?'

'A girl he used to know.'

'How do you know this?'

'It was when I was working at the bridal shop. His sister came in with her to choose the dress.'

Di looked crestfallen. 'It didn't take him long,

did it? Maybe it was on the rebound. But even so, he'll want to hear about the new job, surely?'

I shrugged. 'I doubt it.'

'Well, you should at least try.' Di shook my arm exasperatedly. 'Go on, ring him now. I'll give you some space while I'm doing the washing-up.'

She disappeared into the kitchen and I took out my phone and sat looking at it. Suddenly, I had cold feet. Maybe he'd be out with his fiancée. He wouldn't be interested in what I was doing any more. It would be nice to tell him my news, yet I dreaded hearing the indifference in his voice as he tried to sound interested. I knew Di wouldn't let me get away with feeble excuses so I quickly clicked on his number, hoping that he'd be out or that the number would be engaged.

'Hello, Mark Naylor.'

My heart missed a beat. 'Oh — Mark. It's Louise.'

'Lou! I've been trying to come to terms with the fact that you'd had enough of me. I'd even deleted your name from my phone. How are you?'

'I'm fine — you?'

'Yes, fine. Cathy and the kids moved out a couple of days ago and I'm getting used to having the place to myself again.'

'Oh. You must miss them.'

'I do, but in a good way. You can have too much of being woken up by two little monsters jumping all over you at seven in the morning.' There was a pause and then he said, 'Is everything all right, Lou? You sound a bit — odd.'

'Do I?'

'A bit. Do you have a special reason for ringing me?'

'Do I need one?'

'Well — you tell me.'

'Actually I'm ringing because I've got some news,' I told him. 'Quite a lot of news in fact. I've — '

'*No!*' he broke in. 'Don't tell me now. Let's meet. Are you doing anything tomorrow?'

'I have to go to Patrick Jason's office in the morning. He's my new agent.'

'Right — what time?'

'Ten o'clock.'

'OK if I pick you up from there — say ten thirty?'

'That sounds fine.'

'OK, see you then. And Lou . . . '

'Yes?'

'I've missed you.'

I swallowed hard. 'Me too.'

★ ★ ★

Patrick had the contract all ready for me to sign the following morning. Putting my name to it felt good. The first really important contract I'd signed in my whole career and when I saw the salary Patrick had negotiated for me, my heart gave a leap. It was more money than I'd ever earned.

Patrick looked down at my signature. 'You've signed, Louise Davies.'

'Yes. That's my real name and it's how I want

to be known from now on,' I told him. 'Louise Delmar is dead and buried.'

He laughed. 'Right. I'll make a note of it.'

It was all over and done with by a quarter past ten and I sat in reception waiting for Mark to arrive.

When he walked in, I was surprised at the receptionist's reaction. She looked up with a smile. 'Mark! What brings you out of the woodwork so early in the morning?'

He leant across her desk to give her ear a tweak. 'Less of your cheek, young Sharon. I'm here to escort a lovely lady to lunch.' He turned to me. 'It's terrible the disrespectful way these receptionists treat you nowadays, isn't it?' he quipped. 'You can't get the staff, you know.'

On the way downstairs I asked him how he knew Patrick Jason's receptionist. And he grinned.

'He's my agent too,' he said.

It suddenly occurred to me that he hadn't sounded surprised when I said I had to see Patrick this morning. 'He's *yours* — but . . . ' I looked at him with narrowed eyes. 'I suppose his contacting me wouldn't have had anything to do with you, would it?'

He frowned. 'Come to think about it, I suppose I *might* just have mentioned you in passing.'

'Then it wasn't down to the article in the *Sunday Sphere*!'

'Oh, that!' He laughed. 'I had a good laugh at that. Good on you!'

'I didn't do it for a laugh,' I told him. 'I did it because I needed the money. You didn't have to put in a word for me with Patrick, but thanks all the same.'

'Well, it seems to have worked out. Has he come up with anything for you?'

'He has as a matter of fact. That was what I was going to tell you last night. I auditioned for a part in a BBC soap last week.'

He looked at me. 'And . . . ?'

'And — I got the part.'

'*Great!*' He slipped an arm through mine. 'So we've got something to celebrate. What are we waiting for?'

We had lunch at a small, intimate restaurant quite close to the Savoy, overlooking the Thames. As we were having coffee, Mark looked at me.

'You said you had a lot of news,' he reminded me. 'What else has happened?'

I came down to earth. After the excitement of signing the contract the memory of Susan's revelations had been pushed to the back of my mind. 'The rest of it is a bit more serious.' I looked at him. 'But before I tell you, I think you have some news for me.'

He looked bemused. 'Me? No, nothing springs to mind.'

'Not the little matter of your forthcoming nuptials?'

He burst out laughing. 'That'll be the day! Where did you get that idea from?'

'I did a short stint working in a bridal boutique,' I told him. 'Your sister came in with your fiancée.'

He shook his head. 'My *what*?'

Slightly irritated I went on. 'Come off it,

274

Mark. The name Franny ring any bells?'

His face cleared. 'Oh! Franny! Francesca Barratt. She's an old school friend of Cathy's. She's getting married next month and Cathy has been helping her with the preparations.'

'Oh.' I bit my lip, feeling slightly foolish. Mark laughed softly.

'You didn't actually think it was me, getting married, did you?'

'Well, I . . . '

'And were you at all upset by the news?' I shook my head and he leaned towards me. 'What, not even a little bit?'

'It was an easy mistake to make,' I blustered. 'Was I upset? Not really, no. You deserve to be happy.'

'But we don't always get what we deserve, do we?' he teased.

I looked up at him. 'Will you please stop baiting me?'

'Not until you tell me how you *really* felt when you thought I was marrying someone else.'

'OK, I was . . . ' I searched my mind for the right word. 'I was sad,' I said at last. 'Sad and — OK — a bit jealous.'

His eyes danced. 'Why would you be jealous? You don't love me, do you?'

'Mark — I've got something quite serious to tell you. It's about me — things I only discovered a few days ago — things that might make a difference about how you see me.'

'It all sounds very solemn.'

'It is.' I looked around. 'Could we go somewhere quiet where I could tell you?'

'Of course.' The smile left his face as he beckoned the waiter for the bill. 'You go and get your coat. I'll take you back to the flat.'

* * *

'So that's my background, Mark. Not very inspiring, is it?'

We were seated opposite each other in Mark's sunlit living room. It had been painful, pouring out my past to him. It had taken all my courage and strength and he obviously saw that.

He poured a large glass of wine and put it in my hand. 'It's all so long ago,' he said gently. 'You were still a kid, Lou. It's in the past and what's done can't be undone. Why should it make me see you any other way than I see you now?'

I took a sip of the wine and looked at him. 'Not even the fact that I had a baby at barely fourteen years old?'

He shook his head. 'That was then, Lou. So you made some mistakes — who hasn't? It must all have been sheer hell for you. It's no wonder your mind refused to retain any of it.'

Suddenly I decided to tell him the truth about Karrie. No one else must know but I felt I owed Mark not just some, but all of the truth. 'My baby daughter was adopted by Susan and Frank,' I said slowly. 'Karen is — was my daughter and neither of us has ever been aware of the fact. Susan has asked that it remains a secret and I feel bound to honour that wish, so please, Mark, you are the only other person to

276

know this and it mustn't go beyond these walls.'

He moved to sit beside me. 'I feel flattered that you're prepared to trust me with a secret like that and of course it goes no further.' He slipped an arm round my shoulders. 'Thank you for what you've just confided in me, Lou. It makes no difference to the way I feel about you. You know how much I love you. It's a love that has lasted for years so it's not likely to stop now. I understand so much more about you now and if anything it makes me love you even more.' He searched my eyes. 'Please will you tell me truthfully how you feel, because if your feelings don't match mine this must be goodbye. I couldn't go on, knowing that what I feel will never be returned.'

I put my arms round him and held him close. 'Of course I love you, Mark. I've loved you for years without recognizing the fact. I've been a total bitch to you in the past. I can't understand why you kept on loving me.'

He kissed me. 'Maybe I can make you understand.'

For a long time neither of us spoke and the next time I glanced at the time it was almost five o'clock. I sat up.

'I must go. Di will be home.' I looked at him. 'That's another thing, Mark. It was always Di's flat — never mine. I lied about it. God knows why. I've lied about so many things in the past, but never again. All that ends from today onwards and that's a promise.'

He winced. 'If that's not tempting providence I don't know what is!'

'Well, I believe it anyway.' I looked around the room. 'You asked me once if I would move in. Does that invitation still stand?'

He grinned. 'What do you think?'

I stood up and gathered my coat and bag together. 'Then will you take me to Di's to collect my things, please?'

26

As Susan rang the bell of Karen and Simon's house, she caught Ted's hand and gave it a squeeze. He returned it, looking down at her.

'You are sure they invited me too?'

Susan smiled. 'Of course. I want you all to get to know one another and this is the perfect opportunity.'

Karen opened the door. She looked tanned and relaxed from the recent holiday the three of them had just enjoyed.

'Come in, both of you. Simon is just reading Peter a story. He'll be down in a minute and then we can all have a drink.' She led them through to the living room. Turning to Ted she said, 'I'm so glad you could come. I hope you like steak.'

Ted grinned. 'What man doesn't? It's very kind of you to invite me.'

Simon appeared. 'Phew! Getting away from that young man is like tearing off a plaster.' He smiled and held out his hand to Ted. 'Hi! I'm Simon, as I expect you've guessed. What will you have to drink?'

Karen turned towards the door. 'I'll have mine in the kitchen while I put the finishing touches to dinner. We want to have the meal over and done with ready for the big event, don't we?'

Simon inclined his head towards Ted. 'Whisky?' Ted nodded and Simon poured. He glanced at his mother-in-law. 'Don't need to ask you or Karrie. G and T. Ice and a slice — right?'

Susan laughed. 'I'll take mine and Karen's into the kitchen and see what I can do to help. I'm sure the two of you are dying to talk football.' She took the glasses from Simon and he opened the door for her. Outside in the hall, she paused for a moment to listen but she was soon reassured by the sound of the two men talking. It looked as though they were going to get along. In the kitchen she found Karen tossing new potatoes in parsley and butter. 'I'll put your drink on the worktop, shall I?' she said. 'Now — what can I do?'

'You could put the dressing on the salad, Mum.'

As they worked Susan looked at her daughter. 'You enjoyed your holiday, then? You certainly look well.'

Karen nodded. 'Simon and I have come to a compromise. I can do my tutoring as long as Peter doesn't suffer in any way.'

Susan's eyebrows rose. 'Suffer! In what way?'

Karen blushed. 'Well, you know, being passed round.'

'Being cared for by me, you mean?'

'Not at all! It's just that it's better for him to be in his own home until he's older.'

'So he's not even going to playgroup?'

Karen shook her head. 'Yes, of course he is but . . .'

'I should stop now, dear,' Susan said with a smile. 'You know what they say — when you're in a hole, stop digging.' They both laughed and

Susan went on, 'Actually it's as well you're not going to be asking me to have him very often. Ted and I are going to be really busy, harvesting all the produce from the allotments and manning our stall at the farmers' market.'

Karen smiled. 'Oh, Mum, I'm so glad you're really back together again.'

'Are you? He is still a married man, you know,' Susan pointed out.

'Yes, but it's only a platonic relationship you have with him, isn't it?'

'Mmm.' Susan bent her head to take a sip of her G and T. 'I can't wait to see Louise in this show,' she said, changing the subject.

'Neither can I,' Karen agreed. 'Since she landed that job she's been a different person. In fact you'd hardly know her these days.'

'Yes, and of course she's finally admitted that she loves that delightful man, Mark. She couldn't have a better partner. He keeps her feet on the ground and she might need that if she's going to be a big hit in this show. I understand that the part she's playing is a pivotal one.'

'Yes, so I believe.' Karen handed her mother the potatoes and salad bowl. 'Take these through, will you, Mum? The steaks are done and we'd better get on if we don't want to miss the programme.'

At eight o'clock the four of them were seated in the living room, their eyes on the TV screen. They watched as the initial captions rolled and then it was the opening scene and Louise was seen in the character of Amy, cooking breakfast in her kitchen.

Susan was surprised to see that she was made up to appear at least ten years older than she actually was and as the scene progressed, she could see for the first time what a good actress her stepdaughter was. The character she was playing was just about as different from her own personality as it was possible to be. Watching the scene she soon lost herself in the story, almost forgetting that she was watching her own stepdaughter.

Ted was watching Susan. Her expressions went from surprise to enjoyment and then to pride in Louise's achievement. She was certainly very good in the part. In fact, he thought he could see something of Susan in Louise's development of the character. He looked again at Susan's face and smiled inwardly. She was such a lovely woman. He told himself daily how lucky he was to have met her. He didn't dare to think too far into the future but it was his dearest hope that one day he would be able to ask her to marry him.

Karen watched her sister's performance with interest. Clearly she had worked hard for this and her work had paid off. She was good; very good indeed. This was what Louise had wanted so badly. It had always been her ambition to land an important part on stage or TV and now here she was, fulfilling her dream. Now she could understand some of the reason for her sister's past recklessness, her spiteful, hard-to-forgive actions. They must have sprung from frustration and although they still rankled with Karen, she felt that now she could put them to one side and wish her sister well.

Simon watched the programme with his tongue firmly in his cheek. He didn't like soap operas anyway and he felt that Louise had always belonged in something tacky. She had found her niche and he wished her well of it. Hopefully it would keep her too busy to come and visit and happy enough not to want to cause any more problems.

Giving the programme more attention, he was suddenly aware of something interesting. Louise's portrayal of the motherly Amy was very much like his mother-in-law, Susan. How like Louise to steal someone else's personality for her own gain. He hoped that Susan wouldn't recognize the fact. Surely she would not see it as a compliment. He glanced around the room. Karen and Susan wore rapt expressions and Ted — well, Ted only had eyes for Susan. Good luck to him!

★   ★   ★

I watched my first episode of *King's Reach* full of apprehension and self-doubt. Did I really come across as I'd intended? Did I look right — *sound* right? And that wig! I hadn't been too sure about the make-up or costumes that wardrobe had chosen for me, but now, looking at them from the other side of the screen I could see that they were right.

'So — proud of yourself, Miss Davies?' Mark handed me a glass of champagne and I took it from him, wrinkling my nose.

283

'Not really. Do you think they'll ring tomorrow and say they're terminating my contract?'

He laughed and sat down beside me. 'As if! You're the best thing that's happened to that show in a long time. You bring it to life.'

I leaned across to kiss his cheek. 'I suppose you wouldn't be the teeniest bit prejudiced, would you?'

He looked wounded. 'I hope I'm too honest for that. I'm an actor, remember? And I know good acting when I see it.'

I looked at him. 'What about your career, Mark? Has Patrick come up with anything for you?'

He shook his head. 'To be honest, darling, I'm not that bothered. I was never the actor that you are.' I made to protest but he held up his hand. 'No. I mean it.' He slipped an arm around my shoulders and nestled closer. 'I'm quite happy to bathe in your reflected glory; to chauffeur you hither and thither and be known as the celebrated *Mr* Louise Davies.'

'Don't say that!'

'I will say it because whether you recognized it or not, my darling, that was my fumbling way of asking you to marry me.'

I put down my glass and wound my arms around his neck. 'I don't deserve you, Mark Naylor, and you will never *ever* be *Mr* Louise Davies.'

'Well, OK, but the question still is, will you be Mrs Mark Naylor?'

I kissed him hard. 'I thought you'd never ask,' I whispered. 'And — just for the record, you've got yourself a deal!'

We do hope that you have enjoyed reading
this large print book.

Did you know that all of our titles
are available for purchase?

We publish a wide range of high quality
large print books including:
Romances, Mysteries, Classics
General Fiction
Non Fiction and Westerns

Special interest titles available in
large print are:
The Little Oxford Dictionary
Music Book
Song Book
Hymn Book
Service Book

Also available from us courtesy of
Oxford University Press:
Young Readers' Dictionary
(large print edition)
Young Readers' Thesaurus
(large print edition)

For further information or a free
brochure, please contact us at:
Ulverscroft Large Print Books Ltd.,
The Green, Bradgate Road, Anstey,
Leicester, LE7 7FU, England.
Tel: (00 44) 0116 236 4325
Fax: (00 44) 0116 234 0205

Other titles published by Ulverscroft:

TO DREAM AGAIN

Jeanne Whitmee

The outbreak of war brings mixed feelings for Judy Truman, and it is a relief to get away from the East End and her disastrous marriage. With her two small daughters, she is evacuated to a Norfolk seaside town. Life becomes relaxed, the children flourish, and Judy's confidence returns. But when her husband Sid comes home on leave, he quickly shatters her new self-belief, and his violent jealousy frightens her. A young airman, Peter Gresham, teaches Judy that men can be gentle and loving — but living her life with Peter seems an impossible dream. And when shocking revelations from Sid's past come to light, Judy is horrified . . . With her hopes for the future crushed, Judy must concentrate on looking forward, and use her determination to carry her through.

TRUE COLOURS

Jeanne Whitmee

Frances, Sophie and Katie meet again at a school reunion and discover how their lives have changed. Katie is a successful fashion designer; Frances has a young son and a wealthy husband; Sophie has a happy marriage and a dream home. They resolve to keep in touch, but gradually each of them realises that her friends' wonderful lives are far from perfect . . . Katie is working in a small boutique and struggling to succeed; Fran's marriage to a controlling man is deeply unhappy; Sophie is on the point of bankruptcy and divorce. But old friendships die hard and each of them needs to learn to pocket her pride and reach out for the help and support of her friends.

YOU'LL NEVER KNOW . . .

Jeanne Whitmee

Hazel, Lillian and Ruby might never have become friends if it hadn't been for the war. Hazel is a young teacher with a guilty secret; Lillian is the sole carer to her domineering invalid mother and Ruby is an evacuee waif from the East End of London, abandoned by her feckless mother and left to the mercies of an uncaring and resentful foster family. The three find pleasure and support in one another's friendship. For the three girls the final years of the war bring new, undreamed of experiences, friendship and, for Hazel and Lillian, true love. For each girl, life changes direction. Will it lead to a happier future?

THE WISE CHILD

Jeanne Whitmee

Artistically talented Danielle is resentful when her mother cannot afford to send her to art school. She loses job after job when her temper gets the better of her. Then, when she discovers that her mother gave birth to her as a surrogate child for a wealthy couple but then could not part with her, she decides to go in search of the parents she should have had. However, Danny is unaware of the convoluted difficulties that preceded her birth. Her arrival in the Naylor household and the friendships she forms create problems and almost end in heartbreak for all concerned. But unexpectedly, Danny's fortunes turn around and she emerges a wiser and stronger young woman.

POINT OF NO RETURN

Jeanne Whitmee

When Imogen Jameson is injured in a London bomb blast and mistakenly reported as one of the fatalities, she takes the opportunity to escape from a violent marriage by assuming the identity of one of the victims. Imogen knows that her husband, William, only married her for her money. She leaves London to start again, and meets and falls in love with kind and caring Adam Bennett. But unaware that her new identity is that of an ex-con, Imogen has the criminal underworld searching for her, certain that she knows the whereabouts of a fortune in jewels. And William, a successful heart surgeon, doesn't believe that she was killed in the bomb blast — but he's determined to make sure that she *stays* dead . . . for good.